for Hilary + Cy,
with *[illegible]*
kind *[illegible]*
Best wishes
[signature]
April *[illegible]* '89

BY VICTORIES UNDONE

By Victories Undone

MANOLI OLYMPITIS AND RAYMOND LEWIS

QUARTET BOOKS
LONDON AND NEW YORK

First published by Quartet Books Ltd in 1988
A member of the Namara Group
27/29 Goodge Street, London W1P 1FD

British Library Cataloguing in Publication Data

Olympitis, Manoli
    By victories undone
    I. Title   II. Lewis, Raymond
    823'.914 [F]   PR 6065.L7/

    ISBN   0 7043 2654 X

Printed and bound in Great Britain at
The Camelot Press plc, Southampton

For
John Olympitis
and
Sylvia Margolis

Acknowledgements

To say that this book would not have existed without Norman Mailer would be to state the obvious. Were it not for his unmerited faith in our efforts to entertain, this humble work would never have seen the light of day. We will be forever grateful, not least for his generosity of time.

We would also like to thank for their varying contributions and in no particular order, Miss Valerie Perrine, Mr James Barrymore, Dr Nikitas Theodorou and a host of understanding girlfriends.

MANOLI OLYMPITIS
RAYMOND LEWIS
LONDON
MARCH 1988

E'en victors are by victories undone
JOHN DRYDEN

BOOK ONE

THE OLD BAILEY, LONDON, ENGLAND, 1950

The blindfolded statue of Justice, the golden sword, the scales glinting in the morning sun, was high up there, towering over the chaos – Justice was bored. She had seen it all so many times before. Outside the building crowds seethed on both sides of the street. They were straining for a glimpse of the defendant. The police struggled with nervous horses. They were barely managing to maintain control. A silver Bentley Continental came to a stop outside the main entrance; the chauffeur popped out to open the rear door. Then a fair-haired young man in a blue pinstriped suit stepped firmly out of the car to smile at the crowd before he strode into the cold forum that was the Central Criminal Court.

Inside, Number One Court was in a fever. Anxious ushers and pompous commissionaires barked at reporters. Everybody fought for limited space. The public gallery was packed to capacity with leading lights from high and low society and there were even a few fortunate members of the public who had stood in line all night to be rewarded with the treasure of a seat. Incongruous – in the front row – was a dignified man in tramp's clothing, his quiet, haunted blue eyes gazing out beneath long white hair.

A thrill of anticipation went through the court as the figure of Sir Desmond Fitzgerald, King's Counsel, flanked by three junior clerks, swept through the large swing doors, black silk

3

gown flowing behind him. Pausing while the clerks placed the brief for the defence on the lectern and arranged his famous cushions on the hard wooden bench, our legendary old gladiator looked around the arena. And he beamed.

Three loud bangs from the staff of the Chief Usher reverberated with the Crown's claim to silence and loyalty. Everyone stood. The Lord Chief Justice of England entered. He bowed to the counsel below him and adjusted the ermine collar of his crimson robe. He took his thronelike seat.

The clerk of the court rose from the well to address the young man in the dock: 'Will the prisoner at the Bar please stand. Sir James Clarence Archibald Stuart, you are charged that on the twelfth day of March of this year you did wilfully and maliciously murder one John Herbert Sykes. To this charge how do you plead?'

'Not guilty.' The response was strong and confident.

'Very well,' the judge said. 'Let the trial begin.'

CHAPTER 1
OXFORD UNIVERSITY, ENGLAND, 1947

Gregory Hamilton III had not had a good day – in fact things had not gone well since his arrival in London.

An unscheduled weekend with an aspiring young actress who exhibited a marked preference for oral sex had detained him in New York just long enough to miss the sailing of the *Queen Mary* that would have got him to England in plenty of time. Instead he had switched his reservation to an altogether inferior ship which departed two days later. This would still have enabled him to reach Oxford for the beginning of term had not the paucity of available females on board persuaded him to stay overnight in London. His decision was greatly facilitated by the actress's enthusiastic recommendation of a busty brunette girlfriend who worked as a dancer at the Windmill Theatre. The night had, however, ended unsuccessfully at 5 a.m. at the Embassy Club in Bond Street where he had drunk far too many champagne cocktails and had failed to persuade the girl to accompany him back to Claridge's.

He had awakened the following day with a dreadful hangover which resulted in his missing the fast train to Oxford and being forced to endure a long, uncomfortable journey culminating in a change at Reading where the dining-car had been removed before he had time to lunch. Matters did not improve on his arrival at Oxford Station. Here he found that not only was his luggage halfway to a place called Didcot, but also that his persistent telephone requests for assistance to Perkins, the Head Porter of Christchurch College, were being ignored. By the time he reached the empty Porter's Lodge at the college, Greg was furious and, barely noticing the well-dressed young Englishman behind him, he banged several times on the desk until a spotty-faced teenager emerged from the back room.

'Yes, sir,' he said timidly. 'Can I help you?'

'Well somebody better,' Greg growled, drawing himself up to his full six feet three inches. 'Are you that goddamned fool Perkins?'

'No. In fact his name is Hoskins.' A portly man with silver slicked-down hair appeared. His uniform was immaculate and the highly polished campaign medals from the Great War added to his general air of authority.

'I am Perkins. And you sir, I assume,' he wiggled his veined nose in disdain, 'are Mr Hamilton. It is customary, sir, to notify an Oxford college when you propose to arrive late. Also, sir, I am not normally referred to around 'ere as a fool. Now what exactly is the problem Mr Hamilton?'

'The problem, Perkins, is – as you would have found out if you had bothered to answer your telephone – that my luggage is now in Didcot and I'd quite like it back.' Gregory Hamilton could not abide smart-assed members of staff.

'I see, sir, having a little trouble understanding our railway timetables, are we?' Perkins's nose twitched. 'I'll see what I can . . . Good heavens!' He peered around Greg's broad shoulders. 'Excuse me, sir, but are you Mr James Stuart?'

'Yes, Perkins.'

'Well, welcome to Christchurch, sir.' Perkins shot out from behind the desk, pushing Greg aside. 'Allow me to take you to your room. "Oskins,' he barked. 'Mr Stuart's luggage on the double if you please. I trust you had a nice journey, sir. Thank you very much for your letter. Please follow me.'

'Now just a minute,' Greg broke in, 'what the hell are you going to do about my bags!'

'You'll just have to wait . . .'

'No, no, Perkins, that's all right. Deal with Mr Hamilton

first, but don't take all day.' Jamie turned to Greg. 'I know how you must feel, old man – it's always happening to me.'

At least someone around here has got some manners, Greg thought, his natural good humour returning as he followed Hoskins across the quadrangle. Dark and rugged, he would have looked more like a ranch hand or lumberjack than the son of a leading Boston banker were it not for the deceptive air of wide-eyed innocence he wore about himself. To women, he was a cuddly teddy bear (fortuitously a very rich member of that species) that they needed to mother and could not wait to take to bed. And he adored them, all of them, was only too happy to indulge them, and if Frailty's name was Woman, then women were Greg's frailty.

The Hamiltons had arrived penniless in Boston shortly after the Civil War. Grandfather Hamilton had barely survived his passage to the New World in the stinking hold of an ancient Portuguese trawler but once in the Americas found little trouble in obtaining employment with the First National Bank of Boston. The rest was a classic realization of the American Dream and by the time Gregory Hamilton III was born the investment banking firm of Hamilton and Partners had become pre-eminent in East Coast financial circles and was turning its attention to the international markets. Greg had won a Rhodes scholarship to Oxford for his final undergraduate year and was being groomed to run the newly opened London office of the family bank.

''Ere we are sir,' Hoskins announced.

'Fine. Great. Hey!' The smile vanished from Greg's face as the young porter started down the stairs. 'Hold on a second,' he called after him, 'where are you going?'

'To the basement, sir. That's where your rooms are.'

Two floors above, Perkins was using an old iron key to open the door of a spacious, airy set of rooms.

'I trust you'll be comfortable Mr Stuart, sir. Your father occupied these rooms and so also I believe did Sir Clarence in his time.'

'Thank you Perkins, I'm sure they'll be more than adequate,' Jamie replied. 'Would you put the large bag in the bedroom and close the windows for me please?'

'Of course, Mr Stuart. If there's anything else I can do please let me know.'

There was an extra spring to Perkins's step as he marched down the stairs and bumped into his junior on the way back to the lodge.

'Look sharp young Hoskins, you haven't got all day! You'd better go to the station and get that American's luggage.'

'Yes Mr Perkins. By the way I don't think Mr 'Amilton's very happy with his rooms.'

'Oh he's not eh!' Perkins snorted. 'Bloody cheek. Arriving two days late without so much as a by your leave. Ha! He's lucky to have any rooms at all.'

The reason for James Stuart's late arrival had been the tardiness of the outgoing tenants in handing over the keys to the modest flat he had rented in London's Cheyne Row.

It was taken for granted that Jamie would follow in the family tradition by going up to Oxford but already at nineteen he found the attractions of the capital irresistible and intended to pass as much time there as he could. He had spent most of the twelve months since leaving Eton in the house that his father still kept in Westminster and during this time had come to accept certain inescapable truths about himself – the most basic of these being that he had no intention of fulfilling his father's hopes by entering politics, nor of devoting his life to the administration of Kilpurnie. Scotland bored him rigid, whereas in London he had discovered something that fascinated him. Something that satisfied his reckless, irresponsible nature in a way that nothing else could. Gambling.

Jamie was mesmerized by the whole concept of gambling: everything else paled by comparison. So far as women were concerned they, like a fine old cognac, had their place, a necessary luxury at the right time. And in this respect as well London had provided him with the perfect solution. He had a few months earlier made the acquaintance of one Lennie Landau, procurer and pimp to the aristocracy, whose cellar of bounteous beauties Jamie had tapped on a number of occasions.

Jamie was a gambler who had everything and more, for his grandfather, Sir Clarence Stuart, had possessed an extraordinary gift which Jamie, to a lesser extent, had inherited.

To put it quite simply – it would be presumptuous to approach it in any other way – Clarence had been able to read other people's minds. How he could do this he never understood and where it came from he did not know – the Stuarts were a very old family and neither he nor the archivists could shed any light on his problem. And problem it indeed became. He had no desire whatsoever to understand the thoughts of others. Such knowledge frightened him, not least because of the overwhelming responsibility he felt it placed upon his shoulders, but he was powerless to prevent or control it. In his student days his struggle to cope had manifested itself in harmless eccentricities and a fondness for alcohol, both of which mushroomed to alarming proportions. By the time he was forty he had given up the fight and was suffering from prolonged bouts of what can only be described as madness. He exchanged the privileges and shelter of society for the wet and windy streets of London. Here he was to be found wandering for weeks on end in an alcoholic stupor, dressed as a tramp. Ultimately, during one of his infrequent intervals of lucidity, he summoned up the strength to seek refuge and assistance within the walls of the Headingham Nursing Home.

In one respect, however, Clarence was lucky. Although his wife had died in childbirth, their son had survived and Archibald was everything his father was not. Reliable and hard-working, he had been a promising young Member of Parliament (and for a brief period even a junior Minister) before he had been tragically struck down by polio as he was approaching his prime. Finding he could no longer adequately represent his constituents at Westminster, he returned with wife and baby to the family home at Kilpurnie Castle and devoted himself to those responsibilities which his father had shunned.

It was one of those strange quirks of fate that James Stuart, the grandson, inherited the gift that Sir Archibald had not.

'Shit,' Greg muttered as he left his basement, which had turned out to be between the bicycle shed and the boiler room. He walked disgustedly through the college gates and wandered down the High Street in search of food. Glancing up at the gathering clouds he remembered somewhat ruefully that his new Burberry raincoat had failed to change trains with him at Reading, and stopping outside a cheerful teahouse, he entered. Jamie Stuart, at a corner table by the fire, was the only other customer.

'Hi.' Greg forced a smile. 'Mind if I join you?'

'Not at all. Pull up a chair – if you can find one!'

Greg laughed and sat down. 'I'm starving,' he said to the rosy-cheeked old waitress. 'What can I get to eat?'

'Well, dear, I can do you some nice cucumber sandwiches, a selection of fresh pastries and a lovely pot of tea.'

'Fine. Make that a double portion of everything but,' he winked, 'go easy on the tea.' Turning back to the table, he extended an enormous hand. 'Glad to know you, my name's Gregory Hamilton.'

'How do you do, I'm Jamie Stuart. Have you managed to get hold of your luggage yet?'

'No. It's supposed to be on the way but I don't think that son of a bitch Perkins is trying too hard. He's also given me the worst rooms in the place. Boy, have I had a lousy day!'

'Never mind,' Jamie replied. 'It's probably a good sign. After all, old man, things can only get better. It's always unlucky to win the first hand.'

'I sure hope so.' Greg sighed as his food arrived and they lapsed into silence while he ate.

Munching his way through the sandwiches, Greg examined his fellow student closely for the first time. Jamie Stuart was a couple of inches shorter than he was and, he assumed, about the same age – although he had one of those chiselled, aristocratic faces that was impossible to put an age on. He could have been anywhere from eighteen to thirty-five. He had straight, sandy-coloured hair cut unfashionably long. When he leaned forward it would occasionally fall into his blue eyes and he would carelessly flick it away with a toss of the head. The nose was aquiline and the mouth firm – with just the slightest hint of mockery which was heightened by the clipped manner in which he spoke. He was wearing a perfectly tailored, grey flannel suit with a cream shirt and plain blue knitted tie.

They chatted for about an hour, discovering they had many things in common. They found they shared an antipathy towards all things academic – and Greg wholeheartedly agreed that the fleshpots of London were infinitely more interesting than the cloistered walls of Oxford. He accepted with alacrity Jamie's offer to introduce him to Lennie Landau the following weekend and the frustrations of the previous twenty-four hours faded as he warmed to his new friend.

It was raining heavily when they began to walk back. Greg was reminded of Thanksgiving in Newport as they side-stepped the puddles forming at the junctions of the twisting, cobbled alleyways.

'Feeling homesick, old man?' Jamie looked into his eyes.

'Yes.' A startled Greg stopped. 'We've got a summer place in Rhode Island and I was just thinking about it. How did you know?'

Jamie did not answer but nodded mysteriously and strode on, hands deep inside his pockets, so that Greg was forced to run a couple of steps to catch up with him.

'Fancy a drink later, old man?'

'Sure,' Greg replied. 'Why don't you come down to the basement about nine o'clock and pick me up? You won't have any trouble finding me,' he added wryly.

'Right. See you later then.'

At a quarter to six the following morning a loud banging from the boiler room woke Gregory Hamilton. It was to be a regular occurrence and did nothing to help the headache that was lingering from the day before. Crawling out of bed, he forced himself into his daily routine of push-ups and pull-ups. He remembered from the notice board that the dining-hall did not open until eight o'clock and cast a curious eye over the gas ring and copper kettle nestling in a tiny alcove behind his sitting-room door. After several minutes of applying himself enthusiastically to the alien task of brewing tea he settled back in his armchair, rather pleased with his efforts despite a mouthful of lukewarm tealeaves.

In his far more comfortable rooms upstairs James Stuart had awoken sweating from his recurrent childhood nightmare. He threw open his windows, took several deep breaths and had a cold shower. Cursing the absence of his manservant, he shaved, taking slightly longer than usual to dress by virtue of the fact that his clothes had not been laid out for him. Contemptuously disregarding the gas ring, he set off for breakfast.

CHAPTER 2

'Of course Mr James . . . Absolutely . . . I'm very sorry . . . Of course . . . I'll sort it out and be round at your place within an hour. Yes of course . . . Goodbye Mr Stuart.'

'Christ Almighty,' Lennie Landau said to himself. 'That fucking Maltese slag! It had to be her.'

He angrily reached for the telephone again. 'Angela,' he snapped, 'I've got a problem. That stupid cow Marella ripped off those two punters last night and they're capable of causing a lot of trouble. What's her address? . . . 14 Gerrard Street . . . Right. I'm on my way there now. Don't go out until you hear from me.' He hung up and rushed straight out.

As a book is said to be judged by its cover, so Lennie's Jaguar described him perfectly. Intrinsically a beautiful piece of machinery, it was large, bulky and totally impractical for post-war London and the exigencies of petrol rationing. It had been Lennie's dream motor car ever since he had roamed the streets of Whitechapel as a small-time ponce, running errands for the local gangsters, and he had bought his second-hand model as soon as he had graduated to the smart hotels of the West End. It was his pride and joy. It had been resprayed to his order from a sedate midnight blue to a two-tone chocolate on the day he acquired it and, for a change this morning, the car did not clash with the colour of his suit. Hooting pompously at the cheaper vehicles around him, he squinted over the top of the steering-wheel and waited with impatience for the Oxford Street traffic to move.

He had always felt uncomfortable with Jamie Stuart – though why on earth he should be intimidated by an arrogant kid was beyond him – but Jamie had of late become a valued customer. The girls liked him and he always paid well. When he had called a few days earlier Lennie had gone out of his way to oblige. Especially since Stuart was introducing a rich American customer. But Lennie had felt uneasy: Claridge's was a difficult hotel to get his girls into and he had been forced to grease more than the usual number of palms; furthermore, reliable old Katy had dropped out at the last minute with the curse and Marella, whom he had never quite trusted, was the only good-looking girl available at such short notice.

Number 14 Gerrard Street was a Chinese restaurant with two bedsitters upstairs, neither of which responded to his ringing. Nobody in the restaurant spoke a word of English and, since Lennie's command of Chinese did not extend to the Cantonese dialect, he reluctantly scrambled back into his car and drove off in the direction of Cheyne Row.

On arrival he pulled up directly behind Jamie's Bentley and scampered up the stairs.

'Well Lennie?' Jamie asked curtly as he opened the door to his flat.

'Good morning Mr Stuart sir,' he panted. 'I'm afraid she's not in at the moment but don't worry guv', just give me a couple of days and I'll get it all back.'

'A couple of days? Out of the question! I'm returning to Oxford tomorrow and if I don't have my cigarette case with me I'm going straight to the police.'

'Please Mr Stuart, none of us wants a scandal. I just need a . . .'

'I don't give a damn about a scandal. And what's more, Lennie, unless I get Mr Hamilton's cufflinks and cash as well I'll make sure none of my friends ever comes near you again.'

'Now, now guv', calm down. I know where the girl lives, she's got to come home sooner or later. We can settle this nice and quietly without any fuss.'

'Right. You know where she lives, give me the address,'

Jamies ordered. 'I'm going round there myself after lunch.'

'Oh Mr James. I'd much rather you left it to me . . .'

'Don't argue with me Lennie,' Jamie snapped. 'Give me the bloody address!'

'OK guv', suit yourself,' Lennie said resignedly. 'It's 14 Gerrard Street in Soho, but I really wish . . .'

'Thank you Lennie,' Jamie interrupted. 'That will be all. I'm late for lunch with my mother. I'll be in touch. Goodbye.'

Greg also wished Jamie would let the matter drop. After all Lennie had a much better chance of getting their things back and what was the big deal about waiting a day or two anyway? He couldn't care less about those cufflinks and the lousy hundred pounds, but the last thing he could afford was any kind of scandal with Hamilton and Partners opening a new London branch. He could understand Jamie being upset about his grandfather's cigarette case, but he was overreacting, and Greg had told him so. In any case they'd had a helluva good night and the girls had both been knockouts and great fun. So much so that he had arranged for the redhead, Angela, to come back to Claridge's that afternoon while Jamie was lunching with his mother.

Angela McCarthy was a tall, voluptuous, green-eyed beauty with curly, flame-coloured hair and was in fact that rarest of species, the proverbial whore with the golden heart.

'Oh no!' she cried out when Greg told her of Jamie's intentions. 'We've got to stop him immediately. He won't stand a chance.'

'What? What are you talking about?' Greg asked in alarm.

'Marella lives with Maltese Charlie. He's dangerous. You've got to stop him before he gets hurt.'

'He's probably on his way there now.' Greg looked quickly at his watch and started pulling on his jacket. 'Do you know where she lives?'

'Yes.'

'Right. Let's go.'

The Soho bedsitter contained an unmade bed, two rickety chairs and a wardrobe with a broken door. Dirty cups full of cigarette stubs were everywhere and unwashed clothes littered the floor. It stank of urine, cheap perfume and Chinese cooking. Jamie had never seen a more sordid room.

A thickset swarthy man with several days' stubble on his chin was sitting on the bed picking his nose and listening.

'I don't know what you're talking about,' the girl said. 'Just get out of here and leave me alone.'

'Rubbish! I don't believe you and I can assure you the police won't either.'

'Hey rich boy.' The man spoke for the first time. 'I don't think you hear the lady. Get out! Now.'

'You keep out of this, it's none of your business.' Jamie's eyes turned icy grey.

'Oh but it is my business rich boy.' He jumped off the bed. 'Because her business is my business. Now I don't tell you again. Get out!'

'Don't threaten me, you lout.' Jamie recklessly pushed him away.

As if from nowhere a thin slither of highly polished steel appeared in Maltese Charlie's hand. It gleamed for a second in the dull light of the naked bulb before arching suddenly and viciously towards Jamie's throat. Jumping backwards, Jamie barely managed to escape the blade which slashed his jacket. He tripped and sprawled defenceless in the corner as his assailant moved in for the kill.

The cheap, plywood door of the bedsitting-room was insufficient to withstand the weight of an unpaid landlady, let alone a two-hundred-pound, ex-Harvard football player, and Greg hurtled through it like a thunderbolt. Hardly checking his stride, he delivered a blow to the man's wrist – the switchblade clattered harmlessly to the floor – and a haymaker to the jaw that smashed him into oblivion.

Jamie picked himself up and dusted himself off.

'Most impressive, old man. Nice to see the US Cavalry really does arrive in the nick of time!'

'Never mind the wisecracks,' Greg said shortly. 'Let's get the fuck out of here!'

16

'Just a moment, Greg.' He turned to the sullen prostitute. 'Well?'

'Over there.' She pointed to a handbag.

Jamie picked it up and, turning it upside down, scattered the contents all over the bed. He quickly found the case and links. He looked back at the girl.

'The money?'

'In his pocket,' she said reluctantly.

'For Christ's sake Jamie,' Greg exploded. 'Let's go!'

'Yes, yes, old man. Don't panic.' Jamie removed a wad of notes from the unconscious man's pocket and peeled off two white five-pound notes which he threw contemptuously on the floor.

'For the damage,' he said, and followed Greg down the stairs to where Angela was waiting.

Benjamin Disraeli once said: 'What we anticipate seldom occurs; what we least expect generally happens.' So it proved for Greg the next day. Having arranged to meet Jamie and his cousin Lady Lucinda Campbell-Stuart for a late lunch, he spent a leisurely morning at Claridge's relaxing over the Sunday newspapers and writing home as he had promised to his younger brother Morton and his little sister Jessica. He had a quick Bloody Mary at the bar before walking jauntily across Bond Street to the Coq d'Or restaurant on the corner of Stratton Street and Piccadilly.

'Morning old man, let me introduce my cousin Lucy. Gregory Hamilton . . . Lucy Campbell-Stuart.'

'How do you do.' Greg found himself shaking hands with quite simply the most beautiful girl he had ever seen.

'What are you drinking, Greg?' Jamie smiled.

'Bloody Mary please, extra spicey.'

'Jamie's just been telling me,' Lucy raised an eyebrow, 'that you both had a bit of excitement yesterday.'

'Well.' Greg coloured slightly. 'I suppose it was rather eventful.'

'Eventful! Oh come on, Greg, don't be so modest.' Lucy rested her hand on his. 'I hear you saved Jamie's life.'

'Well I wouldn't go that far.'

'It's all right, old man.' Jamie laughed. 'Lucy and I grew up together. We've no secrets from each other. I've told her the whole story.'

'Everything?'

'Yes Gregsy, you naughty thing,' she chided. 'You don't mind if I call you Gregsy do you? I think it rather suits you.'

'Not at all.' Greg flushed. 'Nobody else has ever called me that.'

'Right, that's settled then. Gregsy you've become and Gregsy you always will be. And, if I was you Gregsy, I would keep away from this rascal of a cousin of mine. He'll only lead you astray, he's been in trouble all his life. Look what's happened to you, and you haven't even known him a week!'

'What about you, Lucy, are you trouble too?'

'Me, Gregsy darling?' she pouted. 'You'll just have to find that out for yourself.'

You can bet your life on it honey, Greg thought to himself. What a fastastic girl: she's a dead ringer for Vivien Leigh. Suppose I'd better be a bit careful, though, she is Jamie's cousin.

'Anyone fancy going to see *Gone with the Wind* this afternoon?' Jamie asked lightly.

'I'd love to, darling, but I've arranged to see an exhibition with Valerie and Davina this afternoon.'

'How boring. What about you Greg?'

Greg looked at Jamie in disbelief. 'I've seen it three times, so I think I'll pass as well.'

Greg was completely thrown and eyed Jamie suspiciously for the remainder of lunch. Luckily his lack of conversation went unnoticed thanks to Lucy, who kept them both amused with the latest social gossip to which Greg anyway could contribute nothing. At the end of an excellent meal the boys decided to make an early start back to Oxford and Lucy readily accepted Greg's invitation to dinner during the coming week.

Jamie as usual drove like a lunatic and Greg – no stranger to fast cars – was more than a little relieved to reach the safety of his basement room. He spent the evening polishing up his essay on Adam Smith's *Wealth of Nations* and went to bed early.

At 5.45 a.m. the boiler as usual entered Greg's dreams. But on this particular morning, and in fact on many others to come, it took on a musical quality – becoming the rich beat of the double bass as he whirled Lucy around the dancefloor of El Morocco's in New York. They had just dined by candlelight at Delmonico's and were madly in love. The bass suddenly hit a false note and Greg woke abruptly, his attempts to recapture the dream failing with the boiler's gathering momentum.

'See you on Wednesday, Gregsy,' she had murmured, gently pecking his cheek. He lay back, luxuriating in that thought. He could hardly wait.

Over the next few days Jamie found it particularly difficult to involve himself in Oxford life. His thoughts also were elsewhere. There was no question that Angela McCarthy was a stunning-looking girl and, unlike most ladies of her persuasion, her enthusiasm for sex was obvious, but he had been far more impressed by the honesty and quick thinking which had undoubtedly saved his life. To Greg's amusement Jamie had resolved to instal her in his Cheyne Row flat as his mistress and had already agreed to meet her and Lennie there on Wednesday night to finalize the arrangements. He too could hardly wait.

It was this spirit of anticipation that led to their decision to cut Wednesday's lectures and drive up to London in the morning. They were having a cheese sandwich and a pint of beer at the King's Arms in Hollywell Street after a turgid tutorial.

'Sod it,' said Jamie. 'If we're skipping Wednesday anyway, let's go up on Tuesday night.'

'We can't, we've got that Freshman's dinner,' Greg replied, ordering another round of drinks.

'So what? It'll be bloody boring. I'm quite happy to pass on that as well.'

'But you'll know a lot of people there, won't you?'

'Yes, I was at school with half of them. That's precisely why

19

I don't want to go. Still, I suppose you're right, we'd better put in an appearance. I'd rather like to get into the university cricket team this summer and I've got to show willing. My grandfather was captain, you know.'

'Really?'

'Oh yes. And played for England a few times as well,' Jamie said proudly. 'Anyway, what sort of car are you going to buy?'

'A Bugatti. I've wanted one for years and I saw a couple in the showrooms in Piccadilly the other day.'

'Very smart, old man! Lucy will love it.'

'I'm not buying it just for Lucy you know,' Greg said, somewhat defensively. 'By the way, where do you suggest I take her for a late dinner?'

'Quaglino's,' Jamie answered. 'Leave it to me, I'll speak to Louis about it.'

'Thank you very much. Oh well, we'd better get moving,' Greg sighed. 'It's two o'clock and our next lecture starts in five minutes.'

Greg was infatuated with Lucy: he would have gone anywhere with her and he happily forsook his preference for the Windmill in favour of Covent Garden and a professed interest in the works of Puccini. Their dinner at Quaglino's was an unqualified success and then they danced until the small hours to the music of Cole Porter and George Gershwin. Lucy was wearing a simple black evening dress which matched her raven hair perfectly, offsetting her white china-doll complexion. With Greg on top form and Lucy at her most effervescent, the evening was only slightly marred by the unwelcome intrusion of Gavin Blunt, a suave, contemptuous young Englishman who did not endear himself to Greg.

'Gavvers darling, you look marvellous. How was the South of France? Do you know Gregory Hamilton? He's a friend of Jamie's from Oxford. Gregory Hamilton . . . Gavin Blunt.'

'Pleased to meet you.' Greg stood up.

'No doubt.' Blunt ignored the proffered hand. 'Lucy my dear, come and have a dance.'

'I'd love to,' she replied, 'if Gregsy doesn't mind.'

'From the look of him I'm sure "Gregsy" would welcome the rest.' Blunt smiled disarmingly and whisked Lucy off to the dancefloor with an irritating familiarity. Wearing an immaculate dinner jacket, light on his feet, he had obviously danced with her many times before.

Outside her parents' house in Eaton Square Lucy had affectionately avoided Greg's overtures as she gently removed his arms from around her shoulders, brushed her lips against his and slipped out of the red Bugatti.

'Darling Gregsy, thank you for a magical evening,' she whispered. 'Give Jamie my love. See you soon.'

There is an oft-quoted saying, emanating from the original coffee houses of the City of London, that 'there is nothing sharper than a Blunt in a hole'. And the Blunts had been in a hole for a very long time.

Blunt and Company was one of those great British trading-houses that had reached its peak during the height of the Empire but had failed to adjust to a changing world. The male members of the family had of late been renowned more for their swashbuckling style and dark, flashing good looks than their business acumen. They had survived on a combination of arrogance, credit and treacherous dealing and it was rumoured that E.W. Hornung's society jewel thief, Raffles, had been inspired by Gavin's father, the rakish Sebastian Blunt. The son had inherited the family looks and style and succeeded in indulging his expensive tastes by supplementing a meagre income with his superior gaming skills. Educated with Jamie at Eton, he had turned down a scholarship to Oxford to become a professional gambler and shortly after returning Lucy to her table had left Quaglino's for Crockford's, the famous St James's club founded some hundred years earlier by the former fishmonger William Crockford. His erstwhile schoolchum was propping up the bar.

'Evening Jamie, how are you?'

'Couldn't be better, old man. Have a drink . . . George, a champagne cocktail for Mr Blunt.'

'Thanks. Playing poker tonight?'

'Yes,' Jamie replied. 'But I'm not staying late, I've got to get back to Oxford tonight.'

'How's it going up there? I dropped into Quag's earlier and saw Lucy with some ghastly American who I find hard to believe is a friend of yours.'

'Well believe it then, he's a very nice chap.'

'Yes dear boy, I'm sure he is.' Gavin smiled condescendingly. 'Anyway I hear you had a big win the other night. Hugo Robard was furious that you called his bluff with a pair of fours. He said that only a beginner or a maniac would have played like that.'

'Huh.' Jamie shrugged. 'An obvious bluff.'

'Excuse me gentlemen, good evening.' Viktor, the *chef de partie*, came up to them. 'The poker game is about to begin. Would you like to take your seats please?'

'Thank you Viktor,' Gavin said. 'We're on our way.'

Moments later Jamie was in seat number six at the horseshoe-shaped table and, lighting a cigarette, surveyed with anticipation the scene that confronted him. His ears tingled to the various sounds: chips clicking as the inspectors scurried around the table, cards whirring as they were shuffled by the dealer, and ice tinkling as the tail-coated waiters served drinks from silver trays. Running his fingertips along the green baize in front of him, Jamie studied the opposition, his thoughts returning to his last visit.

Lucy's unpleasant uncle, the Hon. Hugo Robard, receiving more than his fair share of luck, had dominated the table all evening. The game, as tonight, had been five-card stud and on a crucial hand Hugo had made the largest bet of the evening. Jamie, who had held indifferent cards for some hours, had ended up with only a pair of fours but without a moment's hesitation had called the bet.

'Damn you,' Robard had spluttered. 'If you can call, you win. You must have more bloody money than sense, young Stuart – any pair would have beaten you.'

The game that night was uneventful and ended early. Jamie and the rest of the players had won modestly at the unlikely expense of Gavin Blunt who, not given to losing graciously, unsuccessfully attempted to persuade them to play on for another hour.

'Sorry Gavin, you know I can't stay. I've got an early tutorial.'

'Oh well,' Blunt said resignedly. 'I suppose I'll have to win it back from Hugo at backgammon – shouldn't think he even knows how to spell tutorial!'

Chapter 3

By the end of Jamie's second week at Oxford Angela was firmly ensconced in his London flat. It had cost him far more than he expected to 'sever her contract' – Lennie Landau was in a class of his own in negotiations of this sort – but he was nevertheless pleased with the outcome.

Angela McCarthy was the first child of a large, close-knit family. Her mother, a warm, gentle woman, had seen her own true artistic talents stifled by the necessity of having to work as a seamstress. Her father was a handsome, hard-working, hard-living, Irish stevedore with one major failing – if failing it be – a powerful libido that he found impossible to control. Angela had inherited her mother's nature and the weakness of her father. His fierce pride could not be contained when his favourite daughter unexpectedly won a scholarship to the Bermondsey Art College.

Night after night, in the pubs of London's dockland, he would regale his workmates with tales of his little girl's progress. It was cruelly ironic that big Joe McCarthy, while weaving his way towards the local whorehouse after one such drunken evening in the Watery Grave, should lose his footing and plunge into the murky depths of the harbour he knew so well. His death ended Angela's dreams of a career as an interior decorator and she was forced to leave art school in order to help her mother support her five younger brothers and sisters. It was even more ironic that after a succession of poorly paid jobs in seedy restaurants, she should come upon the good offices of Lennie Landau and thus in one fell stroke solve her family's financial difficulties and discover employment to which she was ideally suited.

With her innate good taste Angela had completely transformed the functional one-bedroomed apartment into a cosy love-nest of warm colours and comfortable furnishings and it became the first real home of his own that Jamie had ever had. Over the months that followed his life settled into an enviable routine. All his weekends were spent with Angela in London and he came down at least once during the week to play poker which, he had quickly realized, was the game most suited to his natural gift and in which he felt he had a built-in advantage.

Though Jamie did not dislike Oxford, he considered it an extension of public school with a little more freedom and, apart from Greg and one or two old friends, he preferred, as usual, his own company. He treated his studies in much the same cavalier fashion as he had done at school – after all, what earth-shattering difference to his future could a degree possibly make? – and did just enough work to pass muster. He was looking forward to the summer term and the beginning of the cricket season.

Greg, on the other hand, loved Oxford life. With his characteristic zest he hurled himself into the multifarious activities that the university had to offer. He debated vigorously at the Union, was a natural at rugby football (winning a place in the Christchurch XV), played the saxophone energetically in a makeshift jazz band, and even attempted on several occasions to enrol in the dramatics society – although Thespian he was not! His only cause for disappointment was that his relationship with Lucy had progressed no further. He had seen her once more for dinner and had found her as tantalizing as ever but she had politely declined the numerous invitations to visit him for the weekend and always seemed to have a prior engagement. Not one to sit around moping, Greg turned his attention to Oxford and soon became the darling of the female set.

26

One day towards the end of term Greg, unable as usual to attract the attention of Clive Perkins, was about to ring the desk bell in the Porter's Lodge for the third time when his ears pricked up at the mention of the name Stuart. The porters were sitting by the fire in the back room and Perkins was settled in his brown leather armchair warming his port in his hands, regarding with disdain his junior's efforts to seal the envelopes of the college Christmas cards.

'Look sharp young 'Oskins, you've got three hundred stamps to go on after that and you haven't yet collected my Christmas box from the wine merchants.'

'I'm doing my best Mr Perkins, I'll soon be finished. But please, Mr Perkins, tell me, what do you mean by Mr James taking after his grandfather?'

'Never you mind 'Oskins, just get on with your work.' Perkins lit his pipe. 'What Sir Clarence got up to is none of your business. I heard the story from old Mr Trotter and 'e would have boxed my ears if I'd asked him questions like that. 'Course he was only junior porter to my grandfather Mr Oswald then, but from what 'e used to tell me Sir Clarence was famous for his eccentricity.'

'Electricity Mr Perkins?' The earnest young lad looked up.

'I said eccentricity you numskull! Where was you educated? Apparently he was a bit too fond of the old whisky and them ladies of the night. Rumour has it that he did strange things when he was drunk – 'e would take ten of them so-called ladies to tea at the Ritz Hotel in London where he would insist on the orchestra playing "Tea for Two" ten times in a row whilst 'e danced with each one of them.'

'Blimey Mr Perkins. No wonder they called him "Fruit-cake Clarence".'

'*Sir* Clarence to you 'Oskins, just remember your place!' Perkins snapped. 'I'll have you know that *Sir* Clarence was one of the best opening batsmen ever to have received an Oxford cap – not that he ever wore it.'

'What's that Mr Perkins, why not?'

''Cause 'e'd insist on wearing a bloody great top hat when he was playing, that's why. Looked like a bleedin' Mad Hatter running between the wickets so they say.'

'Crikey, a top hat Mr Perkins? Well I never.'

'You mark my words, there's a bit of old "Fruit-cake" in our Mr James. He's keeping some tart in London and I've even heard she's living in his place there – God knows what his poor father would say if he knew.'

'Yes Mr Perkins,' the youngster said excitedly. 'And Mr James was captain of the Eton cricket team.'

'Precisely young 'Oskins, precisely. Anyway, enough of your idle chatter or you'll be here till Christmas licking those bloomin' stamps. I suppose I'd better see who's out front.'

But Greg had already left. Deep in thought, he strolled back to his rooms, shivering slightly as he recalled Jamie's words over that first lunch at the Coq d'Or – 'I'm afraid I seem to be following in my grandfather's footsteps.' Though not significant at the time, he remembered that a momentary flicker of fear had seemed to cloud Lucy's sparkling eyes.

Chapter 4

Kilpurnie Castle had been the ancestral home of the Stuarts since before the Norman incursions and like any self-respecting castle it revelled in myths and fables, some more true than others. One such tale, to which many historians had given credence, was that Bonnie Prince Charlie spent the night after Culloden in the now derelict West Tower before fleeing to France. Less veracity is placed in the story that he shared his bed with a local lass, but that in no way prevented the rival claims of the villagers as to the identity of the girl – each family's argument strengthening with the generations.

Kilpurnie Station had been built by Jamie's great-grandfather in the middle of the nineteenth century and a track had been laid from Inverness to the most easterly point of the twenty-five-thousand-acre estate where liveried footmen would await the arrival of weekend guests. Much used by Clarence in his heyday to transport his dubious female friends from London, it had fallen into relative disuse since Archibald's illness.

Greg jumped over the thick, unruly weeds and on to the crumbling planks that served as a platform while the solitary porter struggled with Lucy's luggage. Turning back, he placed both hands around Lucy's tiny waist and lifted her from the carriage, depositing her safely on the platform. They walked over to where Jamie was engaged in conversation with a serious-looking greying man in his mid-thirties.

'Greg, I'd like you to meet Sedgewicke – my manservant and my friend.'

'How do you do sir.' The Scottish burr was faint but recognizable. 'Welcome to Kilpurnie. Lady Lucinda, how lovely to see you again. I trust His Lordship and the Countess are well?'

'Hello Sedgewicke.' Lucy kissed him affectionately on the cheek. 'Mummy and Daddy are fine, thank you. You're looking very well yourself.'

'Right, all aboard,' Jamie said. 'Sedgewicke, you know you're coming back for Mr Blunt tomorrow morning?'

'Yes Mr James.'

Forty minutes later they rounded the last corner of the four-mile driveway and were greeted by three majestic wolfhounds that ran beside them barking excitedly. The vehicle crossed the drawbridge and they entered the pebbled courtyard where the great dogs almost knocked Jamie over in their enthusiasm to get at him. Although he was accustomed to the palatial residences of Newport, Greg was impressed by the grandeur of his surroundings. The gigantic, unyielding battlements towered over him as he walked through the immense, iron-studded doors into the Great Hall. Stunned by the enormity of it all, he stood gazing up at the massive arched ceiling high above him and the ornate minstrel's gallery that ran the length of the hall. The walls abounded with militaria of all kinds – swords and shields, maces and muskets, daggers and dirks.

'This way Mr Hamilton.' Sedgewicke broke into his reverie. Greg followed him up the great staircase, past the polished suits of armour, and was ushered into a modern, comfortable suite of guest rooms.

'Dinner, sir, will be served at half-past eight and Mr James asks that you join him and Sir Archibald in the library for drinks at eight o'clock.'

'Thank you Sedgewicke.'

While Greg and Lucy were being shown to their rooms Jamie had gone straight to his father's private study where both his parents were waiting for him. He knocked once and entered. His father looked frailer than ever. A tartan blanket was wrapped around the shrunken body and he was sitting in a wheelchair, his back to the blazing log fire. Jamie's mother was standing at her husband's side, a loving arm placed protectively around his narrow shoulders. The signs of strain and fatigue in her face were unmistakable and Jamie was shocked. She had aged ten years in the few months since he had last seen her.

'Hello Mummy.' He kissed her on both cheeks as she hugged him tightly. 'It's nice to be home again.'

'Welcome back, darling, the place seems so empty without you,' she said, holding back the tears. 'Now I know your father wants to have a chat with you so I'll run along and make sure Lucy's settling in all right. Please come and see me in my dressing-room when you have finished. I want to hear all your news. See you later, Archie.' She kissed her husband on the forehead and left the room.

'How are you, Father? You're looking fine.'

'That's kind of you my boy.' The voice was still firm. 'Sit down. How's Oxford treating you? Enjoying yourself?'

'Enormously Father, thank you. They've even given me your old rooms.'

'Ah, Perkins still there is he?'

'Very much so.' Jamie laughed. 'One of my house guests can attest to that!'

'Good, good. Best days of your life you know – corny but true. Anyway,' he hesitated for a moment, 'I'm afraid I've got some bad news for you. No easy way to say this, my boy. The doctors tell me that I've got no more than six months left to live and there are certain things we must discuss.'

Jamie closed his eyes as the blood drained from his face and, suddenly feeling very cold, he reached for a cigarette, his fingers trembling. He had always known it was merely a question of time but that did nothing to soften the blow. Somehow he had always expected a miracle.

'Come on Jamie,' Archibald said quietly, 'we've all got to face it sometime or other. In the words of Byron, "'tis not so difficult to die". Now,' his voice became firm again, 'I don't

31

want you to interrupt your studies but your first responsibility is to your mother. I am very worried about her. She will need all the support you can give her.'

Jamie nodded dumbly.

'The second thing I want to talk to you about is your future. As you know, after Oxford I expect you to go into politics. I've spoken to both Winston and Anthony and they assure me there'll always be a place for you in the Tory Party.'

'Yes, Father.' He nodded again.

'The third matter is a little more delicate. It will surprise you to learn that, contrary to what I have always told you, your grandfather Clarence is still alive. It was his wish that you were never to be told and I respected it, but under the circumstances you must know the truth. You are no doubt aware that my father always had difficulty in coping with the pressures of everyday life. Fortunately, while his mind was not yet totally unbalanced he had the strength of character to admit himself to an institution. You will find that a special trust fund has been set aside for his maintenance and support. Needless to say you will replace me as trustee, but you must never try to see him unless he contacts you. Again that is his wish.'

'Very well, Father.' Jamie's mind was reeling.

'Finally Jamie, you too must have a son and heir. Enjoy your youth by all means but do not leave it too long. The entire future of not only this family but hundreds of others on Kilpurnie is in your hands. I know you will not let them down.

Now, I suggest you go and cheer your mother up. Give her the latest London gossip, that'll amuse her. Take her mind off things.'

Greg arrived at the library promptly at eight o'clock and was introduced by Jamie to his father. Sir Archibald was delighted to discover that he had met Greg's father in New York on a political visit many years ago and Greg was outlining the family's plans for the new London office when Lucy and the Robards joined them.

'Gregsy, let me introduce my Uncle Hugo and Aunt Diana.'

Greg smiled politely at the fat, jowly man with his plump,

over-dressed wife. Moments later the group was complete with the entrance of Lady Stuart, whom Greg had already met in London, and the Duke and Duchess of Alderton.

William Alderton was Leader of the House of Lords and looked the part, with his erect military bearing and patrician manner. He had been Archibald's mentor in Parliament and was an urbane, witty man with a dry sense of humour. Greg liked him immediately, but his young wife Edwina was really something special. Tall and statuesque in a figure-hugging dress that left nothing to the imagination, her blatant sexuality was overpowering and, like a moth to a flame, Greg found himself irresistibly drawn to her. By comparison Lucy suddenly seemed a little girl.

Edwina eyed him hungrily up and down. 'Lucy's description didn't begin to do you justice. Are all Americans as big and strong as you?'

During dinner Lucy hardly touched her food. As far as she was concerned, Edwina Alderton was nothing more than a common little actress – and a third-rate one at that – who had tricked the old Duke into marrying her. She dressed and behaved like one of Jamie's whores, the only difference being that she gave it away free. How did she have the gall to wear that dress? The slut couldn't keep her greedy hands off Greg, pawing him every two minutes under the table. How on earth her stupid old husband didn't notice was beyond belief. Even poor Uncle Archie was embarrassed. And look at that hypocrite Greg chatting away to everybody as though nothing was happening and loving every minute of it!

As soon as dinner was over the ladies retired to the drawing-room, leaving the men to their port and cigars. Lucy, determined to hide her jealousy and bored by the thought of women's tittle-tattle, excused herself and went to bed, claiming fatigue from the journey. Jamie, who had not said a word all evening, slipped off to the library alone, armed with the brandy decanter. A few minutes later he was joined by a bored Hugo Robard: 'How about some backgammon, Jamie?'

'Yes, all right Hugo.' At least, he thought, it'll take my mind off things. But it didn't take his mind off what his father had told him and he lost rather heavily before eventually going to bed at around two o'clock. At more or less the same time Greg's bedroom was entered by Edwina, Duchess of Alderton.

Breakfast the next morning was a somewhat fraught affair. Jamie, in a faded tweed suit and woollen tie, was the first to come down. Severely shaken by the conversation with his father, he had found sleep difficult despite the large amount of brandy he had consumed. His nightmare too had been particularly vivid. He had got up at the crack of dawn and, to clear his head, had taken the dogs for a long, vigorous walk. He was sitting at the table smoking his fifth cigarette of the day when a radiant Edwina, her unpinned auburn hair loose about her shoulders came gliding into the room. She picked up a glass of orange juice and kissed him affectionately on the nose as she passed. Shortly afterwards Greg entered, proudly displaying the new check jacket he had recently commissioned from Jamie's tailor in Savile Row. Helping himself to a huge plate of steaming porridge, he sat at the opposite end of the table from Edwina and began to eat ravenously. Little conversation took place and Greg was halfway through his eggs and bacon when a breathless Lucy, fresh from her morning ride and resplendent in her boots and breeches, joined them.

'Sleep well, Edwina?' She glared at Greg who was stifling a yawn.

'Divinely, this Highland air does wonders for me.'

'Careful you don't overdo it. You can catch a nasty cold in the chest,' Lucy said bitchily.

'Well darling,' Edwina purred, looking pointedly at Lucy's little breasts, 'that's certainly something you don't have to worry about!'

'Now, now girls,' Jamie intervened with mock severity as a scarlet-faced Greg nearly dropped his coffee.

'Morning all!' An ebullient Hugo Robard burst in. 'Fancy anything at Ayr today Jamie, or would you rather stick to backgammon? By the way, I give poker lessons too!'

'Really?' Jamie smiled good-naturedly. 'I look forward to my first one. What I particularly need to learn from you, Hugo, is the art of the bluff!'

'Of course my boy, I'm famous for it.' Robard beamed, the sarcasm totally lost on him.

Gavin Blunt arrived in time for lunch and then went off to the races at Ayr with Hugo Robard. Under the circumstances this was something of a relief to Jamie, who was finding it difficult to play host. He asked Lucy, in whom he had as usual confided everything, to look after his guests and was constantly at his father's side. Lucy did her job very well. Greg's weekend was spent in bed with Edwina whenever possible and his public appearances were largely confined to the dining-room. As a result, Lucy was left with Gavin, whom she seduced immediately upon his return from the races, an event which she made quite sure did not pass unnoticed by Greg.

Jamie's mind was in a turmoil. Although he was very different from his father, he loved him and could not accept the fact that Archibald would soon be gone. Moreover the news about his grandfather had greatly disturbed him. As a boy Jamie had been told that Clarence had died young. Strangely he was the only member of the Stuart family whose portrait did not hang above the great staircase and Jamie had never even seen a picture of him. He had always heard that Clarence had been an eccentric but somehow since childhood he had known that this was merely the manifestation of the gift that he, Jamie, had inherited. To learn therefore that his grandfather had been insane for the last twenty-five years terrified him. Was this why he could not face up to his responsibilities? Would he too end his days raving mad in some lunatic asylum?

CHAPTER 5
CROCKFORD'S, LONDON, 1950

The film of perspiration clinging to the forehead of the Hon. Hugo Robard was particularly noticeable that night. Fear gripped his throat as with clammy hands he toyed with the pearl-grey plaques of unusually high value piled in front of him.

On his left in seat number two sat his guest, the sinister shipping magnate Spiros Virakis, through whom Hugo was hoping to bolster his precarious finances by securing the directorship of the Greek's London operation. Reputed to have won his first oil tanker in a card game at the age of twenty-one, Virakis – forty years later – was now the owner of Europe's largest fleet. His peasant cunning, enormous ego and contempt for business ethics were hidden beneath a powerful personality which had removed all obstacles from his path.

Seat number three was occupied by the amateur sportsman and habitual plunger Lord Jeremy Hunter, whose extravagant style of betting Hugo found extremely disconcerting. Next to him was a loud, gross American industrialist named Freddie Singleton. He was not a popular player and got on everyone's nerves with his ponderous style and constant stream of fatuous wisecracks, addressed chiefly to his fellow American, broadcaster and *bon viveur* Larry Collins.

Hugo shifted uneasily in his chair. His eyes alighted upon

the chiselled face in seat number six of Sir James Stuart, whose run of success over the past three years was bewildering. Time after time Hugo had watched Jamie make or call bets which defied all logic.

The remaining player, Gavin Blunt, was a perpetual thorn in Hugo's flesh. Underneath Blunt's languid manner was a razor-sharp brain and nerve of steel that made him a formidable opponent. Although in his early twenties, he was the only professional at the table.

The game was draw poker and since the cards were evenly distributed, there were no spectacular clashes in the first few hours. Virakis and Hunter had set the tone by their aggressive betting and the only significant loser was Freddie Singleton who, though bemoaning his luck, had constantly overplayed his hands. Shortly before two in the morning Singleton attempted a sizeable bluff with two modest pairs on which he had failed to improve. He was instantly raised by Gavin Blunt who was holding nothing more than a pair of sixes. Conceding the hand with bad grace, Singleton demanded a change of cards and dealer which, he loudly predicted, would change his luck.

'Certainly monsieur,' said the ever-attentive Viktor. 'Perhaps gentlemen, a short break would be in order while we attend to it.'

All the players, save one, remained at the table while Paul Bishop, the incoming dealer, unwrapped the new deck, displaying the cards for inspection. Gavin Blunt returned a few moments later and the game recommenced.

Hugo, who had played conservatively all evening and had won only a few minor pots, then picked up the best hand he had seen so far – three kings, the seven of spades and the ten of hearts. Committed to opening the betting, he nervously placed two one-thousand-pound chips in the centre of the table.

'Passo.' Virakis pushed his cards towards the dealer.

'Call and raise,' drawled Jeremy Hunter.

'Thank you My Lord,' said Bishop. 'That will be five thousand pounds to you Mr Singleton . . . Mr Singleton passes . . . to you Mr Collins . . . Mr Collins passes . . . to you Sir James . . . thank you Sir James. Gentlemen, Sir James

38

calls . . . to you Mr Blunt . . . Mr Blunt passes. Do you wish to call Lord Hunter's raise of three thousand pounds, Mr Robard? Thank you Mr Robard. Gentlemen, Mr Robard calls the raise. The pot stands at fifteen thousand pounds. Cards gentlemen please?'

Damn and blast, thought Hugo, discarding two cards. Hunter could be raising me on anything and God only knows what that maniac Stuart's got. He watched impatiently as Hunter took no cards and Jamie changed two. Bastard's been dealt a pat hand, either a flush or a bloody straight, and Stuart must have three of a kind. A sudden wave of elation swept over him and his worries evaporated as he picked up the fourth king. Now, he thought greedily, if Hunter's got his flush and Stuart makes a full house, I've got them both by the balls.

'Mr Robard to bet, gentlemen.' Bishop looked at Hugo who, hoping to lay a trap for Hunter, said calmly: 'Check to the raiser.'

'My Lord?'

'I bet the pot, fifteen thousand pounds.'

'Thank you My Lord, the bet is fifteen thousand pounds to you Sir James.'

It was later argued throughout the gaming-clubs of Europe that this particular hand – and not the more obvious final hand of that memorable night – was the one that firmly established Sir James Stuart as an exceptional poker player.

Jamie had indeed started with three of a kind. He now drew the fourth jack. Ignoring Hunter's bet, he stared penetratingly at Hugo Robard for several seconds.

'I pass.'

'Sir James passes. Fifteen thousand pounds to you, Mr Robard sir.'

Although Hugo was disappointed at Jamie's withdrawal he could still barely contain himself. 'Your fifteen thousand and raise fifteen thousand.'

'Thank you Mr Robard, another fifteen thousand pounds to you My Lord.'

Jeremy Hunter chuckled and held up his arms in mock surrender. 'All right Hugo, I believe you, you win.'

The matter would have ended there and no one would have

been any the wiser had Hugo Robard not been an incorrigible braggart.

'Too bloody right I win!' he snorted, turning over his four kings. 'You obviously had a flush Jeremy, and Jamie was damned lucky he didn't make his full house. Still, no one could have played it better, what?' He gloated while Bishop counted out the pot of forty-five thousand pounds.

'I suppose I was rather lucky wasn't I?' Jamie's eyes twinkled as he revealed his four jacks.

A stunned silence descended over the table, broken only by the spluttering of an outraged, purple Hugo Robard.

'Now you've just proved you're out of your mind, Stuart. How on earth can you pass a hand like that?'

'My dear Hugo,' Virakis interjected, 'I think Sir James finds you a little transparent; now perhaps – with your kind permission of course – we may continue to play?'

'*Sic transit gloria mundi*,' quipped Blunt to a confused and chastened Robard.

As Bishop's deft fingers dealt the succeeding hands the tense atmosphere became further charged – each player's instincts sharpened by the realization that the cards were now red-hot. No one appreciated this more than Spiros Virakis and he continued to force the stakes still higher in an attempt to bully the rest of the table into submission. These aggressive tactics were welcomed by Gavin Blunt who, when confronted by a fifty-thousand-pound bet from Larry Collins on three nines, chose to produce the queen he had palmed during the interval to make an inside straight and steal the largest pot so far.

The hand that was to become a topic of conversation for many years to come, and ultimately brought this celebrated game to its abrupt conclusion, began at five past three with a carefree opening bet of ten thousand pounds by Jeremy Hunter on a solitary pair of kings.

Jamie had been losing consistently. He found himself holding two aces with two queens and quietly raised Hunter a further ten thousand pounds. The betting now turned to a hitherto frustrated Virakis, lying in wait with the remaining pair of aces coupled with two eights.

'Mr Blunt and Mr Robard pass . . . the bet is twenty

thousand pounds to you, Mr Virakis.'

'I call the twenty thousand pounds and raise the pot,' rasped the Greek.

'Yes sir. Gentlemen, Mr Virakis has raised fifty thousand pounds. The bet is sixty thousand pounds to you, My Lord?'

'I rather think not.'

'Lord Hunter passes . . . the bet to you Sir James is fifty thousand pounds.'

'I call.'

'Thank you Sir James. Gentlemen, cards please. Mr Virakis?'

As so often happens prior to a kill, a small crowd of gamblers materialized from nowhere, elbowing each other for space around the red satin rope that surrounded the poker table. Waiters were momentarily distracted from their duties and froze hypnotized. Viktor's deep voice rose above the excitement, insisting upon silence.

'One card.'

'Thank you sir. Gentlemen, Mr Virakis changes one card. Do you wish to change, Sir James?'

'One card.'

'Thank you sir. Gentlemen, both players have changed one card. The pot stands at one hundred thousand pounds and the betting is with you, Mr Virakis.'

The Greek thoughtfully stroked the third eight between his thumb and forefinger. He had made his full house.

'I bet the pot – one hundred thousand pounds I believe?'

Gasps of amazement burst from the spectators and all eyes turned to the young Scottish aristocrat who was making a great performance of lighting his cigarette.

'Thank you sir,' the dealer said with a slight tremor. 'The bet is one hundred thousand pounds to you, Sir James.'

Even Viktor, the official doyen of countless card parties in the Winter Palace of his native St Petersburg, was unprepared for what was to follow.

'Call and raise the pot, three hundred thousand pounds I believe.'

The silence was deafening and Jamie remained impassive, seemingly oblivious to the fact he had just made the largest bet ever seen in a London Club.

'Thank you Sir James.' Paul Bishop could hardly speak. 'Mr Virakis, the bet to you is thr—'

'I also have ears!' barked the suddenly defensive ship-owner. 'With your permission, Meester Dealer, I will reflect on this situation.'

Virakis was already regretting his one-hundred-thousand-pound bet. But, not one to throw good money after bad, his analytical mind was dispassionately examining the combinations by which he could be defeated. He had no doubt that Jamie had made at least a full house and quickly determined that, although three aces was impossible and three kings or queens unlikely by virtue of Hunter's opening bet, his own hand was still eminently beatable. Added to this was the fact that he had earlier seen evidence of Jamie's ultra-cautious nature when the latter had inexplicably passed four jacks.

'No, Meester Dealer, passo. Passo. I don't call. Young man,' he forced a sickly smile, 'may the loser have the privilege of seeing the winning hand?'

'If you insist.' Jamie shrugged. 'But I wouldn't advise it.'

'I do insist.' Virakis was no longer smiling. He reached across the table and overturned Jamie's cards to reveal his original two pairs and the three of diamonds.

All hell broke loose. The Greek, shaking with rage, spat a stream of obscenities at Jamie, deliberately kicked over a drinks table laden with glasses and stormed from the room followed by a worried Hugo Robard.

'Viktor.' Lord Hunter stood up. 'Disgraceful behaviour. I never wish to see that man in this club again.'

'Of course My Lord. I will attend to it.'

The *chef de partie* moved over to an expressionless Jamie and in low, almost paternal, tones said: 'Congratulations, Sir James, on a great win. A historic win. But, with the greatest respect, a very dangerous bluff.'

'Perhaps Viktor, but then you see I *knew* he had a small full house.'

CHAPTER 6

'Wake up, Jamie, wake up . . . Greg's on the telephone. He says it's urgent.'

'What time is it? . . . God I feel awful!'

'It's 4.30 in the afternoon.' Angela handed him the receiver.

'Yes Greg,' Jamie groaned. 'What is it? What's the problem?'

'I've got to talk to you Jamie.' The usually cheerful voice was strained. 'Can you make dinner tonight?'

'Yes, all right. Eight o'clock at the Turf Club?'

'Perfect, see you later.' Greg hung up.

Jamie groaned again and reached gratefully for the pot of steaming coffee that Angela's maid had left on a tray beside the bed. The pungent aroma and bitter taste of the freshly ground beans revived him and, lighting his first cigarette, he felt his mind returning to the celebrations of the previous night. He had gone from Crockford's, with Jeremy Hunter and Gavin Blunt, to the 400 Club, where they had drunk a great deal and then, at Gavin's suggestion, had ended up at the luxurious Duke Street bordello which Jamie had secretly financed on Angela's behalf shortly after leaving Oxford. 'Knaves', under the astute management of Lennie Landau, had rapidly become the most exclusive 'house' in London – famed for the quality and enthusiasm of its young ladies and the lavish hospitality of its enchanting hostess, who had converted the whole of the top floor of the large Mayfair house into her personal penthouse flat.

'Angela, I must get home. Ask Lennie to bring the car around.' Jamie struggled out of bed and began to dress. 'Are the others still here?'

'Hunter is. He's just ordered a huge breakfast and the two Chinese sisters.'

Jamie nodded. 'What about Gavin?'

She hesitated, remembering the tearful and badly bruised French girl whom she had spent the afternoon consoling. With an effort she reminded herself that Blunt was Jamie's friend.

'No. He left around lunchtime.'

'Oh yes, he said something about going to Goodwood. Goodbye darling.' He kissed her on the lips. 'See you soon.'

'Well, well, Sir James.' Lennie glowed with vicarious pride. 'I hear you had a bit of a win last night. Played a real blinder! You're the toast of London, guv'. Congratulations.'

'Thank you Lennie, I was rather lucky.'

'They say luck had nothing to do with it, guv'. As I understand it you turned that nasty little Greek inside out.'

'Well let's put it this way,' Jamie chuckled, 'he won't forget that hand in a hurry!' They drew up outside the wrought-iron gates of Number Six Berkeley Square. 'Cheerio Lennie, keep up the good work.'

Upon entering the house Jamie was confronted by the disapproving figure of Sedgewicke who followed him into the study.

'Good afternoon Sir James.'

'Hello Sedgewicke. I'd like a light whisky and soda, and can you organize a chicken sandwich? Have Louise draw me a bath. I'll be dining at the Turf with Mr Hamilton tonight, please lay out my clothes. Any messages?'

'Nothing urgent Sir James. Lady Lucinda passed by to discuss the flowers for tomorrow and McClintock telephoned from Kilpurnie – he is very worried about a new outbreak of foot and mouth disease.'

'Honestly Sedgewicke, what the hell does he expect me to

do about it?' Jamie said irritably. 'Tell him to contact the vet in Inverness and sort it out. That's what he's paid for.'

'Very well, Sir James; is there anything else?' Sedgewicke sighed.

'No, just my drink please.'

Jamie lay back in the bath sipping his whisky and soda reflectively. Over the last three years his life had changed dramatically. His grief-stricken mother had lost the will to live after the death of his father and had been reunited with her beloved husband a few months later. At twenty years of age Jamie had inherited the title, the estates and over one million pounds. He would have exchanged them all to have kept his mother a little while longer. He had never been close to her cousin, Duncan Campbell-Stuart, Earl of Lochmair, and had no contact with him other than through his daughter Lucy. His only remaining relative was of course his grandfather and, bereft of the love and support that only a family can give, he became a still more solitary figure. His mother's death had removed the last barrier to his leaving Oxford, so when Greg finished his post-graduate year Jamie decided to leave with him.

The rambling, Victorian house within earshot of the Division Bell which his father had acquired as a young Member of Parliament Jamie had sold on the advice of Gavin Blunt, who had persuaded him to move to the playgrounds of Mayfair. He had therefore acquired a suitable house in Berkeley Square, ideal for entertaining, with spacious servants' quarters in which he had installed Sedgewicke, a cook, a housekeeper and Rupert, his chauffeur. The lease on the flat in Cheyne Row he had given to Lucy to use as a studio and Angela had moved into the penthouse in Duke Street.

Knaves had started as an amusing idea when Jamie had been visiting Greg's family in Rhode Island. One drunken evening in a sailors' brothel in Newport they had run across an old schoolfriend of Greg's. It was the one place they were confident of not seeing anyone they knew!

Hank Klenk had embarked on an unlikely (but profitable) career for a graduate of Groton and owned a chain of brothels that stretched from Santa Fe to San Francisco. He was waxing lyrical about the advantages of being in the business and could not have found a more responsive audience.

Greg was now an eminently respectable banker and could not risk exposure, but to Jamie the idea of owning such an establishment for his own amusement was irresistible. On his return from America he instructed Angela (who had always wanted a business of her own) to find and decorate appropriate premises. Lennie Landau, for a sizeable chunk of the profits, had agreed to become the general manager.

Jamie was one of the most eligible bachelors in London – a fact which was not lost on him – but, needless to say, marriage was the furthest thing from his mind. The social-climbing aspirations of debutantes and their mothers left him cold and the numerous invitations to coming-out balls and country weekends that littered his desk remained largely unopened. He preferred uncomplicated liaisons with fun-loving actresses and became a leading member of café society. When not gambling or at Knaves he spent most of his time at light-hearted parties in restaurants and nightclubs.

His links with Scotland had been almost completely severed and during the past year he had spent only one weekend at Kilpurnie, having delegated the running of the entire estate to his trusty factor McClintock. He was well aware that Sedgewicke viewed this as an abandonment of his family responsibilities but Jamie loved his present lifestyle and had no intention of changing it.

Much revived by the hot bath, he wrapped himself in a full-length white towelling robe and passed through his bedroom into the spacious dressing-room where he paused to refresh his drink and pick up that morning's edition of *The Times*. He sat down in a small armchair, scanning the newspaper while Sedgewicke unobtrusively attended to his clothes.

'City news still pretty grim, isn't it Sedgewicke?'

'Yes Sir James, McClintock was telling me that unemployment in Scotland is increasing daily.' Sedgewicke was deeply concerned. 'The people are really suffering – something's got to be done. I understand your uncle, Lord Campbell–Stuart, is addressing Parliament on the subject this evening, and . . .'

'Yes, yes,' Jamie interrupted testily, refusing to be drawn. 'I'm sure they'll sort it out sooner or later.' He turned to the sporting pages. 'The All Blacks match tomorrow should be really close. Would you like to come to Twickenham with me?'

Sedgewicke shook his head in despair. 'No thank you, Sir James. Fortunately *I am* in employment and since we are giving a dinner tomorrow night I think I should remain here.'

'Eighty-five Piccadilly cabbie, quick as you can.' A harassed Gregory Hamilton glanced at his watch.

'Good evening Grace, is Sir James Stuart here yet?'

'Yes Mr Hamilton, he's waiting for you in the bar.'

'Thank you.'

'Hello Jamie. Sorry I'm late, I've been in meetings all day.'

'Quite all right old man.' Jamie was well aware of the demands that the family firm had made on his friend over the last few years. 'What will you have?'

'A very large dry Martini.'

'What's up old man, you look absolutely dreadful.'

'I need your advice Jamie. Remember when I was having an affair with Edwina Alderton . . .'

'Yes. You and the rest of London!'

'I know, I know,' Greg said. 'Well anyway, the summer before last, when we were in America, I wrote her a couple of letters and she stupidly left them lying around. Her maid found them and showed them to some layabout she's been screwing in the village. He kept them and has been blackmailing Edwina ever since. I only found out about it last week and I've agreed to meet him tomorrow evening on Kingston Common to buy the letters from him once and for all.'

'What makes you think he'll give them to you if he wouldn't give them to Edwina?'

'Exactly. She's already paid him several thousand pounds and the bastard keeps asking for more. Quite clearly he intends to string us along for ever. He knows that a scandal would ruin her.'

'To hell with Edwina,' Jamie said contemptuously. 'It's her problem, not yours. Don't get involved.'

'I wish it were that simple,' Greg sighed, 'but I can't afford a scandal either. The bank's doing really well at the moment. You know how conservative the City can be and those letters won't exactly inspire confidence in me. If I go to the police, will the whole thing get out?'

'Probably,' Jamie said carefully. 'That's the worse thing you can do. He'll he charged with blackmail and the newspapers will have a field day. No. Make sure you see the letters first and if he won't sell them to you straight away give him a thrashing he'll never forget and take them off him. Then let *him* go to the police.'

'Yes, I suppose you're right.' Greg nodded slowly. 'There's no alternative, is there?'

'No there isn't,' Jamie said matter-of-factly. 'Just don't be late for my dinner tomorrow night, Lucy's going to be there. She's in London for a few days and is looking forward to seeing you. Now let's go up to the dining-room. I had a big win last night and I'll tell you all about it over dinner.'

'Well done. But do you mind if we eat at my place? We're in the middle of a very important deal and I'm expecting a telephone call from my father.'

'Not at all, old man, let's go now.'

Jamie had a quiet dinner at Greg's rooms in the Albany and went to bed early. He left his house at eleven o'clock the next morning and, standing in the March drizzle, looked up at the dark sky, shuddering at the thought of the mudbath that would be Twickenham. His motor car pulled up and the driver slipped out.

'Jermyn Street please Rupert – my shirtmakers. Then Trumpers for a haircut. I've got to be in the Committee Room at Twickenham for lunch by quarter to one and I want to drive myself there so that you can help Sedgewicke with tonight's dinner.'

An indifferent lunch was followed by an exciting rugby game which Jamie watched in the pouring rain from the anonymity of the terraces, where he always enjoyed the earthy comments of the knowledgeable spectators. The afternoon was not without its frustrations however, and the journey home took three times longer than usual because he had to change a punctured tyre in the already slow-moving traffic. Wet, annoyed, and with cut hands, he barely had time to bathe and **change** into a dinner jacket before the first guests arrived.

CHAPTER 7

The party that evening was in honour of the King of Egypt, a legendary gambler, degenerate and friend of Jamie's. His voracious sexual appetites ranged from pubescent Nubian page boys to brassy American show girls but, although grotesquely fat and dripping with precious stones of every size and description, he was a cultured, gregarious man capable of great charm. Inevitably he attracted much publicity wherever he went and the stories that surrounded him were legion. His own favourite was of the occasion on which he was playing baccarat against the bank in Monte Carlo. On one enormous banco he triumphantly revealed a nine and with pudgy arms gathered in the money. When it was respectfully pointed out to him that he had not shown his other card, he calmly and deliberately dropped it face down into the chute with the other discards.

'It was a king,' he said quietly.

'But Your Majesty,' the flustered *chef de partie* protested, 'it is obligatory to show both cards.'

'It was a king, monsieur,' he repeated patiently. 'Like me. Do you doubt the word of a King?'

'Of course not Your Majesty,' came the hesitant reply. 'Please continue the game.'

He would roar with laughter, tears coming to his piggy eyes as he told the story. His amusement was not shared by the management of the Winter Casino.

Lucy, who always took on the role of Jamie's hostess, had seated the King between a visiting Hollywood actress and a Russian ballerina. She had no intention of allowing his plump, bejewelled hands to wander up her own thighs and had placed herself at the opposite end of the table in between Greg and Jamie. She was flirting with Greg and enjoying herself immensely while Jamie was engrossed in Jeremy Hunter's exuberant description of Juan Fangio's daring victory in the British Grand Prix. Suddenly he felt a discreet tap on the shoulder from Sedgewicke.

'Excuse me Sir James, may I have a word with you?'

Jamie, knowing full well that his valet would never trouble him at such a time unless it were absolutely necessary, rose immediately and followed him into the hall. 'Yes Sedgewicke, what's the problem?'

'There are two gentlemen from Scotland Yard to see you. I've put them in the study.'

'Scotland Yard?' Jamie was incredulous. 'What the hell do they want at this time of night?' He marched down the hallway and into the study.

'Gentlemen, I hope this is important!'

'Good evening Sir James.' A thin, sharp-eyed man in a shabby raincoat jumped to his feet. 'My name is Chief Inspector Norman Foskett and this is my colleague Sergeant Davies.'

'Yes, Inspector?' Jamie nodded peremptorily.

'We're sorry to trouble you sir. I'll come straight to the point.' Foskett fumbled with a handkerchief and extracted a silver cigarette case from an inside pocket of his grubby jacket. 'Does this case belong to you?'

'Yes.' Jamie was puzzled. 'How on earth did you get hold of it?'

'Perhaps I could ask you, Sir James, when you last saw this case?'

'I can't be certain.' A wary Jamie looked thoughtful. 'I mislaid it some days ago. Where did you find it?'

'Do you know a man named Jack Sykes?'

'Never heard of him. What's that got to do with my cigarette case?'

'Are you quite sure you don't know him, sir?'

'I'm absolutely positive!' Jamie snapped. 'Now look here, Inspector, my guests – including the King of Egypt – are waiting for me. Will you please tell me what this is all about?'

'Jack Sykes was found dead earlier this evening by the river on Kingston Common. Early signs indicate that he drowned either during or after a fight. Your cigarette case was found in the woods nearby.'

'I'm sorry I can't help you Inspector,' Jamie replied smoothly. 'I've no idea how it got there but thank you for returning it to me. Now if you'll excuse me I must get back.'

'I quite understand, Sir James, but if you don't mind I'll hang on to this for a while. We'll return it as soon as possible and I hope I won't have to trouble you again. Come on Davies, let's go.'

'Sedgewicke will see you out. Goodnight, gentlemen.'

'Goodnight Sir James. Thank you for your patience. I'd look after that hand if I were you, you've got a nasty gash there.'

'Thank you Inspector.'

The last of the guests had departed when Lucy, Jamie and Greg settled down for a final nightcap.

'Lucy darling, thank you for all your help. The seating was perfect and I think everyone had a good time. If you don't mind I'll have Rupert drive you home. There's something important I need to discuss with Greg.'

'Of course not my love, I ought to leave now anyway. I'm going back to Florence on Friday and I've got to get up early. Gregsy darling, I look forward to dinner tomorrow.' She kissed them both and left.

'Dammit, Jamie, couldn't this have waited?'

'No, it bloody well can't! The police were here earlier and Jack Sykes, who I presume is your blackmailing friend, has been found dead on the river bank at Kingston. What the hell happened?'

'What!' Greg sat bolt upright, his face ashen. 'That's impossible. He refused to give me the letters and we had a fight. Both of us ended up in the river and he managed to get away from me in the water. I saw him climbing out of the river when I left.'

'Did you actually see him get out of the water?'

Greg hesitated. 'No.'

'Well obviously he didn't make it,' Jamie said grimly.

'Why did the police come and see you?' Greg was in shock.

'It appears, old man, that the cigarette case I left in your flat last night was found near the body.'

'Oh no! I had it in my pocket to bring over this morning and I forgot. I must have dropped it there. Anyway,' he buried his face in his hands, 'I still can't believe it. There's no way he could have drowned – I definitely saw him swimming.'

'Well there's nothing we can do about it now. Who else knew that you were meeting him?'

'Only Edwina,' Greg replied dully. 'I must go to the police immediately.'

'Hold on a moment, let's just think this through. There's absolutely nothing to link you with this incident and I've told the police that I lost my case some days ago and that I don't know where. Even though it was an accident there's no point in you dragging yourself through a major scandal simply because some blackmailing lout is dead.'

'But surely the police will believe my story?'

'Yes, they probably will. But it's bound to get out because at the very least there will be an inquest at which you and Edwina will have to give evidence. The best thing you can do is go home and say nothing. When are you leaving for New York?'

'At the beginning of next week.'

'By the time you get back here it'll all have blown over. Scotland Yard have better things to do than worry about a drowned rat they're probably glad to be rid of in any event. Did you get the letters?'

'No. He said he'd hidden them where they'd never be found . . .' Greg's faltering voice petered out.

Jamie was silent for several moments. 'That must be right or the police would already have them. I think we can safely forget about them. Go home, Greg. Keep your mouth shut. Get a good night's sleep. We'll talk in the morning. I'm certain you're in the clear and nothing's to be gained by involving yourself.' He placed an arm comfortingly around his bewildered friend and walked him to his car.

The following two weeks passed without incident. Lucy returned to Italy while Greg – against his better judgement but reassured by the silence from the police – set sail for America. Life for Jamie went on much as usual until one afternoon when he was visited for the second time by Chief Inspector Norman Foskett, who had not come to return his grandfather's cigarette case.

CHAPTER 8

A frown creased the ruddy face of Commissioner Ronald Wilson. He sipped the tepid coffee from the basement canteen of the ugly, imposing edifice on the Thames Embankment that was Scotland Yard and looked across his desk at Superintendent Groves.

'Now Ken,' he said gruffly, 'tell me about Foskett.'

'He's without doubt my best detective. A little unorthodox and a bit of a loner, but a real terrier. Once he's got his teeth into something he'll never let go and he can smell a villain at a hundred yards. The lads call him "Sniffer Foskett". He was the one who caught the Belgravia Butcher. Made mincemeat of the rest of us – if you'll excuse the pun, Chief!'

'Very funny Ken.' Wilson frowned again. 'All right, wheel him in.'

'Yes Chief. By the way, don't be put off by his appearance.'

The Commissioner rose and walked to the large bay window where he stood staring out at a gaily coloured tugboat steaming up the river.

Norman Foskett wished he wasn't wearing an egg-stained tie. His practised eye took in the simplicity of the office with its metal filing-cabinets and framed citations hanging crookedly on the walls.

'Sit down, Foskett. I understand you're in charge of the Sykes case. Tell me everything you know and exactly what Stuart's connection is. You'd better have a damned good reason for questioning him.' Wilson turned suddenly from the window and glowered at the apprehensive Foskett.

'Yes sir. Well,' the detective began hesitantly, 'Jack Sykes was a forty-two-year-old unemployed villain with a total of six convictions. Two for attempted blackmail, one for larceny and three for assault – including a vicious attack on his own wife. She lives in Liverpool with their two children and hasn't seen nor heard of him for over five years. His body was found washed up on the river bank at Kingston Common. The immediate cause of death appears to have been drowning but we're not sure yet. The preliminary pathologist's report shows several bruises around the upper part of the body and a massive blow to the forehead which was probably delivered at close range by a blunt instrument. It is quite clear that he was involved in a fight. An examination of his clothes reveals no bloodstains other than his own, but our investigations at the scene were severely hampered by reavy rain. Time of death was approximately 6.00 p.m. Sir James Stuart's cigarette case was found twenty yards from the body and there were indications that the fight had taken place around that spot. Having identified the crest, I visited Sir James, who told me that he had mislaid the case several days before. He claimed never to have heard of Jack Sykes . . .'

'And naturally you had to choose the middle of a dinner at which that bloody Gippo King was a guest!' The Commissioner glanced at Groves, who was studiously examining the filing-cabinet.

Unperturbed, Foskett continued. 'Yes sir. Although he denied knowing the deceased, subsequent investigations reveal that Sykes was briefly employed in Sir James's household as a handyman and was dismissed by the valet Mr Sedgewicke on suspicion of theft.'

'A handyman . . . I suppose it's possible that Stuart may never have met him,' the Commissioner mused. 'How long did he work there?'

'A total of nine weeks, sir.'

'Uhmm . . .' Wilson pursed his lips. 'What else?'

'When I visited him on the night of the murder I noticed cuts and bruises on his right hand. When I later asked him about his movements on the day in question, Stuart told me that he had dismissed his chauffeur and driven alone to Twickenham to watch the All Blacks game, that he had lunched in the committee box but had watched the match alone from the terraces. He got home shortly before eight o'clock and claims that he was delayed by heavy traffic and a punctured tyre, the changing of which caused him to injure his hand. As you know sir, Kingston is quite near to Twickenham and on the way back to London.'

'I see. Bit thin though?'

'Yes sir, but we may have had a bit of luck. One of my team, young Sergeant Davies' (Groves rolled his eyes to the ceiling) 'discovered a small piece of tweed cloth caught up in the bramble bushes nearby. We are waiting for forensic to come up with their report.'

'What sort of man is Stuart?'

'A gentleman. Very arrogant and very sure of himself.'

'Thinks he's above the law, does he, Foskett?'

'In a way, sir, yes. You know these aristocrats, they're a law unto themselves. Single and aged twenty-three, he's extremely wealthy. Gambles for huge stakes and is reputed to be the best poker player in London. Apart from his own circle he mixes in very dubious company including a well-known pimp and several prostitutes. He's a cool customer and very quick – always seems to know exactly what question is coming next.'

'Right Foskett, carry on, but I want a written report as soon as possible and I want to see you the moment we have the forensic results.'

'Of course sir. Thank you sir.' Foskett left the room.

'You were right Ken, good copper that.' Wilson returned to the window. 'Shame he can't wear a clean shirt.'

Later that afternoon an excited Sergeant Davies burst into the tiny cubicle that passed for Norman Foskett's office.

'I've got it Sniffer,' he panted. 'Forensic have traced the tweed to a supplier in Glasgow that sells to Huntsman's of Savile Row. I've been to see them and they say that they only made one suit and one coat from that cloth – the suit was for some American, but the coat was made for Stuart.'

'Well done my boy. I'm going straight upstairs to see the old man. You make out the warrant and we'll be on our way.'

For the first time in his life James Stuart was worried. The sound advice he had given Greg now seemed to be rebounding to his own detriment as a result of the most ludicrous series of coincidences. He had genuinely failed to recognize the photograph of Sykes and had no idea that the dead man had ever worked for him. Immediately after Foskett's second visit Jamie had telephoned his family solicitor and spoken to Alistair Russell, the senior partner, who had assured Jamie that the evidence so far was purely circumstantial and would be insufficient to support even a *prima facie* case against him.

Jamie had remained in his dining-room after his uneaten lunch and was moodily toying with his coffee cup, filled with apprehension despite the lawyer's advice, when the heavy brass door-knocker shattered his thoughts.

'Yes, Sedgewicke. I know. Show Inspector Foskett into the drawing-room.'

Pouring himself a stiff brandy, Jamie wearily joined his unwelcome visitor.

'Well Foskett, what is it this time?'

'Do you recognize this piece of material, Sir James?' Foskett asked grimly.

'Yes.' Jamie was surprised. 'I have a tweed overcoat that's very similar.'

'Made by Huntsman's sir?'

'That's right – why?'

'Were you wearing that coat on the day you went to the rugby match?'

'I believe I was.'

'May we see it please, sir?'

'I don't see why not. I'll have Sedgewicke fetch it for you.' Jamie rang the bell. 'Sedgewicke, please bring me the brown tweed overcoat that Huntsman's made for me last year.'

'I'm afraid I can't do that, Sir James. I threw it away some weeks ago.'

'What! Why?'

'It was the day of the dinner party for the King of Egypt and you may remember that it was covered in oil stains when you returned from Twickenham. I could see that you would never wish to wear it again.'

'Thank you Sedgewicke,' Jamie groaned. 'That will be all.'

All of a sudden the horrifying recollection that he and Greg had shared the same material dawned upon him. He felt a gentle pressure on his arm from an apologetic Chief Inspector Foskett.

'I'm very sorry Sir James, but I'm going to have to ask you to accompany me to the police station where you will be formally charged with the murder of John Herbert Sykes. I must caution you that you have the right to remain silent but that anything you say will be taken down and may be used in evidence. Please come with us.'

CHAPTER 9

Jamie shivered in the weak morning sunlight, nevertheless grateful for the fresh air. He left Bow Street Magistrates Court and picked his way through the maze of fruit barrows and flower stalls of Covent Garden. Numbed by the experience of the preceding night, he scarcely heeded the words of Alistair Russell telling him that a consultation had been arranged that afternoon with Sir Desmond Fitzgerald.

'Fine Alistair, I'll meet you there. I'm going home to take a bath and get some sleep.'

The previous eighteen hours had been a horror story. Having been charged and searched, Jamie had been unceremoniously bundled into a filthy cell filled with the stench of his drunken companions. He had spent an unforgettable, humiliating night, deafened by the wretched wails of sordid streetwalkers in the cells next door. His appearance before the Chief Metropolitan Magistrate had been brief but successful in so far as he had been granted bail, on condition that he surrendered his passport and reported daily to his local police station.

Clambering out of the taxi cab, Jamie pushed his way through the shouting throng of reporters massed on the pavement outside his home. Once inside, he collapsed on his bed, still unable to grasp the incredible irony of the situation to which the advice he had given Greg had led.

Much as he would have liked, Sir Desmond Fitzgerald KC could not accept his client's story. He had sat quietly throughout the conference, his grey, bushy eyebrows arched sceptically on the massive forehead as Jamie steadfastly maintained his innocence. The legendary Irish advocate said nothing for several minutes and neither Jamie nor Russell dared disturb the ensuing silence.

Removing a gold box from his waistcoat pocket, Fitzgerald sprinkled a liberal measure of snuff on to the oyster of his left hand between his thumb and forefinger. He expertly disposed of the grains into each nostril, rubbed his nose briskly and sneezed violently three times. He lit an enormous cigar and finally turned to Jamie.

'My dear boy, I'm so dreadfully sorry to see you in this terrible predicament. The more so because your distinguished father and I were briefly colleagues in the House many years ago – at least until the good but sadly ignorant citizens of Southport regrettably saw fit to remove me as their representative.' His belly heaved as he chuckled silently. 'Your unfortunate circumstances deeply sadden me my dear and of course I fully accept every word you tell me. But let me explain something to you.' He pointed his cigar at Jamie. 'A workman is only as good as his tools and a simple barrister such as myself is a mere mouthpiece for his client's story. I would not be honest were I to say that the evidence of both your cigarette case and the tweed cloth at the scene of the crime would fail to influence a jury against you. Although your alibi is weak we may still be able to come up with something. But your failure to recognize a former employee – while understandable to me – may not altogether endear you to a jury. I need hardly remind you that you are charged with a capital offence and that I alone stand between you and the hangman's rope. I must therefore stress the need for total frankness with your counsel. We will be spending a great deal of time together under the most difficult circumstances and I don't ask you to like me, but I insist that you trust me.'

With a theatrical wave of his cigar Sir Desmond turned to Russell and, adopting a whimsical tone, lowered his voice.

'You know Alistair, this reminds me of that little blackmail case we did together at the Winchester Assizes many years ago.'

Russell had never appeared at the Winchester Assizes but recognized the gambit. He nodded vigorously. 'Interesting case indeed.'

Fitzgerald swivelled sharply back to Jamie. 'Our client, a prominent stockbroker, was being blackmailed over his fondness for boys under the age of fourteen and refused to meet a payment. This resulted in his being attacked by the scoundrel. In the ensuing scuffle our financial wizard, a former boxing blue with a vile temper, landed more than his fair share of lucky blows, thus extinguishing the flame of life from his small but loathsome tormentor. You will forgive an old hack's immodesty if I claim to have convinced the jury that the murder was in self-defence. Indeed our belligerent broker is still living extremely well on his greedy customers' commissions. Now that's the sort of case I can get my teeth into.' He fell silent again.

Rising with difficulty, the grizzled old advocate limped towards the door. 'Well dear boy, there's nothing more we can do now until we receive the pathologist's and forensic reports. Alistair will be searching for witnesses who may have seen you changing the tyre on your motor car. In the meantime I want you to consider very carefully everything I have said and come back and see me next week. Your trial is due to commence in approximately two months at the Central Criminal Court. We need every minute of that time.'

Jamie left 9 King's Bench Walk with his mind in a blur. He walked through the gateway of Sergeant's Inn out of the Temple into Fleet Street and, turning into the Strand, shakily entered the crooked doorway of the Wig and Pen Club. He found an empty bench in a corner alcove beneath the low, ancient beams, ordered a large Scotch and with a great effort began to collect his thoughts.

Despite his shocked and exhausted condition the full import of his veteran counsel's advice had not been lost on him, including the obvious device of the stockbroker story. He knew the true account that he had given the police had not impressed Sir Desmond, who had effectively told him that he would be convicted of murder. He was enmeshed in a web of damning evidence from which there was no escape other than to inform on his best friend, whom he had persuaded from the beginning not to go to the police. He could wait for Greg to return and make the subsequent confession that he would no doubt insist upon. But if he did he himself would be accused of concealing the facts and Greg, due to the delay of his confession, would appear far more guilty.

On the other hand Jamie was unconcerned with personal reputation, since he had no business affairs to protect, and was a better liar than Greg. The only alternative therefore was to stand trial in Greg's place and tell Greg's story which he was sure he could tell convincingly. Even if he were convicted he knew full well that Greg would not allow him to hang and his friend's confession, corroborated by Edwina, would ensure Jamie's pardon. In any case Greg had saved his life; the least he could do was to try and save Greg now.

At the age of twenty-three, James Stuart – gambler and prodigal son – was about to embark on the biggest gamble of his life.

CHAPTER 10

Gregory Hamilton nestled in the corner of the welcoming London taxi cab. He had disembarked from the *Queen Mary* at Southampton after a successful visit to New York. Having breakfasted on the train to Waterloo, and pleased to be back in England, he was in high spirits as he made his way directly to the office. The chatty Cockney driver lent him the *Daily Telegraph* and, quickly scanning the financial pages, Greg turned to the social columns where he was greeted by a photograph of his closest friend. Smiling, he read the caption with interest:

'Among the guests last night at the opening of Laurence Olivier in Mr Tyrone Guthrie's production of *Richard II* was Sir James Stuart escorting his cousin Lady Lucinda Campbell-Stuart . . .' Greg's jaw dropped in disbelief '. . . Sir James was composed and in good humour but refused to comment on his forthcoming appearance at the Old Bailey for the Kingston Common murder.'

Aghast, Greg rapped on the partition and shouted at the bewildered driver. 'Forget about Moorgate, cabbie. Six Berkeley Square as quick as you can.'

A startled Sedgewicke was brushed aside as Greg ran into the house demanding to see Jamie.

'Of course Mr Hamilton, of course. Sir James is in the study having drinks. I'll just let him know you're here.'

'Never mind about that,' Greg shouted, charging into the

room. 'What the hell's going on, Jamie?' he raged.

'My dear Greg.' Jamie stood up. 'How lovely to see you. Welcome back. Sedgewicke, another excellent cocktail for Mr Hamilton and arrange an extra place for lunch. Take a seat and calm down, old man. How was New York?'

'New York!' Greg exploded. 'I don't believe it. You've been charged with a murder that I committed and you're asking me about fucking New York. Are you out of your head?'

'Well, you were in America old man,' Jamie said mildly.

'America! America!' Greg roared. 'Haven't you heard of a fucking telegram, you lunatic!'

'Now steady on, Greg. Pull yourself together. Let's go in to lunch and I'll fill you in. Everything's under control,' Jamie said soothingly and steered his friend towards the dining-room.

Over lunch Jamie was at his most persuasive and Greg, who had started the meal adamant that he was going to tell the police everything, began to see the logic behind Jamie's argument.

'I don't like it but I'll go along with it for the time being. But, I'm going to leave a sealed confession with my lawyers, to be given to the police in the event of your conviction or of my death before the end of your trial.'

'Delighted to hear it old man,' Jamie said dryly. 'By the way, you'd better destroy your tweed suit in case the police come round – it won't affect anything you say later. When was your last contact with Edwina?'

'I've had none since I last spoke to you about her sending her maid Fanny away. I wasn't about to write to her from America again!'

Jamie frowned. 'I've tried her a few times to tell her that her name won't be mentioned but she hasn't seen fit to return my calls. She's staying well clear of all this.'

'That's typical,' Greg replied bitterly. 'She's always had a highly developed sense of self-preservation.'

'Most women do, old man. They're only around when they want something – at least with a professional whore you know where you stand. Stop worrying, this is one bet I don't propose to lose.'

68

CHAPTER 11
THE OLD BAILEY, LONDON, 1950

Simon Cathcart was an unpleasant man. That he possessed a brilliant legal brain no one could dispute, but he had risen to the rank of Senior Treasury Counsel largely through an innate belief in the guilt of his fellow man which manifested itself in the fanatical conduct of his prosecutions. The more uncharitable members of the Bar – and that august profession is not renowned for its charity – subscribed to the view that this was the result of a massive inferiority complex which stemmed (through no fault of his own, mind you) from an underprivileged background. He was notorious for savage attacks on the character of undeserving witnesses.

Rising, he addressed the jury with relish.

'. . . and so, members of the jury, the prosecution will prove beyond a shadow of a doubt that James Stuart is a cold-blooded, calculating murderer who deliberately set out to take the life of a fellow human being. That he is a man who lied persistently to the police, and a man . . .' his voice trailed off as he realized that the attention of the jury had been focused for some time on Sir Desmond Fitzgerald, who was at that moment exaggeratedly measuring a long line of snuff on a legal casebook in front of him. Cathcart turned with distaste to his adversary but his words were drowned by three loud explosions that were in no way muffled by an enormous red, spotted handkerchief.

'As I was saying, gentlemen of the jury,' he continued, 'a man who lied to the police and no doubt will lie to you throughout this trial in order to save his own neck . . .'

'My Lord, I am shocked.' Fitzgerald's voice boomed as he pulled himself to his feet. 'That is a most scurrilous remark, unworthy of even my learned friend. I'm sure that when the evidence has been presented the jury will be more than capable of deciding the truth for themselves.'

Lord Chief Justice Hammond looked over his spectacles at the prosecution counsel. 'I agree with Sir Desmond. Please confine yourself to the facts, Mr Cathcart. We are not interested in your opinions.'

'As Your Lordship pleases. You will find, gentlemen of the jury, this to be a short trial and there will be only four witnesses for the prosecution. Now with His Lordship's leave I will call the first witness. I call Detective Chief Inspector Foskett.'

Norman Foskett, in an ill-fitting but freshly pressed brown suit, entered the witness box and took the oath somewhat uneasily. He was accustomed to the inevitable publicity attracted by Number One Court and his qualms were caused not by the prospect of facing Sir Desmond Fitzgerald, but by some lingering doubt as to Jamie's guilt which he had been unable to share with his superiors. He gave his evidence-in-chief in a flat monotone much as he had first recounted the story to Commissioner Wilson, and remained motionless as Sir Desmond rose to cross-examine.

'Chief Inspector Foskett, you and I have known each other for many years and we have done battle many times.' Fitzgerald smiled disarmingly. 'May I say that I have always regarded you as a police officer of great skill and of the highest integrity.'

'Thank you sir.' Foskett wondered what the old fox had up his sleeve.

'And may I say from the outset . . .' Sir Desmond paused dramatically, 'that the defence does not dispute one single word of the evidence which you have given us.'

There was a ripple of surprise throughout the courtroom and the judge interrupted. 'Am I to understand, Sir Desmond, that your client admits to killing the deceased?'

'My Lord.' The Irishman drew himself to his full height. 'You are indeed. But we shall show – conclusively and to the satisfaction of every good gentleman of the jury – that Sir James was the subject of a violent and unprovoked attack upon his person by a despicable blackmailer.'

'I see, Sir Desmond.' The judge was busily writing. 'In other words you are pleading self-defence?'

'Precisely My Lord. And in the alternative, that death was *accidental*.' He punched the air with his hand. 'Now Chief Inspector, am I correct in my belief that Sykes was no stranger to the police?'

'Yes sir.'

'Nor to the courts?'

'Yes sir.'

'Nor indeed to His Majesty's prisons?'

'Yes sir.'

'In fact he appears to have been a regular guest of His Majesty.'

'Yes sir, that is correct.'

'Then let us examine together, Chief Inspector, the reasons for these involuntary visits. At the tender age of twenty-one Sykes was convicted at the Liverpool Assizes of larceny from the very same parish church that had provided him shelter for the night. He was detained for three months I believe?'

'Yes sir.'

'And on his release he saw fit to attack and seriously wound the kindly priest and his elderly wife who had given evidence against him. For his little incident he was given two years' hard labour. Am I right, Inspector?'

'Yes sir.'

'And, to the relief of the law-abiding citizens of Liverpool, our delightful friend then worked his passage to Australia where he took up residence in the docklands of Sydney and married an unsuspecting barmaid – one Sheila Pratt. Alas,' Fitzgerald sighed, 'he did not endear himself to the authorities of our Commonwealth brothers and was soon sampling their

71

hospitality as a result of his nefarious smuggling activities.'

Foskett nodded wearily while Sir Desmond poured himself a glass of neat gin from the water jug in front of him. The rich baritone's voice, refreshed, was even more sonorous.

'On his return, Sykes was unable to retain any form of employment for very long and financed his bouts of heavy drinking from his wife's meagre earnings as a waitress. When the unfortunate woman attempted to withhold from him a pittance for their children's clothing, this brutish drunkard beat her senseless with his belt. Thankfully a neighbour intervened in time to save the poor wretch's life. Sykes was apprehended and sent to Dartmoor for three years. Is that correct, Mr Foskett?'

'Yes sir.'

'And finally, having served his sentence, Sykes made his way to London where he discovered his ultimate vocation – the heinous crime of "demanding with menaces". Perhaps, Chief Inspector, you would be kind enough to explain this term to the jury.'

'Blackmail sir,' Foskett replied evenly.

'And the details, Officer, the details – if you please.' Fitzgerald hunched forward on his lectern and glared at the policeman.

'Yes sir. On the twenty-seventh of June 1944 Sykes was sentenced at the Inner London Sessions to eighteen months' imprisonment for the attempted blackmail of his employer, a garage proprietor; on the eleventh of January 1947 he was convicted in this building of the same offence against a local estate agent and was sent to prison for two years.' Foskett closed his notebook.

For an entire minute Sir Desmond Fitzgerald gazed meaningfully at each member of the jury.

'That will be all, Chief Inspector. I thank you.'

Turning imperiously to his junior, Sir Desmond spoke in a clearly audible stage whisper: 'And this is the man, dear boy, whom they claim was viciously murdered by a baronet and pillar of our society!' He sat down abruptly.

'Thank you, Sir Demond. I think this might be a suitable moment to break for lunch.'

'Indeed My Lord, my own sentiments entirely.' Desmond, appreciating the timing, grinned at a discomfited Simon Cathcart.

After lunch the remainder of the prosecution witnesses were called. Sedgewicke's evidence to confirm that he had disposed of the tweed coat was no longer necessary in the light of Jamie's admission; and Sergeant Davies quickly corroborated the unchallenged account of his superior.

Professor Bernard Spillsbury, the eminent forensic scientist, was a difficult and potentially damaging witness to the defence. He had prepared a long and detailed report on the corpse and gave evidence in his normal impressive fashion. His main conclusion was that death was probably caused not by drowning but by a heavy blow at close range to the frontal area of the skull with a blunt instrument.

In an adroit and extremely skilful cross-examination – characterized by a deliberate lack of flamboyance – Fitzgerald was able to elicit the reluctant admission that drowning could not entirely be excluded as a possible cause of death and moved on to his final and most important question.

'Thank you, Professor. Now, you've told us that the deceased was involved in a fight. Is it not possible that he and his fellow combatant fell into the river locked together during the struggle; that they were then separated by the darkness and that, while swimming to the bank against the strong current, Sykes was rendered unconscious by hitting his head against a floating log – or something of that nature?'

'Possible Sir Desmond, but, as I have explained earlier, the angle of the injury to the forehead in relation to the horizontal position of a normal swimmer renders your hypothesis unlikely.'

'But *possible* my dear Professor, *possible*.' Fitzgerald pounced. 'And *that*, gentlemen of the jury, does not mean "beyond a reasonable doubt" – especially in view of the splinters of wood which the good professor has already told us he discovered embedded in the skull.'

A beatific smile on his face, Sir Desmond sat down, satisfied that Spillsbury's testimony had been neutralized. He reached for his glass of gin.

'That witness, My Lord,' Cathcart wound up, 'concludes the case for the prosecution.'

That evening Jamie dined at Greg's apartment with his counsel, his solicitor and Lucy. Sir Desmond had left a sizeable dent in Greg's wine cellar and, moving on to the brandy, addressed himself to Jamie.

'My dear boy, you will forgive a marginally drunken old hack's immodesty if I tell you that as a result of my conduct of your case today you will almost certainly be acquitted. I have no doubt that your performance in the witness box tomorrow will be superb. Just tell the truth and you may safely leave Cathcart to me.'

Jamie nodded and smiled reassuringly at Greg.

While Sir Desmond was enjoying his brandy, Norman Foskett was sharing a stale cheese sandwich with Superintendent Groves in the Scotland Yard canteen.

'Well Sniffer. It looks as though Stuart's going to get off. Don't you agree?'

'Yes Super, I rather do.'

'You don't seem very concerned about it, Norman. Why not?'

'Well Ken, to tell you the truth, my nose tells me that Stuart didn't do it. We've only just discovered that Sykes had a girlfriend who vanished around the time of his death and I've got Sergeant Davies organizing a search for her right now.'

'I see. Well, all I can say is he'd better come up with something fast otherwise it'll all be over by tomorrow night.'

CHAPTER 12

'Members of the jury, I do not propose to make an opening speech for the defence. Nor indeed any speech at all. I do not need to.' Sir Desmond showed no signs of the previous evening's excesses as he downed his first glass of gin.

'The questionable eloquence of an aged hack . . .' his old eyes twinkled . . . 'will do little to persuade you of my client's innocence, but the truth, members of the jury – the shining glorious truth – will become crystal clear when you hear from the only witness I propose to call. I call Sir James Stuart.'

The Lord Chief Justice ordered the doors to be locked and everyone in court sat with bated breath as the young man, on trial for his life, climbed up the steps into the witness box.

'Sir James, will you please tell us in your own words exactly what happened on the afternoon and evening of March the twelfth.' Fitzgerald folded his arms and waited, nodding approvingly from time to time while his client gave his evidence.

'Thank you, Sir James – will you please remain where you are.' Fitzgerald sat down delighted.

From the witness box Jamie was able to see the public gallery clearly for the first time. Out of the sea of faces he managed to distinguish Sedgewicke in the far left corner and a tearful Lucy in the centre being consoled by Gavin Blunt. In the front row and tensed against the rail, he could see the strained face of Greg exchanging a few words with his neighbour – an old tramp whose features were obscured by a shock of silver hair.

'Let me make sure I have your story correct, Sir James.' Cathcart started his cross-examination gently. 'As I understand it you are claiming the following: first that Sykes was attempting to blackmail you. Second that you do not recall ever meeting with him before· – despite the fact that he was employed by you. Third that you agreed to a rendezvous in a secluded wood during the hours of darkness with the express intention of informing him that you would not pay him. And *finally* that he surprisingly then attacked you – which attack you resisted with sufficient force to kill him.'

'Yes,' Jamie nodded.

'Yet you seriously ask us to believe that when you ran off he was still alive and swimming to the shore?'

'That is exactly what happened.'

'Then, Sir James, let us examine these points in a little more detail. First, the blackmail. Was this the first time that Sykes had attempted to blackmail you?'

'Yes.'

'Are you sure that he wasn't dismissed from your household for attempted blackmail?'

'As I've already said, I don't recollect his being employed in my household at all and I have no idea of the circumstances of his dismissal.'

'We'll return to your memory later. What were you being blackmailed about?'

'I cannot tell you,' Jamie said coolly.

'Why not?' Cathcart snapped.

'It concerns a lady's reputation.'

'Oh I see,' Cathcart said sarcastically as a murmur spread through the courtroom, 'a lady's reputation. Of course. How silly of me. In the meantime please tell us why you agreed to a meeting at all, let alone on Kingston Common, if you did not intend to pay him.'

'I wished to make it clear that under no circumstances would I submit to blackmail. Kingston Common was Sykes's choice.'

'A most convenient choice for you, considering your intention to kill him.'

'I strenuously object to that remark, My Lord.' Fitzgerald was on his feet in a flash. 'My learned friend is once again usurping the functions of the jury. No doubt he will graduate to Your Lordship's in a moment!'

'I can assure you he will not,' the judge replied sternly. 'Mr Cathcart, please confine yourself to asking questions.'

'Did it occur to you that your refusal to meet his demands would probably result in an argument leading to violence, Sir James?'

'It did occur to me but I thought it unlikely.'

'But not so unlikely, I suggest, as to prevent you from bringing a weapon with you. Some blunt instrument with which you *battered Sykes to death*.' Cathcart banged on his lectern for effect.

'That's simply not true,' Jamie answered levelly.

'A weapon,' the judge intervened, 'which the prosecution has been unable to produce, Mr Cathcart.'

'Very well, Sir James.' Cathcart ignored the judge's remark. 'Let us return to the subject matter of the blackmail. You say it concerns a lady's reputation?'

'That is correct.'

'And you are obviously unprepared, or unable,' he sneered, 'to produce this lady to corroborate your story. Why is that?'

'I have given my word as a gentleman not to divulge the lady's name.' Jamie scrutinized the jury with care and saw to his relief they they believed him.

'Your word as a gentleman, Sir James?' Let us examine what that's worth,' Cathcart spat. 'You admit that you have lied to the police on more than one occasion.'

'Yes.'

'And naturally as befits a gentleman . . .' He was at his most vitriolic . . . 'you own a large estate in Scotland. How many times have you visited your estate in the last two years?'

'Twice,' Jamie said uncomfortably. 'But I have an excellent factor who manages it for me and I speak to him regularly.'

'And pray tell us what urgent business could prevent a gentleman such as yourself from carrying out his own responsibilities. Gambling and prostitutes perhaps?'

'My Lord, this is intolerable,' Desmond exploded. 'Once again Mr Cathcart is giving us the benefit of his ill-informed opinions.'

'I quite agree, Sir Desmond. Mr Cathcart, I am warning you for the last time,' the judge rebuked him. 'You will confine yourself to cross-examination only at this stage.'

'As Your Lordship pleases,' Cathcart replied unabashed. 'Is it right, Sir James, that you spend much of your time gambling?'

'Yes Mr Cathcart. As you may have heard, many gentlemen do!'

Cathcart flushed and Fitzgerald's belly heaved as the judge gave him a conspiratorial wink.

'But in fact,' Cathcart continued doggedly. 'you are considered one of London's most successful players of poker – a game in which memory plays an important role. Yet you cannot remember a man who worked for you for a period of nine weeks?'

'I'm ashamed to admit that I don't.' Jamie's honesty was apparent.

'Do you know a man named Lennie Landau?'

'Yes.'

'Do you know a woman named Angela McCarthy?'

'I do,' replied Jamie shakily.

'He, I believe, is a well-known pimp and she an equally infamous prostitute.'

'I object!' Fitzgerald was up again. 'My Lord, this has absolutely nothing to do with the case that the jury is here to decide.'

'I'm sorry, Sir Desmond, I'm against you. Such associations may well be relevant to an alleged blackmail.'

'But My Lord, I really must insist. I cannot see how . . .'

'Sir Desmond!' The judge was annoyed. 'I have already made my ruling. Will you please sit down.'

'Certainly – if Your Lordship would prefer me to address you sitting down I will gladly do so!'

Even the judge joined in the laughter and, his objective achieved, Desmond bowed graciously to the gallery.

Simon Cathcart continued in his attempts to blacken Jamie's character but he was beaten. Jamie disposed of the remaining questions effortlessly and, as he left, he could see that the judge believed him as well. His gamble had succeeded.

CHAPTER 13

Shortly before the luncheon adjournment, Norman Foskett, who had been listening intently to Jamie's evidence, was summoned to the police room for an urgent telephone call.

'We've finally found Fanny, Sniffer,' a triumphant Sergeant Davies bellowed.

'I beg your pardon, Davies!' Foskett looked askance at the receiver.

'The girl. Sykes's girlfriend. We've got her here now.'

'Splendid, Davies. Well done. I'll be over in ten minutes to take a statement from her.' Foskett hung up and rushed upstairs to the Bar Mess to warn Simon Cathcart before returning to Scotland Yard.

Forty minutes later Foskett and Superintendent Groves, statement in hand, entered the Commissioner's office.

'All right Ken. What's so important that you had to drag me out of lunch?'

'I'm sorry, but I thought you ought to hear what Foskett has discovered immediately. Go ahead, Norman.'

'Well sir, it's about the Stuart case. We have just found Sykes's girlfriend who was with him until the night he died. She was employed as a personal maid to the Duchess of Alderton and has told us that her mistress was being blackmailed by Sykes over an affair with an American named Hamilton – a great friend of Stuart's. She said that it was

81

Hamilton whom Sykes had arranged to meet that night.'

'Are you saying that Stuart wasn't even there? What about his cigarette case and the tweed coat?'

'We've known for some time that Hamilton had a suit made from the same material and I can only assume that for some reason he was carrying Stuart's cigarette case.'

'Incredible. Why would Stuart take such a risk?'

'I don't know sir.' Foskett shrugged. 'Anyway it seems to have worked; the jury will be sent out this afternoon and they're bound to acquit him. I'm afraid it doesn't end there,' he continued. 'Apparently on the evening of the murder the Duchess returned home around six-thirty drenched to the skin. She gave her dress, which was covered in mud and bloodstains, to the maid and told her to destroy it. The next day the maid was given a large sum of money, instructed to keep her mouth shut and return to her family in Nottingham. This she did, but on hearing of her boyfriend's death, she retrieved the dress and kept it. It's with Forensic now and I'm sure that the blood will prove to be Sykes's.'

'I am certain that it was Hamilton who had the fight with Sykes, that he left him alive in the river and that unknown to both him and Stuart, Edwina Alderton had been watching. She then waited until Hamilton left and murdered Sykes as he climbed, exhausted, up the bank by smashing him on the forehead with something she had found nearby. A large branch perhaps.'

'What's going on at the Old Bailey at the moment?'

'I asked Cathcart to inform the judge of the existence of this witness and to apply for a short adjournment until the statement was taken. Nothing more will happen until they hear from me.'

'Right. Bloody upper-class bastards. Ken, make out a warrant for Edwina Alderton's arrest. I suppose I'll have to clear this with the Home Secretary before we do anything. Foskett, you come with me.'

'My Lord, I would like to ask for a short adjournment. The reason is that during the last hour the police have traced the deceased's girlfriend, one Fanny Harris, and are at this moment taking a statement from her. It is anticipated that her evidence will have a significant bearing on the course of this trial and I may well be making a further application to reopen my case and call this woman as a witness.'

'Very well, Mr Cathcart,' the judge acceded with reluctance. 'I sincerely hope that this is relevant. The court is adjourned but I want to know what's going on in a quarter of an hour.'

Minutes later in the cell below the courtroom, Fitzgerald looked across the wooden table in alarm as his chain-smoking client.

'What is the significance of this woman, dear boy?'

She will send Greg to the gallows, that's the significance, Jamie thought, and ignored the question.

'Tell me, Sir Desmond, is there any possibility of the prosecution dropping the murder charge if I plead guilty to manslaughter? And what sort of sentence would I get if this could be arranged?'

Fitzgerald was stunned. 'What on earth are you talking about? I won't hear such nonsense. I'm not going to allow you to . . .'

'Sir Desmond.' Jamie's voice had become cold and hard. 'We only have ten minutes. I do not have time to explain. Please answer my questions.'

This was a very different young man to the one in the witness box that morning.

'Well, I can only assume that this witness is very damaging to you. Therefore it is extremely unlikely that the prosecution will agree to manslaughter. Assuming they do, however, and I had some reasonable mitigation to put forward, along the lines of self-defence, something I could get my teeth into, then old Hammond, who has always been susceptible to my more emotional mitigations – and likes you anyhow – might be persuaded to keep it down to five or six years.'

'How much of a six-year sentence would I have to serve?'

'You would get one-third remission, which would mean four years.'

'Right. Please try and arrange it.'

'Very well,' Fitzgerald sighed, 'I'll see what I can do.'

'One more thing, Sir Desmond,' Jamie continued. 'My

friend Mr Hamilton is desperately trying to see me. Please tell him from me not to worry and that everything is under control. Just that. Nothing more.'

Lord Glanville, the Home Secretary, was not pleased to be disturbed at the Carlton Club on a Friday afternoon and was even less pleased with the story the Commissioner had to tell him. The thought of the wife of a fellow Minister in the dock of the Old Baily horrified him and he was well aware that, in the present political climate, such a scandal would threaten the very existence of the Government. He sat deep in thought until a club steward informed him that Simon Cathcart was on the telephone, asking for Chief Inspector Foskett.

'I'll take that call, Wilson. I want to speak to him myself.'

Five minutes later Glanville returned.

'We've had a stroke of luck, Wilson.' He rubbed his hands briskly. 'It seems that halfwit Stuart will go to great lengths to protect the life of his American friend. He wants to plead guilty to manslaughter and I've told Cathcart to accept the deal. I'm about to speak to the judge who will give the fool a minimal sentence. Needless to say, you will speak of this to no one. That will be all.'

'Do you mean to say, Minister . . .' Wilson was apoplectic . . . 'that you propose to allow a murderer to go free and an innocent man to go to jail?'

'That is precisely what I propose. What's more, you're going along with it. If you think that I am going to send a Duchess of the Realm to the gallows for the sake of some low-class blackmailing scum, you'd better think again. Now please allow me to finish my lunch.'

'Will the defendant please stand,' the clerk of the court said.

'Sir James Stuart,' the judge began, 'it deeply saddens me to pass sentence on a man such as yourself. You have pleaded guilty to manslaughter and by your plea I am bound to send you to prison. I have listened carefully to the heart-rending mitigation put forward by your distinguished counsel, and am much moved. I fully accept that you were the victim of the lowest type of criminal, whom society is well rid of. You may have the weekend in which to sort out your personal affairs and I will accept your word as a gentleman that you will present yourself to Chief Inspector Foskett at eight o'clock on Monday morning when you will commence a prison sentence of three years.'

Pandemonium broke out. A relieved Jamie stepped down from the dock. He smiled up and shook his head at Greg's protestations. 'See you outside,' he mouthed through the uproar.

A cold chill shot up his spine. The courtroom became a blur. Jamie saw the sad, knowing face of the tramp clearly for the first time. It was the face of his recurrent nightmare – the face of his grandfather Clarence.

BOOK TWO

CHAPTER 1

Bile scalded the back of Jamie's throat and his knees knocked uncontrollably as he moved like an automaton along the wooden bench that filled the reception corridor of Pentonville Prison. He had been hunched for the previous two and a half hours between a stylishly dressed confidence trickster wearing Trumpers' most expensive aftershave lotion and a twitching, emaciated pickpocket who had not washed for several days.

'Stuart. Over here lad.' The uniformed officer did not look up from the list on the metal table in front of him. 'Full name . . . address . . . age. Empty your pockets. Everything in that box. You'll get it back when you leave. Sign here. Right. Off you go.' He pointed down the brick passageway behind him towards a glass door behind which two of his colleagues were waiting.

'Take off your clothes and wait here.' An equally uninterested warder addressed him. Jamie stood shivering until he was directed into a corrugated-iron shed that contained ten rusting baths.

The powerful odour of prison carbolic did nothing to diminish the stench of degraded humanity. Jamie was ordered into a vacant tub with its regulation three inches of dirty, tepid water and a sickening wave of panic enveloped him as he clambered in like an animal into a waterhole. With a shudder he joined the queue of social rejects waiting to be weighed and measured.

Numbly following the reception officer through a labyrinth of gloomy interlocking corridors, Jamie reached the wing to which he had been assigned and was formally placed in the custody of the assistant officer.

'Oh yes, Stuart. Welcome to G wing. I'm afraid we have no one to unpack your cases for you, but do allow me to show you to your rooms. This way number 2819.' The warder spat, prodding Jamie in the ribs and pushing him up the metal steps to a landing. He handed Jamie a battered chamber pot and a soiled green towel and with a mock bow ushered him through an open steel door which he quickly slammed and locked.

Still dazed, Jamie stood in the centre of the small, twelve-foot-square cell. It contained two iron cots, a wooden table, two wooden chairs and a tiny barred window which could only be reached by standing on a chair. A bare light fixed into the ceiling cast a dull shadow over the roughly painted brick walls, covered in illegible scrawl. The pot dropped from his senseless fingers and he collapsed on the unoccupied cot.

He was deprived of his birthright, stripped of his dignity and shorn of his pride. Nothing in his upbringing and experience could have prepared him for the ordeal of incarceration. Sir James Stuart, now merely a number, was the property of the State and his only protection was to be found in his natural gifts.

CHAPTER 2

Jamie's imprisonment was to affect his friends and acquaintances in varied and unpredictable ways.

He had been smuggled out of the courtroom by Sir Desmond through a rear exit and into his Bentley where Greg and Lucy were waiting. Rupert had skilfully driven through the frustrated journalists to the house in Berkeley Square. Still in silence they entered the study. Jamie poured himself a large Scotch, downed it in a single gulp and smiled.

'An acceptable loss under the circumstances, wouldn't you say, Greg old man? Come on you two. Cheer up. It's only three years and I'll be out in two. It could have been a hell of a lot worse.'

'Fuck you Jamie,' Greg replied bitterly. 'It's all just a goddamned game to you, isn't it?'

'Perhaps it is. But the stakes were a bit high this time and I wouldn't want to play that hand again . . .'

'For God's sake, Jamie,' Lucy interrupted in exasperation, tears welling, 'when are you going to grow up? You don't care about anything. You never have. You've killed a man, you're going to prison, and all you can do is make stupid jokes about gambling. Anyway,' she took a deep breath, 'Sedgewicke's already packed your bags for Kilpurnie. I suggest we leave immediately, we won't have much time there in any event.'

'I'm sorry Lucy but I've got no intention of starting my

prison sentence this afternoon. I'm spending the weekend alone with Angela.'

'You're going to spend your last weekend with some filthy whore instead of being in Scotland where you belong? I just don't believe it.' She ran sobbing from the room.

'You really are a prick, Jamie.' Greg shook his head wearily. 'You're sitting here with the only two people in the world who care for you and all you want to do is screw a hooker. Well, you can screw as many of them as you like because I'm going straight to the police and I don't give a shit what happens. I'm glad you had a good time, that the loss is acceptable, and you've still got some chips left for the next hand, but I'm not fucking playing any more and this game's over.' He stood up abruptly and moved to the door.

'For Christ's sake, Greg, just sit down and listen to me for a second. I can assure you that there's nothing I'd like more than for you to serve the two years instead of me. Especially since this was your bloody mess in the first place. But if you go to the police now one of two things will happen. Either they will believe you and you'll be hanged. Or, far more likely, they won't accept your story, you'll make a fool of everyone concerned and create the very scandal we've been trying to prevent. So please stop being stupid and look after Lucy for me while I'm in prison.'

Greg looked down at his friend grimly. 'Jamie, I'm sick of your smooth talk. I should never had listened to you in the first place. I'm going to tell the police the truth and take my chances with them.'

Commissioner Wilson was a man who believed implicitly in justice – he had served it all his life. He listened intently to Greg's agonized confession and thought long and hard.

'Mr Hamilton, there will be no record of this meeting and this conversation never took place. We know conclusively that the charming lady you and Stuart were trying to protect murdered Sykes. Yes, Edwina, Duchess of Alderton murdered Sykes,' he repeated contemptuously. 'And I believe you when you say you saw him getting out of the river. The Home

Secretary has taken the matter out of my hands and refuses to allow me to prosecute her. All the existing evidence plus his own admission has served Stuart up on a plate. That's the way it is and there's nothing any of us can do about it. Believe me, I tried, and if you two silly little children hadn't tried to play stupid games in the first place this would never have happened.'

Greg was beside himself. 'I'm not standing for this! If you can't do anything, I will. I'm going straight to the press. That bitch has got to –'

'I wouldn't bother, Mr Hamilton,' Wilson interrupted with a hollow laugh. 'This is England. The Home Office would never allow the newspapers to print your story and if you so much as open your mouth to them I'll have you on the first plane back home before you can say "Jack Robinson".'

At the precise moment that Jamie was being locked into his cell, Spiros Virakis was ordering breakfast in the Park Suite of the Ritz Hotel. He had occupied the vast apartment since his arrival in London and it had always served as the nerve centre of his global operations. Thoughtfully picking his way through a Greek peasant breakfast of figs, yogurt with honey and thick black coffee, he smiled at the thought of Jamie Stuart starting his prison sentence.

It had been six long months since that black evening on which Stuart had publicly humiliated him. Not only had he, Virakis, lost the largest hand in memory to a *bluff*, but he was sure that his blackballing from Crockford's had been engineered by Stuart. He was convinced that he was the laughing-stock of London's gambling fraternity and the festering sore refused to heal. He was burning for revenge.

He reached for the direct line to his office in St Mary Axe.

'Good morning, Kyrie Virakis.' His personal secretary spoke in Greek.

'Yes Eleni, a very good morning. Please get me that moron Robard.'

'He's in a meeting, Kyrie Virakis.'

'Then save me some money and get him out immediately,

93

eh!' He let out a short nasal laugh and drummed his fingers on the marble table until a gushing and breathless Hugo came on the line.

'Hugo, tell me what is the name of this very pretty red-headed girl that is always with Stuart?'

'Good morning, Spiro,' Hugo panted. 'That's Angela McCarthy – she owns Knavès. Damned good-looking filly, what?'

'I want her to dine with me tomorrow night, please arrange it.'

'Well I don't really know her. But now that arrogant young upstart's in gaol I'm sure there won't be any problem. Your best bet is to have a word with Gavin Blunt at the game tonight.'

'All right Hugo, never mind. Get back to your meeting and try not to talk too much.'

Angela had spent the weekend with Jamie in a pub outside Oxford and, although she had not expected it to be a cheerful occasion, she had been unprepared for the volatile changes in his moods. These had ranged from icy introspection to violent outbursts of temper and had begun immediately after an unexpected visit from Greg on Saturday morning. Jamie had refused to tell her what Greg had said.

All of this she could handle but there had been a significant and shattering change in Jamie's attitude towards her. He had always treated her as a friend and she loved him for it. Indeed she loved everything about him in spite of the fact that he did not love her. All of a sudden that weekend, he had begun to show a contempt towards her which she had never seen before. The hurt this caused was unbearable and for the first time she had to face the painful fact that there had never been any future for her with Jamie.

It was in this dark mood that she sat in her office at Knaves, absently leafing through the forthcoming week's menus. Her thoughts were interrupted by a knock on the door.

'Sorry to disturb you Madam,' the doorman said. 'There's a foreigner out here with a package for you.'

'Tell him to leave it outside, Fred. I'll deal with it later.'

'I'm afraid he's insisting on seeing you personally. Apparently his master is awaiting an immediate reply.'

'Oh all right then, bring him in.'

She instinctively arranged her hair as he admitted a powerfully built, swarthy man with strangely mottled skin.

'How do you do, Miss McCarthy, I am Yiorgio,' he said in faintly accented English. 'My master is Mr Spiros Virakis. He has asked me to deliver this package to you personally and return with your reply.'

'Thank you.' Angela was impressed.

She removed the silver bow and wrappings from the small, red leather box and gasped as she discovered an enormous, heart-shaped ruby pendant on a simple gold chain. Tearing open the envelope she read the handwritten note: 'Please accept this gift and this invitation to dine with me tomorrow night – Virakis.'

Angela looked up at the inscrutable Yiorgio. 'Tell Mr Virakis that I will be delighted to have dinner with him and,' she added with a smile, 'that I look forward to thanking him properly for this beautiful gift.'

'He will be very pleased,' the bodyguard nodded solemnly. 'Would it be convenient for me to collect you at eight o'clock?'

'I look forward to it.'

CHAPTER 3

To the relief of most of his guests Spiros Virakis was in an unusually good mood that night. It was a particular relief to Hugo Robard, who had managed to lose his employer a considerable sum of money earlier that day. Expansively pouring drinks for his guests, Virakis guided them towards a buffet of oysters, lobsters, crabs, cold roast beef, goose and jellied ox-tongue together with various salads and a selection of exotic fruits.

The other poker players were Gavin Blunt, a Yorkshire newspaper proprietor named Henry Murchison, Felix Maggar, the flamboyant Hungarian impresario, and a Jewish property tycoon called Sam Billig. A late arrival was the effete Italian Marquis, Giacomo di Bari, who was also a resident of the Ritz and was infamous among the staff for the procession of handsome young boys that passed through his rooms.

Virakis was more familiar with their personal lives than they would ever have guessed. He possessed a detailed dossier on each of them. He had collected information on the people around him throughout his career, recognizing that knowledge was power.

This evening Virakis was not particularly interested in playing cards. He had formulated the first step in a plan that had become his latest obsession – the destruction of Jamie Stuart. He had suspected for some time that Gavin Blunt was a cheat and was determined to catch him and use the threat of exposure to manipulate Blunt for his own purposes. He had therefore raised no objection to the suggestion that Gavin's bookie friend, Bruce Green, serve as the principal dealer and had secretly enlisted the aid of Sam Billig, who at one time had owned a gaming establishment in the East End.

The game was an hour and a half old. Virakis, having passed his cards, was toying with a string of black worry beads and speculating on the length of time it would take to bed Stuart's whore when his attention was attracted by a cough from Billig.

There were three players left in the pot – Murchison, Maggar and Blunt – the fifth card was still to come, the pot stood at five thousand pounds and the stolid Murchison, showing a pair of queens and the five of hearts, bet three thousand pounds. Maggar called with an open-ended straight to the queen of diamonds.

'Interesting bet, Henry,' teased Blunt who had just received the ace of hearts to accompany the seven and eight of the same suit. 'Let's separate the men from the boys, shall we? Dealer, I call and raise the pot. Fourteen thousand pounds.'

'Men from the boys?' the elderly Yorkshireman grunted. 'All right young lad, I'll see your bet and I'll raise you back another twenty thousand pounds.'

'I think we can safely leave the boys to our dear friend Giacomo.' Maggar smiled charmingly at the Marchese di Bari, whom he knew would not be offended. 'But I call anyway.' He handed his chips to the dealer and ran his fingers exuberantly through his thick brown hair.

'Well, well, chaps.' Gavin sat up with a grin. 'Under the circumstances I won't re-raise, I'll just call.'

Murchison studied his fingernails contentedly, satisfied that his ploy had worked. His closed card was the third queen and his original bet of three thousand pounds had been designed to lure his opponents in. He had not expected Blunt's raise on an obvious pair of aces and was delighted that Gavin's offensive remark had given him the opportunity to back-raise without necessarily exposing the fact that he had three queens. He was the firm favourite to win the hand.

Bruce Green dealt the fifth and final card to each player in turn. Murchison's hand was not improved by the seven of clubs and he was dismayed to see Maggar receive the nine of hearts which appeared to complete his straight. He was unimpressed by Gavin's last card which was the four of hearts, since he was convinced that Blunt could not have been playing for a flush.

'Gentlemen.' The dealer was stacking the chips neatly in the centre of the table. 'Mr Murchison to bet.'

'Check to the possible straight, Felix.'

Maggar had reached exactly the same conclusion as Murchison over Blunt's hand and bet twenty thousand pounds without hesitation, only to be raised a further fifty thousand pounds by a now serious Gavin Blunt.

Murchison, still convinced that Gavin held a pair of aces and was bluffing the flush, nevertheless had no option but to fold his three queens in the face of Maggar's straight.

'I pass,' he said gruffly.

'Well young man.' The impresario's leonine features creased into a warm smile. 'I have no choice; if you have a flush you deserve to win the hand. Call.'

Gavin silently turned up the ten of hearts. 'Thank you Felix,' he said with uncharacteristic modesty. 'I was very lucky.'

'You were indeed my son.' Billig glanced meaningfully at Virakis, who stood up.

'Gentlemen, I have an important phone call to make to my New York Office, perhaps this would be a convenient moment for us to take a short break. Sam, this involves a property situation in which you may be interested. Why don't you join me in the study for a minute? Hugo, perhaps you would take care of our guests in my absence.'

Once inside Virakis wasted no time. 'Well Sam, how did he do it?'

'Easy. Green simply switched decks after the last shuffle. I must say it was nicely done but you'd expect that from a good mechanic.'

'In other words the entire hand was prearranged. No

wonder Blunt raised the opening pair of queens. How could they be so sure that Felix would call?'

'Well, you see,' Billig chuckled, 'that's why they picked on a schmuck like him in the first place. It probably wouldn't have worked on anyone else at the table. But you'll remember that his last card was a heart – so Blunt would have made his flush even if Maggar had dropped out and then *Murchison* would have had to call him.'

Virakis nodded his head in grudging admiration. 'Right. Yiorgio, go into the kitchen and bring Green in here.' He turned to Billig. 'Sam, I will sit behind my desk. I will make Green stand in front of it – you sit in this armchair next to me and please do not say a word. I will handle this.'

'Sure Spiro.' Billig sat down as the door opened and Yiorgio ushered the nervous dealer into the room, pushing him towards the desk.

'Green, you and Blunt have cheated my guests.' Virakis's soft voice was filled with menace. 'There are three of us who have watched you do it and we know exactly how . . .'

'Mr Virakis,' Green interrupted indignantly. 'How dare you . . .' His protestations were cut short by a rabbit punch to the kidneys from Yiorgio and he sank to the floor, moaning in agony.

'Get up, you filth, and speak only when you are told to,' Virakis continued evenly as Green struggled to his feet, clutching his back. 'We know that you changed packs before that last hand and that your association with Blunt goes back many years. You have been cheating together for a long time. You have a simple choice: either you sign a full confession now, or you sign a full confession in five minutes with Yiorgio's assistance.'

Green summoned his last reserves of courage. 'Mr Virakis, you can do what you like to me, but I don't know what you're talking about. Everyone knows that me and Mr Blunt are old associates but that proves nothing and I'm not signing anything.'

Virakis sat back. 'Very well, not only are you a cheat but you are also a fool. Yiorgio, *parakalo*.'

'Hold on a second, Spiro,' Billig broke in, ignoring the

Greek's baleful glance. 'Green, take off your jacket, empty the pockets and give it to me.'

'Of course Mr Billig sir.' The dealer eagerly complied.

'Take off your waistcoat and roll up your sleeves.'

'Yes sir.'

'Really Sam.' Virakis could not contain his impatience. 'This is getting us nowhere.'

'Just give me a little bit longer, Spiro. I don't like violence if it can be avoided. Your trousers please.'

'What about them, sir?' Green's heart sank.

'Take them off.'

'But sir, I, er . . .'

'Take them off!' Virakis screamed suddenly, and in a single movement Yiorgio ripped the trousers from the terrified bookmaker's legs. The three of them watched in fascination as the original pack of cards was revealed strapped to the inside of his thigh.

The rest was easy. Green signed a confession with names, dates and places. It incriminated Blunt totally. The reserve dealer was summoned for the remainder of the game and, after it ended and the unsuspecting guests departed, Gavin proved to be far less brave than his partner in crime. His customary wit deserted him and when he was informed that he could retain his sizeable winnings he too admitted everything in writing.

Virakis was now ready to move on to the next and far more difficult stage of his plan: the assault upon Hamilton and Partners.

CHAPTER 4

Jamie had been in prison for three months when Greg and Lucy decided to get engaged. Since childhood Jamie had been the dominant male figure in Lucy's life and it was natural that in his absence she should come to depend increasingly upon his best friend. The termination of an unfortunate affair with Gavin Blunt had intensified the confusion in her mind and had made Greg seem more solid than ever. Greg for his part had always loved Lucy and his tortured conscience made him feel even more protective towards her.

Greg had gone alone to break the news to Jamie, but it was in a rather depressed mood that he returned to his anxious fiancée, awaiting him at her parents' house in Eaton Square.

'Well darling, how did it go? How is he?'

'Bloody awful.' Greg pushed past her into the sitting-room and began to pour himself a drink. 'He's lost two front teeth, his arm's in a sling, he weighs at least a stone less and looks ten years older.'

'Oh my God . . . But what . . .?'

'How the hell should I know? He certainly won't tell me. He claims to have fallen down the stairs. He refuses to take anything seriously and makes stupid wisecracks about the food being better than at Eton and the company more stimulating than at Oxford. Apparently he's sharing a cell with some con man whom he's become rather fond of. Oh, and by the way,' Greg added caustically, 'he's delighted about the marriage, not least because he will no longer have to worry about you.'

'Worry about me?' Lucy shouted. 'He's never worried about anything in his life, including himself. He's totally self-destructive. Why do you think he spends all his time gambling and chasing cheap actresses and prostitutes?'

'Well, steady, Lucy. He's always loved you, he worshipped his father, and he's been a fantastic friend to me.'

'His father would turn in his grave if he could see him now,' she said bitterly. 'He's the image of his ridiculous grand-father.'

Spiros Virakis would rather have died than admit to the fact that he was nervous. He stopped for at least the fifth time in as many minutes in front of the mirror in the sitting-room and examined himself critically. He frowned as he caught the reflection of his favourite painting, a masterpiece by El Greco, the transcendent purity of the saints' faces contrasting sharply with his own features. He had never been considered good-looking. Short and wiry, he was lighter-skinned than most Greeks. His brown hair was now completely grey and his crooked nose, emphasized by his age, combined with the black hooded eyes to make him look more like a bird of prey than ever. But he knew that few women could resist the raw power that had been part of his personality since his early twenties. Nervousness was as alien to Virakis as scrupulousness was to a fox but over the last few years he had become increasingly disturbed by his growing lack of interest in sex. The marked virility of his earlier years had faded and women had bored him for some time.

The young Spiros Virakis had married the sixteen-year-old daughter of a leading Greek shipowner and although the advantages of this alliance were obvious, they had remained very much in love throughout their marriage despite his well-publicized philanderings. His wife's premature death shortly before her thirtieth birthday had left him grief-stricken and alone without even the solace of the child she had been incapable of bearing him. Since her passing he had escorted many of the world's most desirable women, but they had in the main failed to excite him and he was concerned about the sexual comparison that Angela might make between himself and the young Scot.

Yiorgio's warning buzz announced her arrival and he sat down hurriedly, adopting a relaxed pose.

'My dear Angela. You look lovely. It is very nice of you to come.'

Virakis rose to kiss her hand. He had forgotten how much taller than himself she was. 'I trust Yiorgio's driving was not too uncomfortable for you – he sometimes forgets he is no longer a racing driver.'

'It was perfect. Thank you for your magnificent present.' She slowly caressed the blood-red ruby at her throat and, holding his gaze steadily with her green eyes, she brushed her lips against his.

'Not at all, my dear.' Virakis stepped back, resting the tips of his fingers lightly on her bare shoulders. 'Let me see it properly. Beautiful. But it does not do you justice. Please sit down. A glass of champagne?'

He reached for the small silver bell on the mantelpiece, noting that she was naked beneath a long, black, silk dress, slit to the waist.

'I was very sorry to hear of your friend Jamie's unfortunate situation,' he said. 'Please give him my regards. Have you visited him?'

'He doesn't want to see me. And frankly I'm glad. He's so irresponsible and reckless that I'm better off without him.'

'Mmm . . . reckless . . . really? Yet he is a fine poker player. A most unusual combination. But what about you, my dear? This recklessness, it is something you have also?'

'Only where men are concerned.'

'A serious weakness, unless you know men very well.'

'I know them well enough.' She ran her fingers round the rim of her glass. 'But I hear you're quite a gambler yourself. Is it true that you won an oil tanker in a card game when you were twenty-one?'

'Not exactly an oil tanker my dear,' Virakis said sardonically, pleased nevertheless with the opportunity to tell one of his favourite stories. 'And I was closer to thirty. But it was a ship, that fact at least is true.' He laughed. 'It was in a Turkish restaurant in Piraeus. It had no money – I was a simple sailor – but I won a big hand from a crafty Lebanese merchant who refused to pay me. My shipmate, Yiorgio, and I visited him later that night and explained to him that he could either pay me at the moment – or five minutes later with the additional sacrifice of his manhood. This was a decision he did not find difficult to make, but since he did not have the necessary cash he managed to persuade me to accept a ship in satisfaction of the debt. Unfortunately the word ship was, shall we say, a little euphemistic. It was an almost worthless, rotting, wooden tub that could hardly stay afloat. But Yiorgio and I, we patched her up and she was faithful to us for one final voyage to Benghazi. It was a profitable journey and the foundation of my business, although that ship – the *Artemis* – never sailed again.'

He paused reflectively for a moment and then continued almost to himself. 'You know the first ship is like the first woman – however many you have, you never forget her . . . And now if you are ready, my dear.' His voice grew firmer and he waved towards the dining-room. 'Perhaps you will lead the way.'

Virakis was surprised to feel the stirrings of excitement when in one fluid movement Angela left her chair and swept gracefully past him, luxuriant red hair cascading freely down her bare back. Her pale complexion was illuminated by the flickering candlelight while she waited in the open doorway. His pulse quickened as he took in her magnificent body through the translucent dress, her firm jutting breasts contrasting dramatically with her tiny waist and long willowy legs. He came up behind her to help her to her seat and could not resist stroking the tight, rounded buttocks, a sharp stab of desire shooting through his loins. She turned to face him and gently removed his hands from her bottom. She placed them on her breasts. Kissing him hungrily on the lips, she traced his erection with her long fingernails. Breathlessly they broke apart. Taking his arm, she silently guided him back into the darkened sitting-room to within a few feet of the roaring log fire.

With a shrug of her shoulders, the dress slipped from her body and floated to the floor. She stood naked before him and, removing his jacket and tie, she began delicately to unbutton his shirt. Virakis's need for her was uncontrollable and he tore frantically at his trousers, throwing them carelessly aside. She sank to her knees, taking the full length of his throbbing penis into her mouth, simultaneously stroking his testicles with her hands. Moans of ecstasy came from deep in her throat as he clasped her head tightly against his stomach. Removing one of her hands, she reached feverishly for her swollen clitoris and, massaging it violently, brought herself to a shuddering climax.

Growling savagely, Virakis pushed her on to her back, pulling her legs up around his neck. He grabbed her buttocks and plunged frenziedly deep inside her time and time again.

'Oh yes, yes, fuck me . . . fuck me . . . Oh God, I'm coming . . . I'm coming again!' she screamed and held on to him as if she was drowning until in a succession of violent spasms they orgasmed together.

Two hours later they finally separated and, too exhausted to get up, they fell asleep in each other's arms in front of the dying embers of the fire.

CHAPTER 5

Although the moment that Jamie Stuart was offered the 'book' in Pentonville Prison could be pinpointed without difficulty, those key inmates found their reasons for approaching him less easy to isolate and understand. It is a matter of record, however, that it was offered to him. And that it had never been offered to anyone before. True, Jamie's physical courage had been proved beyond dispute in two well-known incidents; true, his celebrated gambling skills and vastly superior education set him apart from his fellow prisoners, but they not unnaturally lacked the perception to realize that it was the elusive quality of his gift that in fact led them to take such an unprecedented step.

The first incident took place during the morning of Jamie's second day. He had been awakened at 5.50 by the harsh rattling of the lock on his cell door and the command to 'slop out'. Following Alan Shepherd to the recess area on the landing outside, he emptied the contents of his cracked pisspot into the single toilet in the corner and waited his turn to fill his jug with boiling water from the tap opposite. A foetid stench of urine and defecation rose from the toilet as each prisoner disposed of his previous night's excretia, and Jamie returned to his cell to wash and shave with a razor blade that had to be returned immediately afterwards.

'Never mind the ablutions.' The former army corporal stuck his head through the open door. 'You're both on "Governor's" in five minutes. Get moving. On the double.'

'Governor's?' Jamie looked enquiringly at his cellmate.

'We have to report to the Governor – everybody does on their first day,' Shepherd replied. 'Come on. We'd better go.'

The cacophony of banging doors, jangling keys and clattering trays was deafening as they marched along the narrow wing past the other cells and down the metal stairs. Glancing over the railing, Jamie could see the steel safety net that stretched the length of his prison block and was designed to deter those inevitable thoughts of suicide that entered every prisoner's mind.

Jamie's interview with the Governor was short and to the point. He was detailed to sew mailbags and told that with good behaviour he would be released in two years. He was summarily dismissed and instructed to take a shower.

The shower room consisted of one long row of twenty open cubicles shrouded by a dense fog of steam. Stripped and body-searched by the duty officer, Jamie was placed in the charge of a trusty – 'redband' in prison jargon – and was led through the thick swirling steam to the cubicle farthest from the entrance. Although his vision was obscured, he began to sense that while all the showers were operating fully only the first few were actually occupied. He suddenly realized that he was in danger.

He stood alert with the hot water drenching him as the trusty scurried off into the gloom, and within moments a pot-bellied, middle-aged man with brutal features joined him in the cubicle, one hand slowly masturbating a fat, stubby penis.

'Suck it pretty boy,' he hissed, inserting his tongue into Jamie's ear. 'Suck it and swallow it, my sweet. Or you'll never swallow again.'

Jamie bent down and took the tumescent penis into his mouth. He closed his eyes and fought the vomit rising in his throat. Waiting until he felt the man relax, he suddenly clenched his teeth together and bit as hard as he could, his jaw aching with the effort. Hot blood spurted into his mouth and flowed out over his chin, but he hung on to the penis like a mongoose to a writhing cobra. The screams of agony were drowned by the overworked showers and the man slumped to his feet unconscious. Only then did Jamie release his grip and retch violently for several minutes into the lake of blood and water. Slowly straightening, he place-kicked his aggressor three times in the groin before coolly retracing his steps and retrieving his clothes from the nervous trusty.

He spent the rest of the day in shock waiting for the inevitable retribution. He neither noticed nor felt the rusty iron needle lacerating the palms of his hands as he repeatedly forced it through the thick canvas mailbags. He spoke to no one and no one spoke to him and he didn't know whether his fellow prisoners were unaware of what had taken place, or whether for some reason they were unwilling to discuss it. He was therefore somewhat wary when his cellmate broached the subject that evening.

Alan Shepherd was arguably the most brilliant confidence trickster of the day. And, as is always the case with people of such persuasion, had his talents been directed towards legitimate enterprises they would have taken the financial centres of the world by storm. Educated at Harrow and Sandhurst – or so it was said – he had, after a short stint with the Coldstream Guards, made a dazzling début in Shanghai where he persuaded the Chinese government to part with over two million dollars, with the assistance of superbly counter-feited Certificates of Deposit.

Slight of build (and of indeterminate age and looks) he nevertheless commanded great respect among his fellow prisoners and, despite his apparent bonhomie, Jamie did not know whether he could be trusted.

'You seem to have caused a bit of a stir this morning, my old fruit.' Shepherd was delicately mopping the last traces of cabbage from his tin plate with a stale crust and eyeing Jamie's uneaten meal. 'You have become, to say the least, something of a celebrity.'

'I don't know what you mean.'

'Come on Jamie. Everyone in this block including the screws knows exactly what you did to Joe Carpenter. Apparently he's lucky to be alive.'

'I'm sorry Alan.' Jamie did not allow his relief to show. 'I

111

still don't know what you're talking about.'

'Don't worry old fruit,' Shepherd said patiently. 'You're in the clear. Joe's an old lag. He knows his way around and he bribed the redband to set you up and keep the screws in the dark. Unfortunately for him you wouldn't play ball, to coin a phrase.' He chuckled. 'The beauty of it is that no one can say anything. The redband can't admit he was bribed, the screws have to cover it up or they're responsible; and Joe will certainly never grass on you. In fact, as soon as he's better, they'll probably transfer him to another prison. Now, if you are not going to eat your food, pass it over here. There's no point in wasting it.'

Jamie absently pushed his plate across the wooden table. 'What about his friends – am I going to have trouble with them?'

'Definitely not. You've proved you can handle yourself and you've gained everyone's respect.'

Sleep did not come easily to Jamie that night. The lights had been put out at nine o'clock and on Shepherd's advice he had refused the mug of the bromide-laced cocoa that was distributed each evening. His blistered, aching hands and the haunting sounds of prison by night denied him refuge. The sounds grew louder as they multiplied. The spasmodic streams of urine from neighbouring cells; the heavy footsteps of the night warders; the occasional scream for his family of a dreaming man; the barking of the prison dogs in the courtyard and many other noises that Jamie could not identify. As the night grew more still the familiar sounds of clinking glasses and drunken laughter from the pubs closing in the Caledonian Road reached him, reminding him of Oxford and happy, carefree student days that seemed so very far away.

The second incident took place about a month later and was distinguishable from the first – though not in its violence – by the fact that it was instigated by Jamie Stuart in a cold-blooded and calculated fashion. Its origins lay partly in the unique nature of Jamie's gift and partly in the gratuitously brutal manner which typified the behaviour of the enforcer Frank Richards.

Over the preceding five weeks, Jamie had adjusted well to the maddening monotony of his new life. His relationships with both the warders and the convicts were distant but satisfactory and he received no trouble from either quarter. His hands had grown accustomed to the daily labour of sewing mailbags and he had become reasonably adept at rolling his own cigarettes from the meagre ration of tobacco that he was permitted. He became an avid reader in order both to alleviate the boredom and also prevent his mind from degenerating to the level of the vast majority of the inmates (he was helped in this by the fact that Shepherd worked in the library and could smuggle out more than their weekly quota of books). He received regular letters and visits from Lucy, Sedgewicke, and in particular Greg, whose persistent feelings of guilt were undiminished by Jamie's attempts to make light of his predicament.

Although he kept to himself as much as possible, Jamie found one aspect of nightly 'association' appealing and that was the regular game of three-card brag – a simplified, far more basic version of poker which required nerve but little skill. Each participant received three cards face down which he could look at whenever he wished, and for the period during which he was 'blind' his bets cost half as much as those of 'open' players.

The game was controlled with a rod of iron by a grey-bearded, handsome but ruthless gangland chief, called Dirk Brett, who was the undisputed kingpin of the gaol. At the root of his power lay the fact that he was the prison bookmaker through whom all horse-racing bets were placed, and this was the base for a sophisticated credit operation with an attendant, far-reaching network of collectors and enforcers. In the absence of cash the currency for all bets and loans was tobacco.

The events that led up to the incident took place one Friday evening during a brag session and, as always, there were ten players with several others waiting to take the place of those who dropped out. The best gamblers were Jamie, Brett, Alan Shepherd and Frank Richards, whose bloodthirsty savagery Jamie had witnessed that very morning in the mailbag room when he had stuck a needle through the throat of some unfortunate debtor.

Jamie's natural advantage came into play only when opponents ceased to bet 'blind' and thus knew the value of their own hands. Just such a situation arose when Richards, after several rounds of 'blind' betting, picked up his cards to discover that he held a pair of eights and made a largish bet. Jamie then squeezed open his cards and found a pair of tens which he knew would win. He accordingly raised by a sufficient amount to ensure that his bet would be called and Frank Richards obligingly complied.

'What have you got, sonny?'

'A pair of tens.' Jamie turned his cards over.

'You fucking lucky turd.' Richards threw his hand in disgustedly and sat brooding for a while.

'Hang on a minute.' Suspicion turned to anger in his pea-sized brain. 'You made a small fucking raise on a fucking pair of tens knowing fucking well I was going to call it. You must have seen my cards. You cheating little cunt.'

'I can assure you, Frank . . .' Richards's massive fist smashed through Jamie's front teeth, lifting him from his stool and throwing him across the landing.

'Frank!' Brett's voice cracked the silence like a whip as the enforcer hurled himself on to Jamie, reaching for his throat. 'That's enough. Leave him alone.'

A homicidal light burned brightly in Richards's eyes and he struggled to control himself. 'I'm not going to be cheated by this filthy little ponce.'

'Frank! – I *said* that's enough. Don't make me say it again. You weren't cheated.'

Jamie's life hung in the balance for ten long seconds. Richards scowled at the prison overlord who stared back through narrowed eyes, forcing him to drop his gaze. He slouched back to his seat.

With what little strength he had left in his battered body, Jamie gripped the railings and pulled himself to his feet. He stood shakily, blinking hard in an attempt to clear his blurred vision. His face was covered in blood, his lips were split open to the gums and his left arm hung limply by his side. Lurching towards the table he stumbled several times and spat out the remains of his two front teeth. Brett nodded to Alan Shepherd, who immediately got up and helped Jamie walk towards the gangway back to their cell.

'Try biting someone's cock now, you dirty little pansy,' Richards shouted at their departing backs, clowning obscenely with his fingers and mouth to the other players, most of whom joined with him in ribald laughter.

Few of those who bothered to glance at Jamie, however, would forget the chilling look of hatred on his ravaged face as he painfully turned for a moment and stared blindly in Richards's direction.

In the weeks that followed, Jamie ignored both the diminishing respect with which he was treated by his fellow prisoners and the pain of his badly repaired teeth. He was obsessed by a childhood memory of an accident that had taken place in the kitchens of Kilpurnie Castle.

'Alan, how do I get my hands on a couple of pounds of brown sugar as quickly as possible?'

'A couple of pounds. Mmm . . .' Shepherd thoughtfully stroked his chin. 'That's a great deal of sugar. Beady Alfred in the kitchen is your only way.'

'What will it cost?'

'Let me see . . . Alfie will probably want three or four ounces of burn for himself . . . the sugar will knock you back about the same . . . you'll have to pay a redband an ounce to deliver it . . . and if a screw needs straightening you'll have to throw in a pony.'

In other words, I'll need about nine ounces of tobacco and twenty-five pounds in cash. The money's no problem. How much tobacco have you got?'

'A couple of ounces old fruit. Of course you're welcome to it.'

'Thank you Alan, I appreciate that. I've got about the same myself – I'll arrange a loan with Dirk Brett for the balance. How long will it take to get the sugar?'

'Not very long – should have it by tomorrow. Mind telling

me what this is all about?'

'All in good time Alan,' Jamie said through crooked teeth. 'One last thing. Is there anyone we can really trust on this wing, who has a cell between us and the recess area and hates Frank Richards?'

'So that's what this is all about. Everyone's been saying you've lost your bottle. Most people hate Richards but they're all terrified of him . . . Jimmy the Weasel's your man provided you pay him enough. Come on, you can tell me now. What have you got up your sleeve?'

'It's better you don't know at this stage. What I want you to do is set up the sugar deal immediately and I'll need a very simple alibi which I'll explain nearer the time.'

'All right Jamie. When are you planning on doing it?'

'If all goes well, the day after tomorrow.'

Everything did go well. Dirk Brett, who was being released in two weeks' time, was forthcoming with the loan. Alan Shepherd arranged delivery of the sugar and Jimmy the Weasel, in an unprecedented gesture, offered to play his part without remuneration.

Two days later Frank Richards awoke at first bell, stretched, belched loudly and examined the stubble on his chin in the tin mirror at the side of his bunk. It was to be the last time that he would ever see his face. Reaching for his water jug and his personal roll of toilet paper he waited for his cell door to be opened and ambled down the gangway to the recess area. Those prisoners present, including Alan Shepherd, hastily filled their jugs with boiling water and vacated the area, not daring to disturb his customary morning ablutions. He took down his trousers, sat on the latrine and remained alone for less than two minutes, when to his surprise he was confronted by the toothless grin of Jamie Stuart.

'What the fuck are you doing here, you little arse?' He looked up.

'I've come to say goodbye, Frank old man,' said Jamie and poured the sticky, scalding, golden contents of his jug over Richards's head and face.

The entire wing froze in horror as Richards's screams of agony shattered the morning routine. His hands desperately clawed at his face in a useless attempt to prevent the mask of bubbling treacle from penetrating his eyes. Jamie grabbed him by the neck and viciously kicked him in the back, propelling him down the gangway where – trousers still around his ankles – he stumbled sobbing from door to door in a grotesque caricature of a crazed beast. Jamie strolled back towards his cell, casually exchanging his sugar-stained water jug with that of the waiting 'Weasel', who amid the growing confusion then slipped unnoticed into the recess area and thoroughly removed all traces of the incriminating substance.

Jamie meanwhile entered his own cell, slamming the door shut behind him, and half-filled the clean jug with Alan Shepherd's already dirty water. He lay on his bunk and lit a cigarette. He could not remember a cigarette tasting as good.

Richards was not as fortunate as the cook making butterscotch at Kilpurnie had been. He was blinded and his face hideously disfigured for the rest of his life. It came as no surprise that the prison authorities, who were secretly rather pleased to rid themselves of a troublesome inmate, were unable to prove a case against Jamie. Dirk Brett – not least because of his imminent departure – was unperturbed at losing the services of his most effective employee, and after consultation with his closest advisers, decided to offer Jamie the book in exchange for the sum of two thousand pounds to be paid on the outside. Jamie accepted and immediately delegated the daily responsibilities to Alan Shepherd as his second-in-command.

After nine weeks Sir James Stuart Bt – prisoner number 2819 – had become the most powerful man in Pentonville.

CHAPTER 6
LONDON, 1953

The telephone call that Gavin Blunt had been dreading came late one sunny spring morning in his rented house in Curzon Street. His only contact with Virakis since that fateful evening had been at the small marriage ceremony at the Greek Orthodox Cathedral in Bayswater which had been timed to legitimize the birth of the son and heir Virakis had dreamed of all his life.

'Good morning Spiro, how's married life treating you?'

'I want you to have lunch with me at the White Tower restaurant today. Shall we say one-thirty?'

'How kind of you. I'd love to but I'm afraid that's a little difficult. A horse of mine is running this afternoon in the two o'clock at Newbury. How about tomorrow at my club?'

'Tomorrow is too late. Be at the White Tower today.'

Virakis hung up and Gavin resignedly dialled his trainer, groaning at the thought of an indigestible Greek lunch in Soho.

Spiros Virakis was not one for wasting words. Besides, he wished to return to his son.

'I understand your good friend Sir James is leaving the prison today and is to attend the wedding of his cousin to the

119

American banker Hamilton tomorrow. A very social wedding, I believe, and one to which my wife and I were not invited. Eh?' He reached for another plate of olives.

'That's right,' Gavin replied, declining the proffered plate. 'The date was fixed so that Jamie could be there.'

'I hear he made a big name for himself in the prison.'

'Really? I have no idea . . .'

'Well, so I am informed. Anyway I wonder whether he will continue to play poker.'

'Of course he will. It's the only thing he knows, it's his whole life.'

'Precisely.' Virakis refilled his glass with ouzo. 'And he is the finest player I have seen in forty years.'

'That's a matter of opinion.'

'The *finest* I said. But he has two important advantages. One, relatively unlimited funds, and two, a natural talent given by God. This talent only God can take away. But *I*, with your help, will seriously reduce his funds and then we shall see how he plays. I propose to crucify him on the tables in front of everyone.'

'Presumably you want me to cheat him,' Gavin said laconically.

'Certainly not. That is out of the question. Spiros Virakis does not cheat at cards – it is a matter of honour. I will destroy him beforehand, but once the game begins I will defeat him honestly. No. This is what I want you to do.

'There is a certain shipyard in Scotland called Strathclyde Construction which is suffering great hardships as a result of the present slump in the market. In fact it is going bankrupt. The banks have refused to lend it any more money unless it receives important orders to build new ships. Blunt and Company, my dear Gavin, will place such orders with Strathclyde. These will be for six major oil tankers and will amount to a total of eighteen million pounds.'

'You must be joking. Blunt and Company have sold virtually all their ships just to stay afloat. The banks know perfectly well we couldn't commission a rowing-boat at the moment.'

'I know that,' Virakis said contemptuously, 'you will do

120

what you are told and leave the rest to me.'

'OK, suit yourself.' Gavin shrugged. 'But how am I going to convince my cousin, Peregrine, to go along with it?'

'I understand that during his apprenticeship in the East Mr Peregrine developed some Oriental addictions which are rather expensive to maintain. I want the three of us to meet within the next seven days and I will explain everything. Ah . . . here is Yiorgio . . . I must leave now. I will speak with you soon. I hope the wedding goes well.'

The scene at 26 Park Lane was one of domestic bliss. Angela Virakis was in the nursery, playing with her two-year-old son Andreas under the experienced eye of Nanny Peabody. She reflected on the momentous events that had culminated in the marriage which had so dramatically altered her life. She would never know for certain whether her husband would have married her had she not become pregnant after that first night, but she did not doubt for a moment the physical hold that she had over him.

She had entered a world that she had never dreamed existed, a world inhabited by very few people and one which even Jamie Stuart, with all the privileges of his birth, could not afford. This world encompassed private islands in Greece and the Carribbean, a hunting-lodge in Bavaria and homes in New York, Los Angeles, Paris, London and the South of France. She always travelled by personal aeroplane or helicopter and society hostesses, couturiers and jewellers vied for her patronage wherever she went. But above all else, there was power, power to create and corrupt, to destroy and to deify. That all-pervading power – the ultimate aphrodisiac – which was the breath of life to her husband and would one day be inherited by the child in her arms.

'*Angelaki mou.*' Her reverie was disturbed. 'How is Master Andreas? I see he is rather wilful, my darling, just like his father, eh!'

Angela joined in his laughter and got up, placing the baby into her husband's outstretched arms. She kissed him lovingly on the cheek. Watching the proud father play with his son, a glow of satisfaction enveloped her. She was pleased to see that

Virakis at sixty-one now looked ten years younger.

Thank God I've given him a boy, she thought. He'll never leave me now.

'Come, darling.' Her husband returned the child to the nanny. 'Let us leave Andreas to sleep and walk in the garden. It's a lovely afternoon, the roses are almost as beautiful as you.'

They strolled arm in arm out of the nursery on to the lawn.

'Did you do something brilliant today, my love?' she asked affectionately.

'Yes.' He let out a nasal laugh. 'I had lunch with an old friend of yours – Gavin Blunt.'

'Gavin Blunt!' she snorted. 'He's no friend of mine. If it weren't for Jamie he would never have been allowed to set foot in my club. He used to get his kicks from beating up my girls. Lennie and I spent all our time covering up for him. I never understood why Jamie liked him so much – he's absolute filth.'

'You must always remember, my dear, that even filth has its uses and I have a special one for young Mr Blunt. By the way, Stuart was released from prison this morning and will be best man at Hamilton's wedding tomorrow.'

'Good, I'm glad it's all over for him – it's that poor bastard Greg I feel sorry for now. I wonder if he's got any idea what he's letting himself in for.'

'What do you mean, my darling? What is wrong with the Lady Lucinda?'

'It's the best-kept secret in London. That stuck-up little bitch is a raging dyke!'

'Dyke! What is this word?'

'Lesbian to you, Spiro my love.' She stroked his neck. 'Your precious Lady Lucinda has fucked every girl that ever worked at Knaves. Whenever her parents were in the country dear old Leslie had to ferry them round to Eaton Square at all hours of the day and night. That's another thing Jamie never knew about.'

'Really. I can hardly believe this. Most interesting. It certainly does appear that Hamilton's problems are only just beginning. Mmm . . . Dyke . . . Very interesting word. Dyke, eh?'

A week later, and to his disgust, Gavin found himself once more in the White Tower restaurant.

'Mister Peregrine, thank you for coming.' Virakis opened the meeting. 'For reasons which do not concern you I wish to embarrass Sir James Stuart financially. In order to accomplish this it is necessary to ruin the bank of Hamilton and Partners in which Sir James has invested all his available cash.'

Peregrine was taken aback. 'Well Mr Virakis, I must say you don't mince your words.'

'It is a waste of time. This is my plan. The Strathclyde shipyard, despite its fine reputation, is deeply in debt – in particular to its main bank the Union Bank of Edinburgh. It cannot borrow more money without receiving substantial orders to build new ships. Blunt and Company will therefore place an order for the building of six large oil tankers to the value of eighteen million pounds.'

'Mr Virakis, don't be ridiculous!' Peregrine Blunt stared in amazement.

'I am not in the habit of being ridiculous,' the Greek snapped. 'Please be courteous enough to allow me to continue. I will provide you with the ten per cent deposit required for the work to begin and one of my companies will contract to time-charter the vessels from you for five years at very profitable rates.'

'But Mr Virakis,' Peregrine said patiently, 'no matter how generous your contract may be, you must know that we will not be in a position to pay for these ships on their completion.'

'Ah, but you will. This contract will be at the rate of six million pounds per annum, of which the first three years will be paid in advance to enable you to take delivery. Furthermore, in the event of something going wrong, a reputable Swiss bank will guarantee payment to Strathclyde.'

'My God!' Peregrine glanced excitedly at his younger cousin, who remained unmoved. 'This is the deal of a lifetime. It will put Blunt and Company back on the map and no mistake.'

'I regret not, Mr Peregrine, rather the reverse. This little transaction will bankrupt Blunt and Company for ever. Because, you see, you will never actually take delivery of the ships and therefore my contract will be totally irrelevant.'

Peregrine Blunt paled and dabbed his forehead with the yellow silk handkerchief that he habitually kept in his sleeve.

'You can't be serious, sir. Bankrupt the family company! It's been in existence for five generations and I'm certainly not going to be a party to its destruction. Besides, as you yourself said, we'll still have the Swiss bank guarantee.'

'That, I promise you, will turn out to be worthless. But speaking of Switzerland, you will each receive half a million pounds personally, to be paid in advance into the bank of your choice. This is not so worthless, eh? You can purchase many, many opium pipes, with this eh, Mr Peregrine, eh?'

'Well . . . I . . . er . . . don't . . .'

'That's very generous of you, Spiro,' Gavin said swiftly. 'Of course we accept, don't we Perry?'

'Yes . . . er . . . yes . . . I suppose we have no choice. Gentlemen, will you excuse me for a moment?' With visibly trembling hands he pushed himself away from the table and hurried towards the lavatory.

Virakis turned to Gavin. 'We must all answer the calls of nature, however exotic they might be, eh! Have some more of this excellent Turkish Delight.'

'No thank you Spiro, but do you mind if I ask you one or two questions?'

'Of course not.' The Greek waved an arm expansively.

'I realize it's not difficult, but how exactly do you envisage Blunt and Company going bankrupt?'

'You will simply default on your largest existing bank loan at least six months before the ships have been completed. Your bank will have no choice but to start bankruptcy proceedings, which will in turn enable me to declare our contract void.'

'Very ingenious. How is all this going to affect Hamilton and Partners?'

'The Union Bank of Edinburgh do much business with Hamilton and Partners. They have very close links, and in fact one of their senior managers now works for Hamilton's. Strathclyde will need to borrow at least twelve million pounds in order to service your contract. They already owe the Union Bank three million pounds, who will therefore need to share the risks of a new and further loan with another bank. That other bank will be Hamilton and Partners. First, for the reasons I have already mentioned, and second, because Gregory Hamilton's father-in-law, the Earl of Lochmair, is Minister of Industry for Scotland. His main problem is the declining employment in the Scottish shipyards, and he will pressure them into joining the loan. Gregory Hamilton is not a stupid man and will not initially be very impressed by the Blunt order, even though you are a friend of Sir James Stuart. He will, however, be impressed by my contract and the Swiss bank guarantee will make the deal irresistible.'

'I understand . . . so what exactly is the end result?'

'After Blunt and Company go bankrupt and the Swiss guarantee proves to be useless, Strathclyde will be unable to repay their loan and will also go bankrupt. The banks will be left with six ships which under current market conditions will only fetch a quarter of their building cost. Hamilton and Partners will lose around four million pounds.'

'But surely they can handle that sort of loss?'

'That alone, perhaps. But there will be additional and unforeseen circumstances which they will be unable to control.'

'And all this, plus the one million pounds you're giving us, just to beat Jamie at cards?'

'My dear Gavin, you underestimate me. I will then step in and buy the ships for a total of four million pounds and put them to work immediately and very profitably, since of course they will have been built to suit my exact requirements. Yet, it will embarrass Stuart financially, but I will make a great deal of money out of this little transaction.'

CHAPTER 7

The dingy shops and drab pavements of the Caledonian Road sparkled and smiled as the two prisoners stepped through the small wooden door to liberty. They were dressed in the clothes with which they had arrived twenty-eight months earlier. A casual onlooker would have been surprised to discover that both men had served sentences of identical length. Indeed, he would have been surprised to discover that the shorter and older of the two had served a prison sentence at all, such was the perfect fit of his suit.

Jamie's car was waiting and they drove delightedly through the reassuring streets of the West End to Claridge's.

'Well, good luck, old man.'

'Thanks Jamie. Keep in touch.'

Colonel Douglas Barrington-Smythe, alias Alan Shepherd, stepped smartly out of the Bentley, acknowledged the respectful greetings of the doorman and marched through the main entrance straight up to the hotel flower shop.

'Rupert . . .' Jamie leaned across the front seat. 'Would you mind making your own way home from here? I'd like to drive myself.'

'Yes, of course, Sir James.' The chauffeur jumped out and held the driver's door open for him. 'I'll see you later, sir.'

Alone for the first time in over two years, Jamie felt like a child on Christmas morning. His whole being thrilled to the forgotten power and beauty of the great old motor car. The deep rich leather caressed him and delighted his deprived and hungry nostrils with its luxurious, comforting smell. He reached over to the mahogany glove compartment for a packet of his own cigarettes. Breaking the seal, he took one out and lit it with the ivory-topped lighter from the dashboard in front of him. He inhaled the smooth smoke with appreciation and, leaving Grosvenor Square behind him, drove into Carlos Place and on through Berkeley Square. Barely glancing at his own house, he continued up Curzon Street and into Park Lane. He was not yet ready to go home.

After Hyde Park Corner the Bentley found itself following a familiar route down Knightsbridge, along Sloane Street and past the King's Road until it finally entered Cheyne Row. Obediently it came to a halt outside the little flat and Jamie sat there for an hour overwhelmed by memories of lost innocence and youthful folly before remembering that Greg and Lucy were waiting.

Sedgewicke was shocked. Important though it is for a good butler to be a good actor, he was far more than just a butler and was unable to conceal his emotions. Jamie had put on a brave imitation of his old flippant, irresponsible self until Lucy and Greg had left but now he sat in his dressing-room while Sedgewicke drew his bath, his ill-fitting suit hanging loosely around his narrow shoulders, the blue eyes made brighter than ever by the grey prison pallor of his face.

'God, Sedgewicke,' he whispered, 'I'm tired and I stink. As soon as this wedding's over we're going on a long holiday.'

'Of course, Sir James.' The servant hesitated. 'May I respectfully suggest that we go up to Scotland first for a few days. McClintock tells me that . . .'

'Please Sedgewicke, don't start that again. I've just come out of one prison! It can wait until we get back.'

Greg sat at the head of the table and positively glowed with happiness. He had good reason to glow. This was his stag night and tomorrow he would marry the girl he loved. All his remaining family, apart from his headstrong young sister Jessica, had come over for the wedding. Earlier that year she had eloped with an explorer more than twice her age and was somewhere deep in the Peruvian jungle in search of a lost city. His father, brother and even his eighty-six-year-old grandmother were here but he felt a tinge of sadness that his mother was no longer alive.

Opposite him, deep in conversation with his younger brother Morton, who seemed more interested in the erotic picture that decorated the room, was Jamie. What a friend Jamie had been! The debt he owed this strange, remote yet reckless, cold yet incredibly loyal Englishman was incalculable. Somehow, Greg thought, some day, I'll make it up to him.

His eyes moved on around the cosy dining-room to the Adam fireplace where, warming their brandies against the leaping flames, were Gavin Blunt and good old Jeremy Hunter chatting animatedly about the vagaries of the turf. He had always disliked Gavin. The man was untrustworthy, rude and arrogant, but he put up with him for Jamie's sake. Still, he thought grudgingly, Gavin did have indisputable style and, notwithstanding his precarious finances, had generously donated several magnums of vintage Krug to tonight's proceedings.

A discreet knock on the door signalled the arrival of Lennie Landau with the girls from downstairs. Greg began to chuckle at the sight of his brother's bulging eyes as a tall, big-breasted blonde planted herself firmly on his lap. Hell, leave it to Jamie. Who else could own a place like Knaves!

CHAPTER 8

'. . . for a very long time this country was much wealthier than other nations. Our banks financed the world, our industries led the world. Our navy kept the peace. All this changed when things other than ships could cross the seas. While I admire and respect our American friends and allies of two world wars, the United Kingdom must not allow itself to rely on others in its battle against Communism, however much it costs. I mistrust, My Lords, a nation that has the temerity to state openly, and I quote directly from the Communist Party Doctrine: "Bloody wars will be inevitable as the dying Capitalist states turn, like wolves at bay, against the Soviet Homeland."

'I once again draw the attention of this House to the fact that the Russians are maintaining their forces at a level of one hundred and seventy-five divisions and the West remains sublimely indifferent. I urge you, My Lords, to spare no expense, to waste no further time. Britannia must rule the air as it once ruled the waves.'

Lord Glanville had been born to rule an empire, an empire which had once encompassed over half of the world. His grandfather had been Foreign Secretary, his father Viceroy of India. The Glanvilles had been at the heart of British public life for over three hundred years and Britain's declining role in world affairs disgusted him. He was on a personal crusade, a crusade to restore his country to its former greatness, a crusade which he firmly believed could be ultimately successful only with himself as Prime Minister.

Richard Glanville had entered politics at the end of the First World War and his career had progressed steadily and ruthlessly through a series of junior ministerial posts to Home Secretary and more recently to Minister of Defence – an office for which he had been handpicked by the Prime Minister in order to persuade Parliament to approve a massive increase in the defence budget.

Later that day, in the library of his country home, he cursed as he waded through an interminable pile of household bills – the custodian of Britain's future had more important things to do with his weekends. Would his stupid wife never learn to distinguish between the essentials and the luxuries of life? His dwindling family income, itself insufficient to support Glanville Hall, was hopelessly incapable of sustaining the additional burdens of high office and he had recently been forced into the final indignity of arranging a mortgage on the estate and an overdraft with the local bank. Moreover, since the sudden departure of their butler two weeks ago, he had been compelled to assist his scatterbrained wife in the running of the household. Cursing aloud, he flung aside a final demand from her milliner, stalked out of the room and into the driveway, where his official car was waiting to take him to London.

'Good night My Lord.' The new butler handed him his briefcase. 'I hope you have a pleasant journey.'

'Thank you Thomas.' He barely glanced at the little Welshman. 'I trust that you are equal to the task of balancing Her Ladyship's accounts!'

Daily Telegraph
16 May 1953

GLANVILLE RECEIVES STANDING OVATION
by our parliamentary correspondent
The Minister of Defence roused the patriotic fervour of a packed House of Lords last night in an impassioned speech

which opened the debate on the proposed increase in the military budget. It is the first time that a senior Cabinet Minister has openly warned of the possible dangers of reliance upon our allies . . .

Jamie handed the newspaper back to the barman at Whites with evident distaste.

'I'll give that bastard standing ovation,' he muttered.

Greg nodded but said nothing. He was under no illusions as to the effects of prison on his friend. Although Jamie was outwardly fit and tanned after a few weeks in the South of France, Greg had seen a frightening change in his personality. On a number of occasions he had dramatically overreacted to the everyday irritants of life, but this, Greg supposed, was understandable and in time would pass. What worried him more was the fact that Jamie was at times unable to distinguish between the law of the jungle and the rules of civilized society. From time to time during Jamie's incarceration Greg had made discreet enquiries as to his wellbeing (after all, Virakis was not the only one with private sources of information) and was deeply disturbed at the reports he received. But Jamie never talked about prison and Greg never asked.

'You see old man, "an eye for an eye, a tooth for a tooth". Forget that and you're finished. You've lost respect.' Jamie's voice took on a chilling edge.

'Ye. . .e. . .s. But calm down, old pal. Just take it easy. Between us we'll figure out a way . . .'

'Take it easy!' Jamie shouted. 'Take it *easy*! I'll get that pompous prick if it's the last thing I ever do.'

'Sure, sure,' Greg said soothingly, 'and I told you I want to help . . . What about that slut Edwina? She's the one who's really responsible.'

'Absolutely. She'll get what's due to her as well. But she's easy. First things first. It's Glanville I'm after at the moment and I want him *now*.'

The Minister of Defence was tired but exhilarated. In a masterly display of parliamentary skills he had achieved his

133

aim. It had not been easy. Not only had the opposition parties fought tooth and nail against his Bill, but he had had to contend with several months of sustained resistance from backbenchers within his own party, which had at one time threatened to break into open rebellion. The country itself had been passionately divided on the issue and anti-nuclear demonstrations had taken place in most cities, culminating in a huge march on Trafalgar Square. Pickets had surrounded his London residence daily and he had received a great number of poison-pen letters. His forceful oratory in the House, however, and the arrogance of total conviction, had served him well. The Bill had passed into law late that afternoon with a surprisingly large majority and the Prime Minister had taken him aside personally to congratulate him on a job well done.

So good was his mood that night that even the persistent nagging of his wife failed to irritate him. They were dining in their small house in Pimlico and, oblivious of the day's momentous events, she was complaining bitterly over his failure to replace her unreliable old motor car. Her monologue was interrupted by the entrance of the butler with coffee.

'Thank you Thomas,' Glanville said. 'Please bring over the cigars.'

'At once My Lord.' He cut the tip from a fine old Havana and expertly held a lighted match to the end before passing it to his master.

'May I take the liberty of congratulating Your Lordship on a marvellous victory. If I may say so, My Lord, the country is in your debt.'

'You may indeed Thomas. Thank you. That will be all, take the rest of the evening off.'

'What's he talking about, Richard? What have you been up to?'

'Oh nothing, Louise. Nothing for you to concern yourself with.'

For the first couple of days Jamie was surprisingly happy to be back at Kilpurnie. Far from imprisoning him, the ancient castle walls guarded and protected him as they had his forefathers. He wandered for hours alone through the hills and climbed trees, on the trunks of which his faded initials were still carved. The realization, however, that his parents were gone for ever finally sank in and this saddened him greatly. He sorely missed his mother's loving warmth and his father's sound counsel, but thanked God that they had not lived to see him go to prison. On the other hand, the belief that Jamie had killed a blackmailer in defence of a lady's honour had made him a folk hero. Though faintly embarrassed by all the fuss, he accepted the drinks and handshakes with good grace.

Before long he became restless. McClintock, an efficient but humourless man, bored him stiff with the endless problems associated with running the estate; Sedgewicke's usual lectures on duty and responsibility made him feel guilty and served only to depress him; Greg, who at the last minute had come up for the weekend with Lucy, was mooning around like a bear with a sore head and was drinking more than ever. As if all that was not enough, his companion – a pushy blonde actress with the absurd name of Lulu Lejeune – was driving him mad. Her sexual expertise had been most welcome in the South of France but her ludicrous attempts to ingratiate herself with the staff and tenants annoyed everyone. He could not wait to get back to London.

Greg's problems were of a very different nature. He had come to Scotland in order to discuss with the Union Bank of Edinburgh a possible loan to the local shipyard on which his father-in-law had approached him some weeks earlier. He had also hoped that the return to Scotland might revive the early promise of his sexual relationship with his wife. During their engagement he had found Lucy to be a willing if inexperienced lover and he had taken for granted that it would not be long before a mutually fulfilling partnership would result. He was wrong. Although the perfect wife in every other respect, she had, since their return from honeymoon in Kashmir, consistently found some excuse to avoid his overtures. He attributed this to post-marital depression and resolved to be patient. The weekend, however, had solved nothing. He had been gently but firmly rejected three times in as many nights and was rapidly losing interest.

CHAPTER 9

Richard Glanville was determined to waste no time in implementing the mandate his government had been given by Parliament and had immediately invited the country's five leading aircraft manufacturers to submit their designs, specifications and prices for a new prototype of aeroplane. The existing series of 'V' Bombers – Vulcan, Valiant and Victor – were limited in their range and load capacity. He had spent many weeks deep in consultation with the department's military advisers and the Joint Chiefs of Staff and had agreed with their unanimous conclusion that these aircraft would soon be obsolete.

Since taking office he had eaten, slept and dreamed bombers. No one could have done his homework more thoroughly. He had hunched in uncomfortable cockpits, been shunted from draughty hangars to endless wind-tunnels and argued for hours with dogmatic boffins over such complexities as reverse thrust and vertical take-off. The five folders in front of him each contained revolutionary designs that were the product of the country's most brilliant scientific minds. He was well aware that the company to which he awarded the contract would be receiving the most valuable and prestigious order ever placed by a British government and was determined to examine each bid with the utmost care and impartiality. He had therefore decided to leave his wife in London for a few days in order to reach his decision in the peace and solitude of the English countryside.

It was snowing lightly as the DC3 began its decent to Geneva Airport. Spiros Virakis reluctantly handed the controls back to the captain and walked back to the lounge area where Angela was mixing herself a drink at the bar.

'Where is Andreas?' he asked sharply.

'Nanny Peabody is dressing him in the bedroom.'

'It would be nice if his mother dressed him occasionally instead of drinking at eleven o'clock in the morning. We will be landing in ten minutes. A car will take you and Andreas straight to the Richemond. I have a meeting but I will join you at the hotel in time for lunch.'

'Whatever you say, my love. How long are we staying in Switzerland?'

'I am not sure. Perhaps two or three days, perhaps a week. We are on, as you would say my dear, a shopping expedition.'

'Shopping, darling? How exciting! What are we buying this time?'

'Ah *Angelaki mou*,' he chuckled. 'One only buys three things in Switzerland. Chocolates, cuckoo clocks and banks. Which one do you think we are buying, eh?'

Doctor Julius Schlumberger, Chairman of the Managing Board of the Crédit Banque de Genève gazed out over the lake and sighed.

'Very well, Herr Virakis, we accept your offer. We would be foolish if we did not.' He turned and walked slowly back to the boardroom table. 'This is a sad day for me. I have worked in this bank for fifty years. Since the day my grandfather founded it. It has been my whole life and if, like you, I had a son I would never sell – whatever the price.'

He sat down and, taking off his glasses, examined the Greek shrewdly. 'If I may ask, Herr Virakis, why did you choose our bank? We are a small community here and news travels fast. I know that you have had discussions with at least two other banks in the past few days.'

'Very simple, Herr Doktor, I wanted a bank with not only a first-class reputation and excellent management but also one with a solid asset base.'

'I am very flattered, but the others also have fine reputations and in fact, far greater deposits than we do.'

'Correct my friend, but we Greeks are old-fashioned and not as sophisticated as some of our more modern European neighbours. I have always distinguished between deposits and assets. A bank's clients can always remove their deposits but only the owner of the bank can remove its assets. The greater part of your assets are your valuable properties and I believe in the safety of property.'

'I see.' The old man nodded sagely. 'But why a Swiss bank?'

'Because of your secrecy laws. I do not wish anyone to know that I own this bank. This is why it is part of the deal that you and your staff remain here.'

'Of course Herr Virakis, that is understood. No one will ever know.'

'My Lords, I would like to assure this House that there is no truth whatsoever in the scurrilous and scandalous allegations contained in today's edition of the *Daily Mirror*. Neither I nor my wife has ever owned any stock of any kind in United Aerodynamics Limited and have certainly not profited by one single penny during the recent surge in their share price. Furthermore, I have just instructed my solicitors to issue a writ for libel against the editor and the proprietors of this irresponsible newspaper and, since the matter is now *sub-judice*, I have been advised that save for this denial I should make no further comment.' Glanville bowed and hurriedly left the chamber of the House of Lords to keep the appointment with his solicitors Montague, Silman and Partners.

'I am afraid the news is not good, Richard. I spoke a short time ago to your brokers Heath and Co, and Michael Heath swears blind that he took instructions to buy the stock from you personally the day before the announcement that United Aerodynamics had been awarded the government contract. He says there is no way he could have mistaken your voice on the telephone and that you specifically requested that the shares be purchased in your wife's name.'

'What the hell are you talking about?' Glanville was beside himself with rage. 'Michael's gone stark raving mad, I haven't given him an order for six months. Someone's playing a trick on the bloody fool – probably some bloody newspaperman.'

'I'm afraid it goes a bit deeper than that, Richard. According to Heath he asked you why you were buying UAD and you just laughed and suggested he buy some for himself. Apparently you bought ten thousand shares at two pounds ten shillings.'

'That's ridiculous, Monty. I can't possibly afford twenty-five thousand pounds.'

'Well it would appear you can now, Richard. According to Heath you spoke to him again two days later and gave him instructions to sell at six pounds. I make that a profit of thirty-five thousand pounds. A rather benevolent joke for someone to play on you.'

'This is absolutely insane. I'd better speak to that halfwit myself. How am I supposed to have paid for this, anyway?'

'Under no circumstances should you contact Heath directly. I've already asked him about payment. Apparently the firm received a cheque from you and they've been in touch with the bank who are going to send it to me as soon as they trace it. Obviously,' he arched his eyebrows, 'it will turn out to be a forgery.'

'Good.' Glanville snorted. 'The sooner this bloody mess is sorted out the better. I've got to go and explain all this to the bloody Prime Minister now.'

Thomas the butler had been given a few days' leave by Lady Glanville in order to visit his dying mother at her home in the small Welsh village of Tonnypandy. The truth of the matter, however, was that Thomas the butler – whose real mother had passed away some twelve years earlier in the genteel spas of Baden-Baden – had never set foot in the green but unprofitable pastures of Wales. Moreover his erstwhile employer would have found it impossible to recognize him, such was the miraculous transformation in his appearance. Gone were the green contact lenses, gone the pencil-thin moustache and gone the jet-black hair. Most of all, gone were the mellifluent lilting tones of the Welsh valleys as he stopped and poured himself another glass of champagne.

'. . . So you see, old fruit, once I got the old dear's confidence the rest was easy. She was more than happy to leave the household accounts to me and would sign anything I put in front of her. I'd served his broker at a dinner party and heard the way they spoke to each other, and I'd discovered which company was going to get the contract from the papers he was working on that last weekend. I always typed up the cheques on his typewriter. The first one she signed was to pay for the shares and the second one paid off the mortgage on his estate. That's the one that'll finish him off.'

'But Alan, how are you going to get away with it? You'll have Scotland Yard breathing down your neck in no time.'

'Yes Jamie. But they'll be looking for my old friend Evan Thomas of Tonnypandy, who indeed answers to their description but in fact died between jobs in America last year. Whatever the police think, the press will never believe Glanville's story and from what you've told me he's not going to get very much help from Commissioner Wilson.'

'Alan, you're a fucking genius. I don't know how to thank you.'

'No need to, old fruit. I can assure you that I made a bit of a killing out of UAD myself. The next bottle of champagne is on me. Waiter, another Dom Perignon please!'

Alan Shepherd was right. The final nail in Glanville's coffin was the receipt by the building society of his wife's second cheque clearing their mortgage. Michael Heath continued to insist that he could not have mistaken his old friend's voice. Three days after his denial to the House of Lords, Richard Glanville resigned. He kept the money, divorced his wife and was never heard of in politics again.

Chapter 10

Jamie now began to pick up the threads of his former life. He had made a decision to distance himself – apart from the occasional weekend – from the affairs of Kilpurnie and told Sedgewicke this in no uncertain terms. He regularly played tennis with the coach at Queens Club and quickly regained his former fitness, although he began to suffer from intermittent headaches which his doctors told him were a result of the beating he had received in prison. Poker remained his first love and, in the way of gamblers everywhere, Jamie had little time for relationships with women. Which is not to say, of course, that he no longer enjoyed sex. Far from it. If anything, he spent more time at Knaves than ever, but this was at his convenience – either during the afternoon or in the early hours of the morning and often after a game. His days were spent lunching in various clubs and going to the races with chums such as Blunt, Hunter and occasionally – when office hours permitted – Greg, who was now also to be found regularly at Knaves.

The brothel itself had changed hardly at all since Angela's departure. It was still a closely guarded secret that it had originally been financed by Jamie who, not wishing to profit from the peccadillos of his fellow man, had sold the operation to Lennie Landau at a bargain price.

'Sir James, if you've got a moment, I'd like a word in private.'

Jamie had just arrived after an uneventful poker game and was looking forward to unwinding with one of the girls and a bottle of champagne.

'Of course, Lennie. What's the problem?'

'It's about Mr Blunt,' Lennie said hesitantly.

'What about him?'

'I'm afraid it's a bit delicate guv'. Miss Angela always insisted that we never tell you. But he's gone too far this time and we had to throw him out last night. I've told him never to come back.'

'What on earth's going on Lennie? What the hell's he been up to?'

'He beats up the girls sir. Always has done. Trouble is this time he chose the wrong girl.'

'What! Nonsense, Lennie. I don't believe it. Mr Blunt's been a friend of mine for twenty years; he'd never do anything like that. The girl is obviously lying; she probably got beaten up by her boyfriend and is trying to get money from Gavin.'

'Oh no sir, I wish that were the case. I'm afraid Mr Blunt's been doing this for years. We only put up with it because he's a friend of yours. But this girl's different and I've got a lot of straightening out to do.'

'The whole thing's unbelievable, Lennie. Gavin of all people! Who is this girl anyway?'

'You don't know her guv', she's a nineteen-year-old Whitechapel girl called Shirley Knight and thank God her family don't know she's working here. They're a very powerful and dangerous lot. She certainly won't tell them the truth and I just pray that they don't find out. But I'm not having Mr Blunt here again, Sir James, I'll tell you that.'

Dawn was breaking, the last customer had gone to bed, Lennie was doing the accounts and the black pianist from New Orleans was folding up his music when the front door came violently off its hinges, the lock skidding across the floor.

'Well, well, well, if it isn't little Lennie Landau, our smart little jewboy from the Commercial Road.' Dirk Brett walked in and stopped in the centre of the room. 'You've done very nicely for yourself. Very nicely for a little yid who used to pick blind men's pockets down Petticoat Lane. Boys, let me introduce you to the charming Mr Landau, a gentleman who has come up in the world. A gentleman who would sell his own mother for a salt-beef sandwich. Wouldn't you, Len?' Brett walked over to the quaking clubowner and with one hand lifted him off the ground by the throat. 'A gentleman who sells our Shirley to rich cunts who stub cigarettes out on her stomach. My own sister's little girl!'

He dropped Lennie suddenly and kicked him viciously in the crotch. Screaming hysterically Lennie fell to his knees clutching his groin. A sweeping backhander broke his nose. Seconds later Brett grabbed him by the hair with both hands and with a brutal head butt split his forehead open like a watermelon. Lennie lay sobbing at Brett's feet.

'Please Dirk, please,' he whimpered. 'No more, you'll kill me. Please, Dirk, I beg you.'

'You're bloody right I'll kill you, you scumbag cunt, unless you tell me what filthy pervert did those things to our Shirley.'

'G...G...Gavin Bl...Blunt,' he gasped before passing out.

'Gavin Blunt,' Brett spat. 'Well you can tell him from me whoever he is he's a dead man. Right boys, I'll leave you to get on with the redecorations.'

He turned to the petrified pianist, who had been watching rooted to the spot. 'And as for you, nig-nog, you'd better go home and keep your black mouth shut or you'll never play with your prick again, let alone your piano!'

Leaving the Tower of London behind him, Jamie turned left into the Whitechapel Road. His car, conspicuous among the carts and vans of the Cockney traders, was forced to pull up in the early-morning traffic. He had been dragged – bleary-eyed after only two hours' sleep – to the Middlesex Hospital by the shaken pianist and there found Lennie Landau receiving treatment for three broken ribs, a broken nose, multiple bruising and severe shock. Though barely conscious, Lennie had managed to tell him of the night's devastation and Jamie, in an attempt to save Gavin's life, was *en route* to see Dirk Brett. He weaved his way through the cheerful commotion towards the converted warehouse which had served as the gangster's headquarters since the end of the war.

The Golden Gloves gymnasium had been the home of many legendary fighters and was part of the folklore of the East End. Brett had spent his childhood in and out of the ring and a promising career as a light heavyweight had been prematurely ended by a slightly detached right retina and a continual disregard for the Marquess of Queensberry's rules. His rapid and early rise to the highest echelons of London's underworld was a result of a shrewd mind and a love of violence. In later years he consolidated his position by balancing his hair-trigger temper with an innate sense of justice and an unswerving loyalty to those who followed him. His criminal activities extended to protection, gambling and loan-sharking and included a recent spate of daring robberies which had captured the public imagination. He also owned a number of genuine companies centred around the dockland area whose principal use was the laundering of his illegal gains, and he was actively seeking to legitimize them completely.

'Where do you think you're going, son?' Jamie's entrance was barred by the wrinkled hand of an unshaven caretaker.

'I'm here to see Mr Brett.'

'Oh yeah, and who might you be?' The old man was unimpressed by Jamie's appearance and accent.

'Just tell him James Stuart would appreciate a few minutes of his time.'

'Hold on.' The caretaker stepped back into his cubicle and muttered a few words into the telephone. 'All right, go through the doors, straight to the end of the gym and someone will meet you at the bottom of the stairs.'

Feeling rather out of place, Jamie strode through the long gymnasium, avoiding the hostile glances of sweating boxers in training and the suspicious stares of old lags as they recounted tales of glory to wide-eyed youngsters.

'This way, Mr Stuart.' A large greasy-haired youth in a black leather jacket led the way up the stairs to a plain wooden door, upon which he rapped three times before they both entered.

'Jamie. Good to see you.' Dirk Brett, clad in a tracksuit, got up from the centre of a crowded card table. 'Boys, this is Sir James Stuart, an old friend of mine from the 'Ville. You've all heard of him, now you can meet him.'

'How do you do? Pleased to meet you.'

A chorus of greetings arose from the players.

'Pull up a chair, Jamie. What can we offer you? Coffee? Tea? A drink? Some breakfast?'

'Hello Dirk. Thanks very much, coffee will do fine.' Jamie nodded to the others and sat down.

'Blimey mate, you look a lot better than the last time I saw you. What are you doing slumming it down here?'

Jamie, sipping his coffee, looked around and began tentatively. 'It's a rather delicate matter, old man. I've come to ask a favour . . .'

'Say no more. Boys, leave us alone for a while.'

Jamie lit a cigarette uneasily as the room emptied.

'All right mate, what's your problem?'

'Gavin Blunt,' Jamie replied quietly.

'Gavin Blunt!' Brett turned white with rage. 'He's a dead man. Don't tell me that piece of shit's a friend of yours.'

'Yes Dirk, I'm afraid he is and . . .'

'I'm sorry Jamie,' Brett shouted. 'I've just told you, he's a dead man. You should see what state my sixteen-year-old niece is in before you come asking favours like that.'

Jamie shifted nervously in his chair. 'I know, Dirk, and I couldn't agree with you more. She's not my niece but I'm as disgusted as you are. I've known Blunt for twenty years and I would never have suspected he was capable of anything like this. I can still hardly believe it. He obviously needs medical help. He's my oldest friend. Please give me a chance to get him to a psychiatrist before you do anything.'

'Jamie, I respect the fact that he's your friend.' Brett was calming down. 'But there's nothing I can do. You know the code and what's more it's family. I can't let it go. I'm sure he's sick but that's not my problem.'

'Come on Dirk,' Jamie pleaded. 'You're bigger than the code. You're the only one who could let this go. There's got to be some other way to make him pay. At least think about it and let me talk to him.' Jamie held his breath and waited.

'All right mate, I'll think about it for forty-eight hours.' He reached out and ruffled Jamie's hair affectionately. 'You're a gutsy boy, Jamie, and he doesn't deserve a friend like you. I'll be in touch.'

'Dirk, I can't thank –'

'Don't thank me yet, I haven't done anything. And by the way don't let him get any funny ideas about doing a runner, I've already got two men on him.'

'I won't.'

'Off you go Jamie,' Brett said gruffly, 'and take care of yourself mate.' He sat motionless, deep in thought as he watched the younger man vanish down the stairs.

Lucy was miserable and frustrated – nothing seemed to be going right for her. It was mid-morning and as the maid removed the remains of her breakfast, she lay back against the pillows wondering whether she could be bothered to get up. Greg had been in Scotland for three days negotiating some boring deal with a local shipyard and even with their problems she felt lonely without him. Their short-lived sex life had ended when they returned from honeymoon and despite her genuine affection for her husband their subsequent attempts at lovemaking had been disastrous. She could no longer bear to be touched by him.

The previous day, while shopping at Fortnum's, she had unexpectedly run into Amanda from Knaves and against her better judgement had agreed to have tea at the Fountain restaurant. The pert little blonde had flirted outrageously with Lucy and on kissing her goodbye had brushed her breasts suggestively against Lucy's own. Lucy had thought of nothing else since – she was desperately in need of the release that only a woman could give her.

Curzon Street and its residents do not take kindly to being awoken much before lunchtime. Gavin Blunt's part-time butler had not yet arrived and it took Jamie several minutes of persistent ringing and knocking to summon a dishevelled, hungover Gavin to the front door.

'Bloody hell, Jamie, it's half-past nine. What on earth are you doing here?'

'Trying to save your miserable life. And I'm not joking.'

'Frightfully decent of you, old chap, but isn't it a little early for melodramatics? Anyway, since you're here you'd better come in.' Gavin shivered and, tightening the sash of his silk dressing-gown, led the way downstairs to the kitchen and put a pot of coffee on to the stove. Jamie sat in silence, watching Gavin lace his cup with a shot of brandy.

'Well my dear chap.' Gavin swallowed his coffee gratefully. 'What's all the excitement about?'

'The excitement, my dear chap, is simply that the most dangerous gangster in this country wants you killed.'

'Come on Jamie, we're in Mayfair now, not in prison. Your imagination's running away with itself. What could such an esteemed gentleman have against me?'

'What he has against you Gavin,' Jamie said matter-of-factly, 'is that the girl you assaulted at Knaves last night happens to be his niece.'

'Don't be ridiculous. That girl was covered in bruises before I even touched her. You know these sluts as well as I do, they'll lie about anything.'

'No Gavin,' Jamie spoke quietly, 'you're the liar. You've been beating up girls all your life.'

'All right, what of it? I pay them very well,' Gavin said haughtily.

'Shut up and listen!' Jamie shouted. 'You may be my friend but you sicken me. The facts are that Lennie Landau is in the intensive care unit of the Middlesex Hospital, Knaves has been smashed to pieces and there are two gorillas with orders to kill you parked outside.'

Gavin darted out of the kitchen and returned a moment later, his face sheet-white beneath the overnight stubble. 'Christ Almighty, the bastards are on my bloody doorstep.' He reached shakily for the brandy bottle. 'What am I going to do?'

'I don't know yet. We can thank your lucky stars that I *did* go to prison. This man's called Dirk Brett and I knew him in Pentonville. I've managed to persuade him not to kill you for a couple of days on the basis that maybe, just maybe, you can make it up to him in some way.'

Gavin breathed a deep sigh of relief. 'So it's money he's after. How much?'

'He can buy and sell you a hundred times over.' Jamie looked at him wearily. 'You just don't understand. You beat up his niece and these people take family very seriously. Very seriously indeed. He's agreed to a meeting and, let's face it, you've got nothing to lose.' He gave a hollow laugh. 'Put it this way – it's the last hand of the night, so you might as well draw to an inside straight.' Jamie got up to leave. 'Sit tight and wait until you hear from me. Just don't try anything smart.'

Gavin was close to tears as he followed Jamie out and grasped him tightly by the arm. 'Before you go Jamie, there's something I must tell you. You're the only real friend I've ever had and I'm not making an excuse but there's something wrong with me. The only way I've ever been able to have sex properly is by slapping the girl around a little bit first. Nothing serious, Jamie – just a little bit. But it's been worrying me for some time and,' he lied, 'I've started seeing a psychiatrist. It has made my life a nightmare. I really loved Lucy,' he choked, 'but why do you think I broke off the engagement? I had to protect her from myself. Whatever happens to me I want you to know that.'

'Yes, yes, Gavin,' Jamie said, not believing a word but desperately wanting to, 'just leave it with me.'

The Lucky Horseshoe in Shaftesbury Avenue was not typical of the gaming establishments generally frequented by James Stuart and Gavin Blunt. It was, however, owned by Dirk Brett, who had told Jamie to bring Gavin there at midnight.

They waited apprehensively in the centre of the garishly decorated casino and watched the frenzied movements of the small-time gamblers as time and again they compulsively risked their entire week's wages on the spin of a wheel or the turn of a card. Their faces distorted by greed, they jostled and fought to place their wagers. For such people life extended only as far as the next bet and the final release came with the loss of the last chip. This was gambling in its crudest form.

'Good evening, Sir James, please follow me.' Mike the greasy-haired youth from the Golden Gloves, had exchanged his leather jacket for a vulgarly embroidered tuxedo. 'Mr Brett's waiting for you both in the restaurant.'

'Unbelievable.' Gavin grimaced as they crossed the mauve neon-lit dining-room – its gaudiness magnified by the mirrored ceiling – towards Brett, sitting alone at a corner table. He lowered his voice, 'You don't think he expects us to eat here as well?'

'Shut up you idiot,' Jamie hissed. 'This could be your last supper.'

'Jamie mate.' Brett rose to greet him. 'Come and sit down. What are you drinking?'

'Whisky please Dirk.'

'Right. Angelo.' He snapped his fingers at the attendant waiter, ignoring Blunt completely. 'A large malt for Sir James.'

Gavin gingerly pulled up a chair while Brett continued chattily, 'Ran into an old friend of yours the other day – Alan Shepherd. He's just had one off – something to do with a *killing* in the market.' He laughed nastily and looked for the first time at Gavin.

'Really?' Jamie said innocently. 'Good for Alan. Anyway, cheers Dirk.' He raised his glass.

'Yeah mate, cheers.' Brett grunted and turned to Gavin. 'Well scum, this is what's going to happen. I've decided to spare you your little life because luckily you've got something I can use.' He began to prod a white-faced Gavin painfully and repeatedly in the chest. 'Your family seems to have a good thing going with that 'Bubble' shipowner. Now it just so happens that I've got a few straight businesses of my own that could do with a bit of a facelift. You're the one who's going to give it to them.' Brett emphasized his last remark with yet another prod and sat back for a moment as Jamie smothered a grin at Gavin's discomfiture.

'Blunt and Company,' Brett continued, 'will take over my businesses and give them the so-called respectability that I'm told they need.' He leaned forward suddenly and with a

151

particularly violent poke in the stomach left Gavin gasping like a stranded fish. 'Though God knows . . .' he shook his head sadly, 'it's a sick world when gits like you are considered respectable. The purchase price for my businesses will be your entire shareholding and you will be my representative on the board. And if you ever try to do a number on me, sonny . . .' the prodding finger was poised for action, 'your feet won't touch the ground. Is that understood?'

'Yes.'

'And one more thing. You will go round to my sister's house tomorrow morning – Mike will give you the address – with a very large bunch of flowers and get down on your knees and beg her to forgive you for laying your filthy hands on her daughter. You will also leave an envelope for our Shirley with ten thousand pounds in cash in it and a letter of apology. Understood?'

'Yes.'

'Now get out of my sight before I change my mind.' He beckoned to Mike and Gavin was escorted out.

'Well Jamie, mate, how about a game of cards for old times' sake?'

'Love to, old man, and while you're organizing it, I think I'll try my luck at your dice table.'

'I wish you would.' Brett laughed. 'At least the odds will be on my side for a change.'

'To hell with the odds,' Jamie replied. 'I'm a gambler like everyone else out there.'

Humiliated but relieved, Gavin Blunt pushed his way through the throng of Saturday-night theatregoers and headed towards Cambridge Circus in search of a taxi. It was not until he was safely ensconced in the comforting surroundings of the bar at Crockford's and had disposed of two very large Stolichnayas on the rocks that he began to evaluate the significance of Brett's demands. Yes, his life had been spared. There was no denying that. There was also unfortunately no denying that Jamie had been responsible for saving it – although he still could not understand why he had found himself in this ridiculous situation in the first place. So what if he *had* beaten up some common little whore? He had paid her, hadn't he? And there was certainly no reason for Jamie of all people to turn sanctimonious and then sit there smugly in that disgusting place while that common lout was poking him like some bloody pig. 'Christ,' he cursed, examining the grubby piece of paper the greasy yob had given him. Tomorrow he would have to go down to the Mile End Road of all places with *flowers* for some smelly old woman and give her sluttish daughter – who was a lousy lay anyhow – ten thousand pounds. Ten thousand fucking pounds. That really hurt.

Still, it could have been worse. He was alive and unharmed and little did Brett know what he'd let himself in for. In a few weeks' time his stock in Blunt and Company would be worthless, Brett's own sordid little businesses would go under and if that bearded thug had any complaints he could take them up with Virakis. Ha! Let him try to poke Virakis in the ribs!

He finished his drink, wandered out of the bar and up to the nearest roulette table where he absently placed his usual bet on 'nineteen and the neighbours'.

'*Quatre rouge et pair.*' The voice of the croupier brought him back to earth with a start and his heart skipped a beat as he realized that he had made a winning bet. Four was next to nineteen on the wheel. Several pieces of evenly measured chips were smoothly pushed across the table to him by the croupier's rake.

'*Faites vos jeux mesdames, messieurs, s'il vous plaît.*'

Gavin swiftly doubled his original bet and watched mesmerized as the gleaming ball skimmed around the periphery of the spinning wheel.

'*Rien ne va plus.*' The ball began to drop and jumped jerkily from slot to slot before settling firmly and surprisingly for number twenty-one. Gavin grinned broadly at the croupiers and graciously accepted the murmurs of appreciation from the other players. Conscious that all eyes were upon him, he doubled his bet yet again and with studied casualness folded his arms and stood back from the table. There was no mistaking the ball's intention this time. It was as though nineteen was the only number on the wheel and the ball was in a race against time to get there.

'*Dix-neuf, rouge, impair – felicitations Monsieur Blunt. Un grand coup!*' His back was heartily slapped several times by those surrounding him and he smiled delightedly at them before gathering in his winnings.

'Thank you very much François, please cash me in. I think I need another drink!'

'*Bien sûr, Monsieur Blunt.* Ten thousand three hundred and fifty pounds *exactement.*'

CHAPTER 11

'My dear Gavin, good evening. I'm glad to see you've helped yourself to a drink. To what do I owe this unexpected pleasure?'

'Hello, Spiro. There have been some unforeseen developments and I may need some help. But don't worry, it doesn't affect your plans.'

'Believe me, I am very far from being worried. But go on. What has happened?'

'Well it's a personal matter and I won't bore you with the details. Suffice it to say that I have had to surrender my shares in Blunt and Company to a villain called Dirk Brett whose dubious enterprises we have recently been forced to acquire. Nothing changes as far as you're concerned. I'm staying on the board and retaining all my voting powers, but Brett's going to be very unhappy when we pull the plug and he discovers that his stock is worthless and that his own companies will go into receivership as well.'

'Mmm.' Virakis crossed the room to the drinks trolley and poured himself an ouzo, ignoring Gavin's empty glass.

'He will not exactly be a satisfied investor, eh Gavin, eh! But tell me, what induced you to part with such a priceless birthright in the first place?'

'The bastard was going to kill me,' Gavin replied bitterly. 'I had no choice. He thinks we're going to make a fortune out of your contract. Under the circumstances. I made a rather good deal.'

'Who is this Brett? Why did he want to kill you?'

'He's a gangster friend of Jamie Stuart's – they were in prison together. I was involved in an unfortunate incident with his niece and he rather overreacted.'

'Overreacted with a vengeance one might say! Eh Gavin, eh! Ahaa!' Virakis's laughter increased at the sight of the pained expression on Gavin's face.

'Do forgive me, my friend.' He could barely conceal his contempt. 'So your problem is that in approximately one month's time he will again want to kill you and you need my protection. Of course you have it. We are partners and I do not intend to invest half a million pounds in a corpse. Besides, as you well know, any friend of Stuart is an enemy of mine. Yes, my dear Gavin, you can safely leave your Mr Brett to me.'

Maximillian was more like a Paris couture house than a fashionable ladies' hairdressers. Late as usual, Lucy hurried through the over-elaborate marble entrance hall with its pretentious neo-Roman pillars and ascended the sweeping staircase to the first floor. Maximillian himself greeted her effusively in a pronounced Viennese accent which belied his Bethnal Green origins and introduced her to a pretty young apprentice called Sarah who led her into a small private room. The girl busied herself arranging towels and testing the temperature of the water while Lucy sat waiting dejectedly – her thoughts turning to the dismal failure of her marriage.

She was in the midst of a major depression. She had succumbed some weeks before to the advances of Amanda White and had found in their subsequent affair both a refuge from the tedium of her marriage and the physical fulfilment that her body demanded. Amanda's sudden and inexplicable disappearance a few days ago had left her devastated. They had arranged to meet as usual in the little studio in Chelsea which Lucy used for their afternoon lovemaking, but for the first time, her inamorata had failed to arrive. Her telephone calls had remained unanswered and she had waited in vain at the studio every afternoon that week. Finally, and in desperation, she took a taxi to the flat in Bayswater where Amanda lived with her mother, only to be told by an irritable landlord that they had gone abroad and left no forwarding address.

Moreover, she had no evidence, but was fairly certain that Greg was seeing other women and frankly could not blame him. At least he was discreet and whenever they were together, his kindness and consideration could not be faulted. She had dreaded that he might one day learn of her affair with Amanda but that danger, she reflected ruefully, had now passed. Not that there had been much chance of that anyway – he was totally submerged in his work and was spending a great deal of time in Scotland where he was increasingly concerned over the loan which her father had persuaded him to make. She had recently learned that Gavin Blunt, of all people, was in some way involved. No wonder they were having problems!

'Excuse me, Lady Lucinda,' Sarah's childlike voice broke in. 'Everything is ready for you now.'

Lucy leaned back in her chair, arching the nape of her neck over the sink. She brightened as she looked up into the eyes of the young shampooist whose face was barely six inches from her own. She turned her head slightly to one side and hungrily took in the gentle swell of the small breasts under the flimsy cotton housecoat. My, my, she thought, what a sexy little thing we are.

'You simply must tell me all about yourself, my dear . . .'

Though the Blunts were never in the same league as the Jardines or the Mathesons, they had nevertheless been a force to be reckoned with in their time, a fact to which their boardroom bore testament. The oval teak table had been carved from the prow of the first schooner that had set sail from Southampton in 1823 under the command of Captain Horatio Blunt. The walls were panelled with sandalwood from Ceylon and covered with paintings of the numerous brigantines, clippers and steamships that had over the years constituted the family fleet. Mementos of the days of empire were everywhere – ivory tusks from India, squatting Buddhas from Burma, hand-carved jade from Hong Kong.

All this was of no consequence to Gregory Hamilton, who was eyeing Gavin Blunt suspiciously. 'Forgive me, Gavin, but since when did you become the spokesman for the company? I thought the only time you came to the office was to collect your director's fees.'

'Well thinking never was your strong point, was it, Greg? Now perhaps you'd be good enough to allow me to continue.'

'Yes, yes, all right. Go on.'

'Thank you. So you see, Gordon,' Gavin said to the manager of the Union Bank of Edinburgh, 'the monsoons came three months early this year and our entire position in the rubber market was wiped out. Our losses meant that we couldn't meet our obligations to the Midland Bank and we have been forced to default. We simply don't have any money. We're broke. After one hundred and thirty years, Blunt and Company is out of business.'

'And at the worst possible moment,' Peregrine finally broke in. 'Just when we were on the brink of our biggest deal ever.'

'Well actually,' Gordon McKay spoke for the first time, 'all is not lost. That's exactly why we're here, Mr Blunt. You will appreciate that it is very much in our interests for your company to remain a viable entity so that our clients – the Strathclyde Shipyard – can complete and receive payment for your ships without which they too will become insolvent. Mr Hamilton and I are agreeable to advancing you sufficient funds to meet your current obligations. We are confident that you will be able to repay us from the proceeds of your contract with Mr Virakis.'

'I am sorry to have to tell you this.' Gavin shook his head sadly. 'But you're too late.'

'What do you mean?' Greg sat bolt upright.

'What I mean, Greg, is that that slimy Greek bastard has already welshed on his contract. God knows how he found out so quickly, but within half an hour of our default, I received a call from that clown, Robard, informing me, and I quote, "In view of your present financial situation we regret that we have no alternative but to repudiate our contract." When I tried to reach Virakis himself, I was told that he was cruising in the Greek islands for the next three weeks and could not be contacted under any circumstances. I immediately telephoned our solicitors who advised us that he is entirely within his rights. There is nothing we can do, gentlemen. We're absolutely fucked, and by tomorrow morning, the whole of the City will know it.'

'Well, well.' Greg broke the ensuing silence. 'We have been a busy little businessman, haven't we, Gavin? I suppose that's that. Come on Gordon, let's go. Thank you both so much for your time.'

The two bankers left the building and hurried down Cheapside to the headquarters of the Union Bank of Edinburgh in Princes Street.

'Well, thank God, we've got the Swiss bank's guarantee; I suppose we'd better contact Geneva immediately.'

'Yes, Gordon, but this whole thing stinks,' Greg replied sourly. 'I've known Gavin Blunt far too long and nothing would surprise me now.'

He would, however, have been extremely surprised – as would Dirk Brett – had he known that at that very moment Gavin and Peregrine Blunt were sitting in the back of Spiros Virakis's Rolls-Royce en route to London Airport. Gavin's signed confession to Virakis was safely tucked away in his inside jacket pocket.

CHAPTER 12

Needless to say Spiros Virakis was several thousand miles from the Greek islands. He was in New York in his permanent suite at the Pierre Hotel and on the telephone to E. F. Hutton.

'. . . General Motors are up two and a half points, IBM are up two, AT & T are holding firm at six dollars fifty but railroad stocks are taking a bath right now and Union Pacific is down fifteen per cent since you bought them. By and large, I'm very pleased, Mr Virakis. Your portfolio is showing a net gain of twenty-three per cent over the last month.'

'Excellent, Stanley, thank you very much. Sell the Union Pacific and buy for me one hundred thousand Standard Oil of New Jersey – I have a feeling that the oil sector is a little undervalued at the moment.'

'Certainly, Mr Virakis.'

'Now, Stanley, there is one more thing. An important and delicate matter. Give me a price on Hamilton and Partners, the bankers.'

'Just a moment sir, I'll check on it right away . . . Unchanged at four dollars, Mr Virakis. Yes, if you're thinking of adding some bank stock to your portfolio, Hamiltons are a good buy right now.'

'No, Stanley. I wish you to sell them short. What is their issued capital?'

'One minute, sir.' The broker consulted his records again.

'There are ten million shares outstanding with a par value of one dollar. The family and their associates control twenty-seven per cent and various institutions – primarily British – control another thirteen point eight per cent. But I really don't think it would be wise to . . .'

'Stanley, I know what I am doing. We will make this stock go down and down. And even further down. I wish you to start by selling say . . . five hundred thousand shares today . . . and continue to sell at your discretion each time the price falls by twenty cents.'

'Christ on horseback, Mr V, what the hell's going on? They're a reputable outfit. How low are they going to go?'

'Very low indeed. Please put all my transactions through one of your nominee companies and naturally you will keep this information to yourself. Do you understand?'

'Of course, Mr Virakis – leave it to me. By the way, how long will you be in New York? My wife and I would be honoured if you would dine with us one night.'

'Most kind of you. I will be staying about three weeks, but unfortunately I am very busy and I also have my son with me. Perhaps we can do it on my next visit.'

'Of course.' Virakis's obsession with his son was well-known. 'I quite understand. I'll be in touch with you daily on the Hamilton situation.'

'Thank you. Goodbye.'

Virakis immediately placed calls to three other prominent Wall Street stockbrokers with whom he held identical conversations (and declined three further invitations to dinner). The diabolical plan which he had initiated by engineering Gavin Blunt's defection was entering its final phase. Blunt and Company was already in the hands of the official receiver and its proprietors had received their pieces of silver. The Strathclyde Shipyard was in a similar position and if all went well, Hamilton and Partners would soon go the same way. Jamie Stuart would be ruined and not only would he, Virakis, pick up the ships at bargain-basement prices, but he would also make a further fortune from his shorting of Hamilton shares.

He was in the middle of placing a final call to Hugo Robard

in London when his son burst into the room, the nanny close behind him.

'Daddy, Daddy, we've just been to the park. I saw Alice in Wonderland and I climbed up on her and I talked to the White Rabbit and I played with the Mad Hatter.' The words tumbled out breathlessly as the child jumped into his father's arms, knocking the receiver from his hand.

'Yes, Andreas. Good. Wonderful. But you must sit down nicely and keep quiet – otherwise I'll have to ask nanny to take you into another room. Daddy is talking to the office in London.'

The boy obediently sat still until his father had finished the conversation and then climbed back into his lap.

'Daddy, are all the offices really going to be mine one day?'

Virakis hugged his son tightly. 'Yes, my little soldier, and the ships and the factories and the houses. Everything.'

'But Daddy, what about the cars? I want to be a racing driver like Uncle Yiorgio.'

'No, Andreas,' he replied gravely. 'You have more important things to do. You are a Virakis and you must never forget this. One day, my darling son, you will be one of the richest and most powerful men in the world.' He put the boy down. 'Now, before you have your lunch, we must telephone Mummy in Paris and stop her spending all of our money on dresses!'

The Grill Room at the Connaught Hotel was packed. Jamie, at a relatively secluded table, was staring moodily into his second dry martini, cursing Lucy and Greg for being late as usual. He had lunched on humble pie while Dirk Brett had ranted and raved over the Blunt bankruptcy and Jamie had been hard pressed to persuade him that he knew nothing of Gavin's disappearance or present whereabouts. Moreover, the sudden slump in Hamilton and Partners' share price over the last week was costing him close on five hundred thousand pounds. He was in a foul temper.

'Can't you ever get anywhere on time!' he snapped when Lucy and Greg finally arrived and, brusquely dismissing their apologies, he ordered a round of drinks. 'Now, Greg, what the hell is going on with your bloody shares?'

'Oh God, Jamie.' Greg looked and sounded exhausted. 'I wish I could tell you. All I know is that there is a major seller of our stock in New York. I have no idea who it is or why, but it has started a panic. OK, so we lost four million pounds in the Scottish deal and it hurts, but we can handle that sort of amount. It has to go much deeper than that. Somebody is deliberately setting out to ruin the bank.' He finished his drink and picked up Lucy's glass. 'Not only that, but talking about the Scottish deal, I'm convinced there's a conspiracy between your great friend, Gavin Blunt, and Virakis. Why else would Virakis have broken that contract so quickly and Gavin have disappeared? And how else could the Banque de Crédit have mysteriously become worthless overnight? By the way,' he added, 'we've started proceedings for fraud in Switzerland, but their secrecy laws are so complicated that we'll probably never get to the bottom of it.'

'There's no need to tell me about Gavin,' Jamie said bitterly. 'So you think Virakis is behind all this?'

'Not behind the run on our shares. No. But I'm certain he's manipulated the whole Scottish situation so that he can pick up the ships cheaply. I've never met the man. You know him, what do you think?'

'What the hell are you asking me for, I've only met him once! Robard brought him to a poker game and he lost a lot of money. He's a bad-tempered little bugger and he made such a scene that Jeremy Hunter had him banned from Crockford's. Apart from that and the fact that he married Angela, I know nothing about him. You're the bloody banker, you should have done your fucking homework.'

'On top of everything else,' Greg continued shakily, 'there seems to be a personal vendetta against me. An article appeared in the *Wall Street Journal* yesterday implying that I'm an alcoholic, no longer fit to run the bank and that I only went into this deal because of my father-in-law.'

'Well, you are drinking too much.'

'That's very unfair and disloyal of you, Jamie.' Lucy jumped to her husband's defence. 'Gregsy's going through hell at the moment and he needs all the support he can get.'

'Huh, a bit late in the day for you to talk about loyalty and support,' Jamie responded cruelly. 'A lot of help you've been to him the past few years.'

'Come on, Greg, we've leaving. We're not going to sit here and be insulted by some irresponsible gambler, even if he is my cousin!' Lucy stood up and stormed out of the restaurant.

'I'm sorry, Jamie,' Greg said sadly, getting to his feet. 'I'll talk to you in the morning when we've all calmed down a bit.'

'Damned right you will,' Jamie replied coldly and turned away as Greg left.

In the days that followed the shares of Hamilton and Partners plummeted and by the end of the second week had halved in value. Business journalists on both sides of the Atlantic were united in their criticism of Greg's leadership of the bank and editorials began to appear calling for his resignation.

As so often happens in the financial marketplace – that cruel barometer of fear and avarice – those well-aimed pebbles that Virakis had skilfully scattered had started a merciless avalanche.

That this would exact a terrible toll on Greg was inevitable. He was a wreck both mentally and physically. Utterly powerless against the onslaught, he snapped like a reed in the wind and sought refuge in the bottle. For the first time in their marriage, Lucy rose to the occasion, discovering within herself unsuspected reserves of character and courage. But alas, her valiant efforts to revive her husband's broken morale were futile.

Spiros Virakis executed his *coup de grâce* late one Saturday morning through the unwitting agency of the postman who cheerfully presented Greg with a registered package. In keeping with his normal practice, Greg took his mail along to his study to read over breakfast, and opened the parcel first.

For the next six hours, he sat silently at his desk, his head buried deep in his hands. He had locked the door and given strict instructions that he wished to be alone. The rest of his mail remained unopened as he stared sightlessly into space, mechanically working his way through a bottle of whisky.

The first photograph showed Lucy naked on her hands and knees, her head buried between the splayed thighs of a blonde hooker from Knaves whom he had screwed himself. There were several more photographs of his wife with this girl. In some, she was grabbing Amanda's breasts from behind, rubbing herself greedily against the blonde's buttocks; in others she was lying on her back across a bed in total abandon, Amanda's entire hand inside her. And in one picture, the two girls were simultaneously sucking each other off. The photographer had captured perfectly both the look of ecstasy on Lucy's face and the knowing smile of the prostitute staring coldly into the camera. The final and most sickening photograph of all was of a pretty young girl, barely sixteen years old, wearing a hairdresser's housecoat which she was holding up around her breasts as she leaned forward over a chair – her face contorted in pain. Lucy, a grotesque dildo strapped to her crotch, was entering her savagely from behind.

One of the curious aspects of alcohol is that the more desperate one is to become paralytically drunk, the more difficult it is to do so. And so it was that Greg emerged from his isolation stone-cold sober. He went straight to the kitchen, where he meticulously burned the photographs, and then to his dressing-room. Ignoring Lucy, he changed for dinner. The engagement was unavoidable. It was in honour of the new American ambassador and their attendance was *de rigueur*.

Dismissing his driver and limousine, Greg drove Lucy in his old red Bugatti to Winfield House where he consumed at least as much alcohol as he had before and to no noticeable effect. People were afterwards to remark that he was on particularly good form that evening and seemed to have put his troubles behind him.

They left at about 11.30 p.m. and precisely three minutes later, as they were leaving Regent's Park, Greg swerved to avoid a drunken motorcyclist. He drove straight into a tree at forty miles per hour. He and Lucy were killed instantly.

CHAPTER 13

'Excuse me, Sir James. Sorry to disturb you.' Sedgewicke entered the bedroom. 'Mr Robard's on the telephone from London again.'

'All right, Sedgewicke,' Jamie said listlessly. 'I'll be down in a minute.' He put aside a volume of his father's first edition of Sir Walter Scott and slowly walked down the great staircase through the old armoury to the estate office.

'Yes, Hugo. What is it?'

'Jamie, I've been telephoning you for days. You might have had the decency to return my calls. Stop feeling sorry for yourself. Lucy was my niece, after all, and if she hadn't married that stupid American friend of yours, she'd still be alive. Now I've got a job to do. Virakis has been in London for the last month and is driving me mad to organize a game. He insists on you playing, so when the hell are you coming back to town?'

'When I feel like it.'

'Yes, but when? What do I tell Virakis?'

'I don't give a damn what you tell him!' Jamie snapped. 'I'll be back in London when I'm good and ready. Now if that's all, Hugo, goodbye.'

He wandered aimlessly into the great hall, hesitated at the foot of the staircase and for the first time in weeks felt the need to breathe some fresh air. So he went tentatively out through the keep and into the courtyard.

From his customary post at the head of the drawbridge, Hannibal pricked his ears. Sensing the faint stirrings of a change in his master's mood, he bounded over, determined to encourage it. Jumping up on his hind legs, he placed his massive paws on Jamie's shoulders and began to lick his face enthusiastically.

'Get down, Hannibal, you ridiculous creature. Go away.' Jamie half-heartedly avoided the dog's embrace and made a pretence at pushing him away. But Hannibal knew better. He dropped down, circled his master playfully a few times and set off across the moat. Seeing that he was alone, he stopped sharply in the middle of the drawbridge, turned and barked commandingly over his shoulder.

'All right you stupid dog, I'm coming,' Jamie laughed and followed obediently.

It was two months to the day since the police had dragged him out of bed in the middle of the night to identify the charred and mangled bodies of his cousin and his best friend. He had stood shaking in the mortuary of St Mary's Hospital, unable to speak and unable to believe what had happened. 'A bit late in the day for you to speak of loyalty and support.' The memory of those words would haunt him for ever. The last words he had ever spoken to Lucy. He was consumed with guilt. Why couldn't he have telephoned her? Just the once? Why couldn't he have gone to see her? She was his cousin, his sister, she was his childhood. She had lied for him when he was a boy; she had cried with him at his father's grave; she had stood by him when he was in prison. She had even married his best friend. He could still hear her voice at the wedding, 'Jamie, darling, Gregsy and you and me, we're all going to be so happy together . . .'

And poor old Greg. Poor, dear, big-hearted Greg, so warm, so decent. And always so unlucky. Why had he been so selfish? So insensitive? He had known exactly what Greg was going through and, far from being supportive, had brutally criticized and abandoned him. Abandoned his closest friend. How could he have behaved like that? He of all people. How many times since his release had Greg warned him to get his values and priorities back into perspective? He had wept unashamedly as he watched Greg's coffin being loaded into the hold of the aeroplane that would take him home for the last time. The image of the Greg he had seen at the Connaught was etched indelibly in his mind – grey, haggard and trembling. So different from the young Oxford athlete who had burst into Jamie's life with such freshness and vitality so few years ago.

And even Gavin. Where the hell was he? Despite everything – even though Lucy, Greg and the others had been right – he missed him. After all, who else was there? What other friends did he have? Angela? Even she had gone. Gone to a man who saw everything in terms of dollars and cents. He was completely alone.

Hannibal barked and tore off in pursuit of a grouse breaking cover. It was a hopeless chase, but the dog would not give up while there was breath left in his body. He was a thorough-bred. Well, neither would he, Jamie, give up. For once that slob Hugo was right. He had to stop feeling sorry for himself and face reality. He would return to London and damn well play in that Greek swine's game. So what if he was nearly broke? Since when did Jamie Stuart need money to win at poker? He was the best there was.

'Hannibal,' his voice rang out firmly across the Highlands. 'Here boy, heel! We're going home.'

CHAPTER 14

There are 2,598,960 different poker hands in a deck of cards. The chances of being dealt a pair are 1 in 2; of a straight, 1 in 255; and of a four of a kind, 1 in 4,165 – to name but three of these possibilities. Such permutations are well-known and can be mastered by anyone, much as a child memorizes his multiplication tables. To the simple percentage player, these and other similar mathematical calculations are the cornerstone of the game. His golden rule is that he will not make or call a bet if the odds tell him not to. Unable to understand why these percentages will not ultimately shield him from the vagaries of fortune, he continually finds himself bewildered and demoralized. He will always lose.

The good player knows that the only rule is that there are no rules. He has learned the percentages early in his career and soon after has learned to discard them. He is a psychologist extraordinaire. He has a deep understanding of the human mind – its twisting paths and blind alleyways. He has learned to recognize the cruel creatures that inhabit this terrain – these animals are the poker players' adversaries and he respects them. Their bluffs and counter-bluffs, their raises and re-raises. Like the wary hunter, he is always on guard against the unexpected and knows full well that, whatever his weapons, he can never kill every creature in the jungle.

The great player has an instinctive, indefinable gift that enables him totally to dominate the game and everyone in it. He is born and not made.

Most poker players consider themselves good or even great – why else would they play this most egotistical of games? But they are not. The vast majority of them play poorly and only a few are capable of assuming even the mantle of mediocrity. They regularly blame bad luck for their losses, yet do not claim good luck in their infrequent victories. Thankfully for the Gavin Blunts of this world, they will never accept that, in the long run, Lady Luck plays no part in the art that is poker.

Spiros Virakis of course knew all this. He also knew that the good player with a lot of money in front of him has a built-in advantage. His own aggressive game was a perfect example of this precept. It allowed him to apply the maximum amount of pressure around the table while permitting him to withstand the occasional and unavoidable setback. This is not to say, however, that a very rich man is less likely to go to pieces under pressure than the man in the street. Indeed, it is one of the ironies of poker that the loss of one or two major hands at the wrong time will destroy anyone's confidence.

'Good evening, Sir James.' Virakis's voice betrayed no emotion. After six long years revenge was at hand. 'How good of you to come. I was terribly sorry to hear of the tragic death of the Lady Lucinda and her husband. You were very close to both of them, yes?'

'Yes.' Jamie forced himself to accept the handshake. 'Very.'

'I believe you two know each other.' Virakis gestured edgily towards his wife who hurried over to them.

'Of course.' Jamie smiled tightly. 'How are you, Angela? You're looking marvellous.'

'Thank you, Jamie. It's good to see you, it's been far too long.' Angela was shocked by Jamie's appearance. She had not seen him since he'd gone to prison and the intervening years had not been kind. The aristocratic good looks were still there, but the face was much, much older. The skin was stretched even tighter over the cheekbones and the blond hair was flecked with grey. The creases around his eyes had become deeply carved lines and the eyes themselves, colder than ever, contained a profound sadness. He was surrounded by an aura of isolation.

'Jamie, come and talk to me.' She took him by the arm and gently pulled him aside, leaving her husband to greet the other guests alone.

'I was really upset about Greg and Lucy. He was such a lovely man. You know I always adored him.'

'Yes I know, Angela, thank you.' Jamie was pleased to see Angela and was touched by her concern. But he loathed her husband. Although he did not directly blame him for Greg and Lucy's death (he had no idea of Virakis's involvement in the demise of Hamilton and Partners), Jamie knew that he had instigated the Strathclyde débâcle which was at least partly responsible for the subsequent events. His own huge losses had left him angry but unmoved. He was born with that carefree attitude towards money that was characteristic of his class and, besides, to a gambler money is simply the tool of his trade. His accountants had salvaged enough, so they claimed, for him to live on reasonably comfortably for the rest of his life. *Provided*, they had stressed, provided that he was careful.

Over Angela's shoulder, Jamie could see that everyone had now arrived. He had played with them all before with the exception of Ben Wyatt, a gangling oilman from Texas and a very big gambler.

'Gentlemen, if you are ready, I suggest we start the game. Please take your seats,' Virakis announced unctuously.

'Well, Angela, it's been lovely seeing you again.'

'You too, Jamie my love,' she whispered softly in his ear as he kissed her on the cheek. 'Break a leg!' For an instant she was reminded of the old Jamie as that familiar smile flickered briefly across his face and he boyishly brushed his hair from off his forehead. The memories came flooding back. Jamie casually throwing her the keys to the flat in Cheyne Row; Jamie at Oxford laughing hysterically when Greg fell into the river trying to fish her out; and Jamie flushed with elation after his first big win, presenting her with a pair of diamond earrings.

She was a good wife to Virakis and had pulled off a marriage beyond her wildest dreams, but she would always love Jamie.

No one could ever take his place. Her husband could sense this and she was afraid for Jamie. She knew what Virakis was capable of and the terrible lengths to which he could go when he felt threatened. She also knew that tonight's game held a special significance for him. How could she ever forget Lennie's excitement when he had burst into her bedroom at four o'clock in the morning with the news that Jamie had won the biggest hand ever seen in a London club. And from a Greek shipping millionaire! Only now it was different. Thanks to that stubborn, unswerving loyalty of his, Jamie had no money. He could not afford to lose and he could expect no mercy at the hands of her ruthless husband. She watched him taking his place at the table – lonely, isolated, without a friend in the world – and prayed that he would win.

Jamie took out Sam Billig first. It was just before the dinner break and the ex-casino owner – a percentage player if ever there was one – was already groggy from the previous hand in which he had been brutally outdrawn by Felix Maggar. Before he had time to lick his wounds, he was dealt a pair of sevens back-to-back.

Jamie was high card with a ten and had a jack in the hole. In keeping with the aggressive style which he had adopted from the beginning, he made a hefty opening bet. Two people called before Billig, testing the waters, raised.

'Re-raise,' Jamie snapped.

The two other players passed and Billig warily called, reading him for a probable pair of tens.

'A jack to the ten, a four to the seven. Jack, ten to bet.' Paul Bishop glanced enquiringly at Jamie.

'I check.' Jamie did not bother to look up.

Billig swiftly concluded that Jamie would not check with a pair of tens and therefore must have an ace, or possibly a king, in the hole. His pair of sevens were winning.

'I bet the pot.'

'Call.'

'Thank you, Sir James. Gentlemen, the pot stands at £4,800.' Bishop smoothly dealt the fourth cards. 'A five to the jack, ten and a nine to the seven, four. You to bet again, Sir James.'

'Check.' Jamie still did not look up.

'Pot,' said Billig unhesitatingly, determined not to allow Jamie to outdraw him cheaply.

'Call.'

'Thank you, Sir James. Gentlemen, the pot stands at £14,400. Last cards. A jack to the jack, ten, five and a seven to the nine, seven, four. A pair of jacks to bet, Sir James.'

'Check.'

Billig thought carefully. He reasoned that effectively nothing had changed. He had made three sevens and Jamie had either a pair of jacks only or, as seemed more likely in view of his last call, two jacks and two tens.

'Fourteen thousand pounds,' he said confidently.

Jamie looked up for the first time. 'Call and raise the pot.'

'Thank you, gentlemen. We have a pot of £84,800 and it is £42,400 to you, Mr Billig, if you wish to call.'

Billig was taken aback. The last thing he had been expecting was a raise. A moment ago he had been on the attack hoping Jamie would call him and certain that his three sevens were well in the lead. All of a sudden, the roles had been reversed. He was on the defensive, facing a huge re-raise within minutes of having lost a big hand. Was this why Jamie had raised? Was he bluffing, pretending to have three jacks? Or did he really have them . . .? No . . . No, he couldn't. He would never have re-raised at the beginning with ten, jack. The best he could have was jacks and tens.

'Obligatory call, my son. What have you got?'

'Three jacks,' Jamie said coldly.

Billig slumped back despondently as Paul Bishop passed the chips – £127,200 in all – to Jamie. He had been taken from beginning to end – 'stitched up like a kipper'.

'Deal me out boys, I've had enough.'

Jamie talked to no one over dinner. Over the next few hours, he won some small pots and consolidated his position. He was saving himself for the major clashes which he knew were inevitable.

The next to go was Felix Maggar at the pudgy hands of

Hugo Robard. For reasons best known to himself the stylish Hungarian had suddenly taken off in the most extraordinary manner. He had exercised for some time an unusual degree of restraint and was bored. The sight of a single ace filled him with a divine inspiration. His moment had come!

Unfortunately, Hugo, playing like granite, had been dealt kings back-to-back and followed him all the way. Felix was on a suicide mission. He raised, re-raised and came to grief in spectacular fashion. 'It is not enough to be Hungarian; one must also have cards. I seem to have done it again!' Maggar signed his cheque with a flourish. 'Thank you for the game. By the way,' he smiled charmingly, 'as far as my wife is concerned I had a modest win! And now, I bid you all a very good night.' Everybody liked Felix and laughed warmly with him as he left.

'Thought I played that rather well, don't you, chaps?' Hugo said smugly.

'Hugo, you are an idiot,' Virakis observed nastily. 'You did nothing. My four-year-old son could have played that hand just as well. Get on with the game.'

'Yeah.' The Texan was in no mood for small talk; he had been losing steadily. 'Come on, Paul, deal the cards.'

'Really, Spiro, that's a little unnecessary. By the way, chaps, I'm not saying this because I'm winning, but it's nearly five o'clock. What time are we finishing?'

'Shit, Hugo, if you wanna go, go. Where I come from when a man sits down at a poker table, he sits down to play.'

Ben Wyatt had grown up playing cards in the saloons of a West that had seen little change since the days of the frontiersmen and as a penniless wildcatter had played countless marathon games. He was a tough, uncompromising player and for him the game was just beginning.

'Exactly,' Virakis agreed. 'Don't worry, Ben, Hugo is going nowhere. I suggest we play until eight and then break for a couple of hours' rest.'

'Yep, that's fine with me. How about you, son? You up to it?'

'I'll play as long as you like.'

'Or as long as your money lasts! Eh, Sir James, eh!'

'You're welcome to try and take it off me, Virakis. You

couldn't do it last time and you're still not good enough.'

'We shall see,' Virakis replied softly. 'We shall see.'

At the breakfast break Jamie was winning exactly one hundred and twenty thousand pounds, Hugo was desperately trying to protect the fifty thousand which he was ahead and Wyatt was losing the same amount. Virakis had held indifferent cards all night and was doing well to be breaking even, but was disconcerted at the confident manner in which Jamie was playing and was annoyed that he had built up a cushion. However, the game was young, and he was sure that Jamie's financial instability would soon tell.

'My friends.' Virakis stood up. 'We reconvene at eleven o'clock. Please make yourselves at home. Order breakfast, use the guest room – anything you wish.'

Paul Bishop slipped downstairs to the servants' quarters, grateful for the bed and hot bath that were awaiting him. He was tired, but by no means exhausted. Having once dealt for three days without a break, he was no stranger to long games and was proud of his reputation as London's top dealer.

Virakis, who throughout his life had survived on three hours' sleep a night, joined his wife and son for breakfast in the nursery wing.

'Good morning, my dear.' He nodded to Angela. He kissed his son. 'And how is my little soldier today, eh? What are you eating? Mmm, those sausages look good!'

'Fine, Daddy. How are you?'

'Very well, Andreas, thank you.'

'How's the game going, darling? Are you winning?' Angela looked up.

'Not yet, my dear. But I will.'

'Yes, I'm sure. Who is winning at the moment?' she asked a shade too quickly.

'Don't worry, my loyal little wife, your friend Stuart is well ahead.'

'Don't be so silly, Spiro. I couldn't care less what happens to Jamie. You know that.'

'Of course you don't, my dear. After all, he no longer pays the bills, eh!' He turned his back on her and spoke to his son,

'Well now. Might I enquire whether Andreas Spiros Virakis proposes to go to school today?'

'No, Daddy. I don't want to. I want to watch you playing cards. Is that fat fool, Hugo, playing with you?' the child asked in earnest.

'Andreas! Don't be so rude,' Angela scolded.

'But, Mummy . . . Daddy calls Hugo a fat fool all the time,' he protested. 'If he worked for me, I'd sack him.'

'One day, my son, I am sure you will,' Virakis chuckled. 'But you must go to school and learn all the things that Daddy did not have a chance to. You will have plenty of time to play cards when you are older. And me, I must have a little rest.'

Jamie slept for two and a half hours. He bathed, shaved and changed into a grey flannel suit and cream shirt. Hesitating for a full moment in front of his tie rack he deliberately selected the Christchurch tie that had belonged to his grandfather. He smiled grimly at the symbolism and returned to the game colder and more determined than ever.

'Call and raise.'

'Thank you, Mr Wyatt, that's £7,500; it's £12,500 to you, Sir James.'

'Call.'

'. . . to you, Mr Virakis.'

'Call.' Virakis had lost a large hand to Wyatt shortly after lunch, but this did not bother him – it was Jamie he was after.

'A three to the ace, king. A four to the jack, ten. A six to the eight, seven. Ace, king to bet, Mr Virakis.'

'I check.'

'Waall now, shooter.' The Texan chewed on the end of his cheroot. 'How much is the pot?'

'£35,000 sir.'

'That's the bet.' Wyatt casually threw his chips into the centre of the table.

'£35,000 to you, Sir James, to the possible straight.'

'Call.'

'Mr Virakis?'

Virakis came to life. 'I call and raise.'

'Shit. Looks like I've walked into a pair of aces.'

'Or kings,' Jamie added dryly.

'Sure. Anyway what the hell. I call.' Wyatt had jacks back-to-back and would not be shaken off yet.

'I call as well.'

'Thank you, Sir James. Last cards. A three to the ace, king, three. A seven to the jack, ten, four. A two to the eight, seven, six. Mr Virakis, the pair of threes to bet.'

Virakis smiled openly at the sight of Jamie's busted straight. Jamie had put in all his profits and more. He was behind for the first time. 'I bet £400,000.'

'Son of a bitch. Goddamned jacks always cost me money. Pass!' Wyatt slapped his cards face down angrily.

To everyone's astonishment Jamie did not pass his cards immediately. He began to stare penetratingly across the table, his hard blue eyes focusing on a point deep inside the Greek's head. His concentration was frightening. Several minutes later he relaxed; he had made up his mind. Virakis was bluffing.

'I call,' he said crisply. 'I've got a pair of eights. If you have more, you win.'

All eyes turned to Virakis who struggled to retain his composure.

'A very good call, Sir James. You win. An inspired call in fact.'

'Not really, Virakis,' Jamie said unpleasantly. 'Your hand was easy to read. It was Ben I was worried about.'

'Fuckin' right, son! I passed the winning hand,' the Texan said in disgust. 'How the hell were you so sure Spiro didn't have it?'

'Lessons come extra. You know that, Ben.' Jamie winked.

Three deals later, Jamie hit Virakis again. He was playing like a man possessed.

It was not for a great deal of money, it was not a particularly notable hand. But it was a bluff – and all the more humiliating for it. A bluff that shattered Virakis's already eroded confidence.

On card five, Virakis with an open pair of kings bet the pot into yet another possible straight. This time there was no hesitation on Jamie's part.

'Very dangerous bet, Virakis,' he sneered. 'I call and raise the pot.' He deliberately showed Wyatt his hole card. 'Still, no doubt Professor Hugo will advise you.'

'Yes. Well, actually I'm sure he has got—'

'Shut up, Hugo! Passo.'

'Wrong again, Virakis.' Jamie taunted him by revealing his useless hidden card.

Virakis fought to control himself and, realizing that he was about to crack up completely, called for a break. They had now been playing for twenty-four hours and Jamie was in an almost unassailable position.

The hand that finally broke Virakis came immediately after dinner. There had been two rounds of heavy betting, Wyatt had dropped out in the beginning and by the fourth card, Hugo had made a pair of aces with two eights. Jamie also had two pairs – queens and jacks – but was in third position. Virakis was way ahead of both of them with two tens and a nine showing and the third ten in the hole. He made the maximum bet. Jamie called rather recklessly, but with the confidence of the gambler who knows the cards are running his way. Hugo's greed got the better of him. After agonizing for some time, he concluded that he was probably in the lead and reluctantly threw his hard-earned winnings into the pot.

Paul Bishop dealt the final card. 'A nine to the ace and pair of eights.' Virakis glared as Robard took the nine that would have given him a full house. 'A two to the nine and pair of tens. A queen to the queen and pair of jacks. Two pairs to bet, Sir James.'

'Pot.'

'Blast you, Stuart, you lucky bastard,' Hugo swore. 'I fold.'

'You to call or raise, Mr Virakis.'

Jamie had an obvious full house and Virakis should have known better. But he was completely gone and called with the desperation that is the hallmark of the heavy loser.

'Full house,' Jamie said. It was all over.

'Full house, eh! . . . Full house! . . . Of course full house!' Virakis's voice quavered insanely. 'Eh, Hugo, eh! You bloody fucking moron. What are you doing in this pot, eh? You imbecile!'

'Come on, Spiro. I had aces up, I though I was in the lead . . .' He ducked suddenly as Virakis took a wild swing at him. 'What do you think you're doing?' he spluttered, blows raining down upon him from every direction.

'Thought you were in the lead so you take my full house!' Virakis was on his feet, incoherent with frustration and rage. 'Take my full house and give him one. You fat, stupid parasite!'

'Ouch, Spiro, please control yourself! Ouch!' Hugo yelped in pain as the Greek kicked him viciously in the shins. He ran from the room chased by his demented employer.

'Waall, I guess that's that,' Wyatt stood up, grinning at Jamie. 'Helluva win, son. Come on, I'll buy you a drink.'

Chapter 15

Win, lose or draw, sleep does not come easily to the gambler. And when it does, it is a shallow, twitching thing filled with blurred images of spiteful playing-cards laughing and chattering as they tumble from the dealer's chalk-white hands.

Jamie spent the whole of the next day in just such a state. He awoke in the early evening still weary, heavy-lidded and strangely empty of elation. It was while he was dressing that the pains started again. Moaning in agony, he clapped his hands to his head and sat involuntarily on the floor. His fingers scrabbled across the top of the dressing-table for his pills, but within seconds the pain had reached such blinding intensity that he heard himself screaming in terror for his mother before crumpling to a heap.

'Don't worry, Jamie, it's all over now.' Clarence smiled through the swirling mists. 'You don't know how lucky you are, it would have destroyed you.'

'But Grandfather, help me,' Jamie whispered.

'I am helping you,' he replied. 'You must understand it's over now.'

'Where am I, Grandfather? Am I dead?'

'Certainly not, Sir James, very far from it.' Clarence's voice was firmer but more alien now. Jamie squinted through the thinning haze, trying to focus on the features that were fast replacing Clarence's.

'Go away!' he shouted. 'Leave me alone. Where's my grandfather?'

'Please relax, Sir James,' the doctor said in a gentle voice. 'You've been very ill, but you're in good hands now. My name is Harcourt. You are in the London Clinic and you've had a stroke. You're not in any danger, but you do need to rest and Sister here will give you an injection to help you sleep. I'll be back to explain everything later.'

'But, Doctor, my grandfather . . .' Jamie struggled to form the words but lapsed into a deep unconscious void.

The next time he woke up he was still exhausted, but his mind was clear. He knew where he was and what had happened to him. His mouth was parched. With an enormous effort he reached for the water jug on the locker to the left of his bed and half filled the perspex tumbler. With even greater difficulty, he brought it to his mouth and drank, a few drops dribbling down his chin. He stopped, breathless, and balanced the glass precariously on his chest for several minutes, amazed at how weak his body had become. Gathering all his remaining strength, he transferred the water to his right hand. But the hand was not there. It would not move. Helpless, he watched the tumbler roll slowly to the side of the bed and fall with a dull thud to the ground. He cried out with horror as the shocking realization dawned on him that he could not feel his right leg either. He blacked out again and came to – he knew not how long later – soaked in a sweat of fear.

'Ah, jolly good, Sir James, glad to see you've surfaced. Let me introduce myself; I'm Giles Harcourt and this is Sister Robinson.'

Jamie nodded weakly. 'Yes, Doctor, I remember.'

'Ah, you remember. Excellent.' Harcourt's voice exuded confidence. In his late sixties, he was very much a doctor of the old school, right down to the fresh carnation in the buttonhole of his pinstriped suit. The most eminent neurologist of his day, he had cancelled a lecture tour of America at the personal request of his old friend, the Earl of Lochmair, in order to attend to his new patient.

'Now I don't want you to be alarmed. You've had what appears to be a mild stroke, but we don't yet know the extent of the damage.'

'Doctor, I'm paralysed. I can't feel the whole of my right side,' Jamie said desperately.

'Calm down, old boy. Loss of feeling does not mean paralysis. Your system's had a bit of a jolt and it's bound to take time to recover. I'm going to start with some simple reflex tests and that'll give us an idea of what's going on.'

Harcourt nodded to the nurse who pulled back the bedclothes obediently.

'I want you to tell me what you can feel and what you can't.' He began to push, pull, prod and tap various parts of Jamie's anatomy, sometimes provoking a reaction and sometimes not.

'Aha,' Harcourt exclaimed jubilantly, 'so you've got some feeling in your right toes. Try and wriggle them about a bit. Excellent. There you are, that's not paralysed is it? I wager you couldn't have done that twenty-four hours ago. Most encouraging. Now let's just have a quick look at your eyes.' He took out a penlike torch and examined Jamie's pupils. 'Look up . . . down . . . left . . . right. Follow my finger . . . good . . . everything seems to be normal there. Right, that's all for today.' He straightened up and put the torch back in his pocket. 'I'm very pleased and there is no need to panic. Tomorrow we'll do some proper tests and then I'll be in a position to give you a prognosis. But as I've said, the signs are good and in the meantime, the most important thing you can do is rest and get as much sleep as possible. Sister will give you a tranquillizer shortly and Dr Grumbar, my registrar, will check on you this evening. Is there anything else I can tell you at this moment?'

'No, Mr Harcourt,' Jamie answered in a tired voice. 'Thank you very much. I can see I'm in good hands.'

'Righto old boy, sleep well and I'll see you tomorrow. Thank you, Sister, that will be all.'

Jamie spent most of the next few days sleeping. During his waking hours his mind was alert, but, physically handicapped as he was, he had to suffer the indignities of assistance with his basic bodily functions. He was subjected to numerous tests: he felt alternately like a child that had just entered the world and an old man about to leave it – and wished that he were one or the other instead of the piece of human furniture that he had become. Despite the continual reassurances of Harcourt and the enthusiastic Grumbar he was very frightened.

Late one afternoon while Jamie was struggling to turn the pages of *The Times* on the clipboard in front of him, the jovial Harcourt burst into his room.

'Ah, jolly good. Glad someone's got time to read a newspaper. Anything interesting going on in the world?'

Jamie gave a wry grin. 'My old friend, Jeremy Hunter, has just won the Cheltenham Gold Cup by eight lengths and I wasn't around to put on a bet. He told me yesterday Formula One would skate it.'

'Wish he'd told me,' Harcourt said ruefully. 'I had my money on that Greek's horse – bloody nag fell at the last.'

'Yes,' Jamie replied. 'Virakis always was an unlucky gambler.'

'Anyway, dear boy.' Harcourt pulled a chair up to Jamie's bedside. 'It's time we had a little chat. There are some questions I need to ask. But first, let me tell you what we do know. There are two ways in which a stroke can be caused. The first is by a sudden rise of blood pressure which leads to the bursting of a blood vessel and haemorrhaging in the brain. The second is when a clot is formed that prevents the blood reaching some part of the brain. In your case, we have established that your stroke was caused by the former.'

'Is that good or bad?' Jamie asked anxiously.

'Well, that's not the point,' Harcourt replied. 'You've been lucky: the blood vessel has sealed itself and the bleeding has stopped. It may be difficult for you to appreciate this, but I'm confident that relatively soon – and with a lot of hard work – you will make a good recovery.'

'What exactly does that mean?'

Harcourt brought the tips of his fingers together to form a pyramid and leaned back. 'I would say – and it varies from patient to patient – that you'll be with us for about another three weeks, and within three or four months of intensive physiotherapy at home you should be more or less back to normal. When I talk about a good recovery there may well be some small residual impairment such as stiffness in your right arm or shoulder, or perhaps a facial twitch or even a slight limp. Any of these may be with you for the rest of your life – we just don't know. It depends largely on you; strokes are strange things, the most important thing is the individual's mental attitude.'

'Thank God.' Jamie exhaled deeply, his head flopping back on the pillow.

'Yes indeed,' said Harcourt, 'but what is much more important is to establish why someone of your age should have had a stroke in the first place so that we can try to prevent it from happening again. Because, quite frankly, if there is another one it will be much more serious.'

'What do you want to know?' Jamie pulled himself up with the help of the metal bar in front of him.

'I've been through your medical history. Your blood pressure has always appeared to be normal and we can rule out any hereditary conditions. But I understand from your own doctor that you've been complaining of severe headaches?'

'Yes.'

'When did they start?'

'As you may know, I spent some time in prison and . . .'

'Er . . . yes, old boy,' Harcourt cleared his throat. 'I was going to come to that. I'm afraid their medical records leave an awful lot to be desired.'

'I'm sure. Well, anyway,' Jamie continued, 'while I was there I was badly beaten up. I spent a few days in the prison hospital with some head injuries, a broken arm and a few missing teeth. That's when the headaches started. The prison doctors told me that I had been concussed, there was no brain damage and that the headaches were to be expected.'

'That's all?'

'Yes. They gave me a few aspirin and told me to go away. That was their standard treatment. Chap I knew had a burst ulcer, they gave him a few aspirins too and he died the next day!'

'It doesn't surprise me,' Harcourt shook his head, 'but describe the headaches to me – were they sudden, sharp pains or did they start as dull aches?'

'Sudden, sharp pains.'

'And whereabouts in the head did they occur?'

'Mainly in my temples and eyes.'

'Hmm.' Harcourt re-arched his fingers thoughtfully. 'Were there no other injuries from this incident?'

'Yes. I fractured a rib and had severe bruising around my lower back and kidneys.'

'Kidneys.' Harcourt sat up. 'That's interesting. Did they examine or treat them? A blood transfusion, for example?'

'No,' Jamie said dryly, 'just a few more aspirins.'

'Did you ever pass blood in your urine?'

'Yes, for several weeks.'

'But didn't they do anything about that?' Harcourt was amazed.

'Nothing. It was a common trick among prisoners to eat a lot of beetroot and claim they were passing blood in order to get into hospital for a few days.'

'I see. Did the headaches occur with increasing frequency?'

'Yes.'

'One final question,' Harcourt said gently, seeing that Jamie was tiring. 'What was the last thing that you remember before passing out?'

'An excruciating pain in my head.'

Harcourt stood up. 'Well, I think we may have found the answer. We'll have to do some more tests, but my guess is that your kidneys are scarred and this can often cause short periods of very high blood pressure. The headaches that you thought came from your head injuries are symptomatic of this – the severer the headaches, the higher the blood pressure. Now I'm going to let you rest and I'll see you again tomorrow. I want to start you on physiotherapy in the morning.'

'If you're right about my kidneys, is there anything that

can be done?'

'One thing at a time, old boy, let's get you back on your feet first. But in most circumstances, a simple operation can remove a lot of the scar tissue.'

Jamie's physiotherapist was a North Country girl called Sue Merryweather. Plain-looking and sensible, she took her work seriously and drove him hard.

'Good morning, Sir James.' She had poked a cheerful head around the door on her first day. 'I'm your physiotherapist. Just wanted to tell you we'll be starting work in an hour, so don't make any other plans.'

'What a nuisance. And to think I was going for a run round Regent's Park this morning!'

'Don't worry,' she laughed, 'like it or not, we'll have you doing that soon enough.'

It was not an idle threat. Attacking both sides of his body with equal vigour, she methodically twisted and pulled his ankles, knees, shoulders and elbows. She maintained a steady stream of irrelevant but comforting chatter centred mainly around her latest litter of cocker spaniels, a subject on which she was obviously an authority.

'You got dogs then, have you dear?' she enquired as she produced a resounding crack from his good shoulder joint.

'Yes,' Jamie winced.

'What kind?'

'Wolfhounds . . . Ouch, that hurt!'

'Don't be such a baby, you'll soon get used to it. Wolfhounds, that's an interesting breed. Can't have them in London though, they need room to run around and lots of exercise.'

'Yes, I suppose so.' Jamie grimaced again. But he fervently wished that he could transfer just a little of the pain to his right side.

The only other people Jamie saw were the two doctors, a rather flirtatious Australian night nurse and Sister Robinson, who clucked and fussed around him like a mother hen. And of course, Sedgewicke. Good old Sedgewicke who had brought him to the hospital in the first place, and practically moved in. He had not been permitted to see Jamie for the first couple of days, but had remained devotedly outside his room interrogating every member of staff that entered. When he was eventually allowed in, he was a pillar of support during Jamie's darkest moments, steadfastly refusing to accept that his master would remain handicapped for long.

As the week progressed, Sue's unrelenting efforts began to have some effect and Jamie's condition showed a slow but distinct improvement. He could just manage to move his right fingers as well as his toes and the numbness had receded to the limited extent that he could feel a pinprick in his right arm. Under Harcourt's cheery supervision, Jamie started to recover his spirits and the natural optimism that is the essence of the gambler reasserted itself.

.The nights were nevertheless still bad. As in prison, they were the most difficult times. His mind kept jumping from one tragedy to another – the trial, prison, Lucy and Greg, and now his stroke. Jamie, who had always despised self-pity, was wallowing in it. The arrogance was crumbling, the reserve had gone. The faintest image from the past would trigger uncontrollable weeping, his fierce pride alone forcing him to stifle his sobs beneath the pillow.

It was as though a trapdoor in his mind had sprung open, releasing a Pandora's Box of tormenting, alien emotions. What had he done with his life? Who would have mourned for him apart from Sedgewicke? He had no family, he had no friends, he certainly had no children. He had lost millions and won millions, yet to what purpose? Self-indulgence. Pure and simple self-indulgence. He was the last of the Stuarts and had failed lamentably in his duty as the custodian of centuries of hard-earned position and respect. A week in hospital and hardly a visitor – an impressive commentary on the first twenty-eight years of Jamie Stuart's life!

Hours later, emotionally exhausted, he would succumb to a deep, merciful sleep such as he had never experienced before. The tormented dreams that had plagued him since childhood were no more. The tortured visions of his grandfather had disappeared.

By the beginning of the second week, Jamie had taken his first faltering steps with male nurses supporting him under each arm. His initial revulsion at the sight of his lame, dragging leg only served to reinforce his determination to walk normally again. He soon graduated to a walking-frame and at last felt the luxury of pain cutting into his arm and shooting down his right leg.

It was early one evening, midway through the third week, and Jamie had just been round the block on crutches for the very first time, accompanied by Sedgewicke who had left him to sleep. He was drained, lying fully clothed on his bed, too tired to undress himself and without the energy to ring the bell for assistance. His muscles and joints were on fire and he was in agony. But it was the joyous agony of the marathon runner entering the stadium for the final lap. His head fell forward as the rapturous applause of the crowd faded from his ears. Moments later he was fast asleep.

'Wake up, Jamie! Wake up!' The night nurse was whispering excitedly into his ear. 'You've got a visitor, love. I've seen her picture in all the magazines. Come on, we'd better smarten you up a bit.' She straightened his tie and pulled at his waistcoat as he propped himself up on his elbows, rubbing his eyes.

'Who is it?'

'Angela Virakis. Come on.' She helped him to his feet. 'Let's get you into the armchair, we can't have such important guests seeing you like this.'

'I wouldn't worry about Angela,' Jamie laughed, 'she's seen me in every conceivable position.'

'How nice for her,' the nurse said sarcastically and showed Angela in.

'Jamie, darling, I'd just got back from St Moritz when I heard last night. I'm so sorry, I had absolutely no idea.' She knelt in front of him and took his head in her hands, covering his face with kisses. 'Thank God, you're all right. That nice

Doctor Grumbar said everything's going to be fine.'

Jamie's voice was charged with emotion. 'You don't know how good it is to see you, Angela.'

'I simply can't believe it, darling.' The tears were rolling down her cheeks. 'First Greg and Lucy, now you. What's going to happen next?'

'Nothing, Angela. Don't worry about me, I'm OK. Anyway, tell me about you. How's your lovely son?'

'Oh, he's well.' Angela burst into a fresh flood of tears.

'Come on, Angela. Pull yourself together. There's nothing to cry about. You'd better not let your husband catch you here. I shouldn't think he'd be very pleased. The last time I saw him, he looked as though he was the one who was about to have a stroke!'

'Oh to hell with him,' she replied miserably. 'Do you know, Jamie, I was thinking only the other day about Greg and Oxford and all the good times we used to have together. Why is everything so complicated these days? What happened to us all?'

Jamie put his arm around the back of her neck and pulled her face gently to his chest. He could feel the wetness of her tears through his thin cotton shirt and turned his own head away. He did not wish her to see that he was crying too.

'What happened, Angela,' he said sadly, 'is that everyone grew up. Everyone except me. Greg, God rest his soul, loved poor Lucy more than anything else in the world. He loved his job, he loved the bank. He took pride in everything he did. And however things turned out, at least he tried. And you, look at you, my darling. You married well, you've got a wonderful son. You've got everything you've ever wanted out of life . . .' His voice trailed off and they hugged each other in silence for several minutes.

'You know, Angela,' he continued as she kissed the tears from his eyes, 'I think that once this is all over I'm going to go away for a while. I'm so very tired. There's nothing left for me in this country except memories now. I need a change of scenery.'

'Yes, I understand. Where will you go?'

'I'm not sure yet. Somewhere different. The Far East

perhaps. America. Anywhere I can get a decent poker game,' he laughed ironically. 'By the way, talking about poker, how is your husband?'

'The same as ever,' she said, 'but he really hates you, Jamie. Why?'

'God knows. Just a bad loser, probably.'

'Yes, but it goes much deeper than that and it really scares me.'

'Well, I don't know, perhaps it's got something to do with you. Anyway, I'm a cripple now, I'm sure he's lost interest in me.'

'Don't talk that way, Jamie. Of course you're not a cripple, that absolute nonsense. You're going to be fine.'

'Perhaps, perhaps not. In any case, my darling, please don't think me ungracious. It's been wonderful of you to come here, but I really am most awfully tired . . .' His head fell back against the chair and he was fast asleep.

Angela sat at his feet for a while watching him snoring gently. There was something different about his face under the pallor of sickness, a softness that had never been there before and a peacefulness – a sort of understanding. She got up quietly, kissed him on the forehead and slipped away.

Spiros Virakis was playing chess with his son. He was no match for the boy and, glowing with pride, he turned over his king and conceded defeat.

'Bravo, Andreas, I am no longer a suitable opponent for you. I can see that our business will be in good hands.'

'Now let's play cards,' the boy said excitedly.

'No. It is time for you to do your homework.'

'But, Daddy, you promised,' he pleaded.

'I'll play cards with you later,' Virakis said firmly. 'Off you go and finish that story you showed me.'

He sat back and finished his ouzo. It had all been worthwhile. All the lying and the double dealing on the way up. All the manipulation, bribery and trickery to remain at the top. All the sweat and anxiety to build and maintain an empire. Yes, it was worth it. Even marrying that whore had been worth it. He had a magnificent son. Bright, handsome and charming. Everything he had always wanted his son to be – an English gentleman in fact. His mood changed.

'Hello, darling.' His wife breezed past him, followed by her chauffeur who was defying all known laws of gravity by maintaining his balance, an assortment of boxes piled high within his arms. 'Take those up to my dressing-room please, Metcalfe.'

'Certainly, Madam,' the driver grunted and groped for the door handle, losing his cap in the process.

'Had a good day, Spiro?' She threw her sable coat over the back of a divan. 'Where's Andreas?'

'Andreas is upstairs writing a composition on the French Revolution,' Virakis answered smoothly. 'Which for your information, my dear, is not a new style by Dior, but a period in the world's history when useless aristocrats were sent to the guillotine.'

'You would have been quite safe then, wouldn't you?' Angela retorted.

'Ahaa,' he cackled, 'I can see these important shopping expeditions have sharpened your wit. Tell me, *Angelaki mou*, what did you buy at the London Clinic? A useless aristocrat, eh?'

She coloured slightly. 'What do you mean? How do you know where . . .'

'How do I know? You stupid whore, I know everything! How else do you think I survive with everyone plotting against me? Eh!'

'You're sick, Spiro,' she said contemptuously. 'You need your head examined.'

'Sick . . . Sick!' he screeched at her departing back. 'Me? . . . sick! You talk to your friend Stuart about sick. Ask him about his grandfather if you want to hear sick! Get out of my sight . . . *poutana!*'

Virakis was convinced that ever since they had stopped sleeping together his wife had turned to other men for her physical needs. It was only to be expected. She was young, desirable and highly sexed. She had been followed for some considerable time now and it was a source of continual frustration to him that his army of private detectives had failed to produce a single scrap of evidence of infidelity. The simple truth that she had never been unfaithful to him – if only out of fear – he refused to accept. As indeed he had refused to accept throughout his life the simple truth about anything (and how well it had served him).

His greatest frustration, however, was as always Jamie. Against all odds and with his world crumbling about him, Jamie Stuart had played the game of his life. Every move had been inspired. Virakis had been outclassed. He would never play poker with Jamie again. The years of meticulous preparation had not been entirely wasted – he had made a fortune by shorting Hamilton's stock and a further huge profit when the value of the ships that he had picked up cheaply from Strathclyde had soared as a result of the Suez crisis. But Jamie had escaped him and through his timely stroke had robbed him of any further opportunity for revenge. After all, what satisfaction was there in beating a dead octopus that someone else had caught?

'*Skata!*' he swore and hurled his glass against the wall.

BOOK THREE

CHAPTER 1

'Sedgewicke, I'm thinking of doing some travelling,' Jamie began with apprehension.

'Yes, Sir James.' Sedgewicke nodded disconsolately. He was disappointed. It was over two years since Jamie had been wheeled out of the hospital and he was now firmly back on his feet.

Sedgewicke welcomed the changes that had appeared in Jamie's character – incredible though it seemed, the stroke had actually helped him. He was a man finally at peace with himself. More relaxed than at any time since his schooldays, he no longer spent his nights gambling or in the company of dubious women. He had begun to take out young ladies of suitable background and was even showing a serious concern in the affairs of Kilpurnie. All the indications had been that he would face up to his responsibilities, marry and move up to Scotland where he belonged.

'Cheer up, Sedgewicke. I'm not going for ever. I just want to see a bit of the world before it's too late. I propose to start in America. I must pay my respects to Mr Hamilton's family and I've got to tie up one or two business affairs there. Now I very much want you to come along, but I'm not going to force the issue. The house will remain open here and of course, you can always go up to Kilpurnie.'

'My place is with you. Of course, I will come, but couldn't we . . .'

'Good.' Jamie rubbed his hands together. 'That's settled then. Let's have a drink on it.' He walked over to the sideboard, his right foot dragging slightly.

'There you are.' He handed him a glass of sherry. 'Cheers. To America. Think of it, Sedgewicke, America, The brave new world! What fun we'll have. What marvellous things we'll see.'

'Yes, let's hope so,' a taciturn Sedgewicke replied. 'But won't the doctors . . .'

'Don't talk to me about doctors, Sedgewicke, I'm sick of them. We're going and that's that.'

'Very well, Sir James.' There was no stopping Jamie in this mood. 'Might I enquire when this foreign adventure will begin?'

'As soon as possible. I was thinking in terms of straight after Ascot. How does that suit you?'

'Whatever you wish.'

'Your enthusiasm knows no bounds,' Jamie chuckled. 'Never mind, Sedgewicke. You'll enjoy it once we're there, you'll see.'

'Of course, sir. Now if you'll excuse me.' He put down his glass. 'I have several matters to attend to.'

'Yes, yes, Sedgewicke, off you go.' Jamie waved his arm airily.

He was relieved. Since his stroke, Sedgewicke had become more indispensable to him than ever and in the early days of his recuperation had been a godsend. One day when walking home to Berkeley Square from his shirtmaker in Jermyn Street – a path he had trodden for over ten years – Jamie had inexplicably got lost. Several hours later he had been found by Sedgewicke wandering like a stray child outside Greg and Lucy's old house in Eaton Square, unable to remember even his name.

There had been another occasion on which Sedgewicke had come to the rescue. Jamie had arrived at his club for a doctor's appointment and had persistently refused to accept the porter's alarmed protestations that White's was not in Harley Street and was certainly not a doctor's surgery.

These had been isolated incidents and Harcourt had warned

him that there might be periods of confusion. There had been no recurrences, but the prospect of travelling alone to America made him nervous.

The real reason, however, for his decision to travel and (if the truth be known) to start a new life, was a discovery of shattering proportions, a discovery which had shaken him to the core and which, by definition, must change the shape of his life to come.

His gift was gone. He had lost it.

It had taken some time and a number of poker games for him to realize it, but at the end there was no doubt. His instinct for reading his opponents' cards was no longer infallible. His ability to predict their reactions was flawed. In short, he had lost his peculiar genius for cards.

Mark you, he was still an exceptional player and could more than hold his own in any game. But for Jamie Stuart, that was not enough. He had tasted greatness in his chosen vocation, had accepted it as his right, and could not live with anything less.

That he had been warned of this loss was now obvious to him. He no longer suffered from his nightmares, no longer saw his grandfather's twisted face in his dreams and Clarence's final words from that last dream in hospital were now crystal clear to him: 'Don't worry, Jamie, it's all over now . . . it would have destroyed you.'

Perhaps it was a fair exchange. A gift that would have destroyed him for a stroke that had changed his life. Only time would tell.

CHAPTER 2
NEW YORK, JULY 1958

New York City in the summer was no place for a gentleman, nor for that matter a gentleman's gentleman. Not that Sedgewicke needed the weather to put him in bad humour. He hated New York and everything about it; its architecture, its *arrivisme*, its brashness, its belligerence. He could find a lament for every letter of the alphabet. He sat shivering in the air-conditioned suite of the Plaza Hotel while for the third consecutive day yet another illiterate Puerto Rican waiter laid out the wrong breakfast order.

'No, no, no,' he said testily. 'How many times do I have to tell you? I asked for cornflakes, C...O...R...N... F...L...A...K...E...S.'

'*Si, señor*, I breeng you pancakes.' His colleagues in the kitchens had warned him of this difficult guest and the waiter smiled indulgently.

'For God's sake, man,' Sedgewicke exploded, 'cornflakes. Cornflakes! They're a bloody cereal!'

'*Si, si señor*. Me understand, ees OK . . . I bring you seerup already,' the waiter said soothingly. 'Ees here, beautiful seerup for the pancakes.' He removed the top of a silver dish with a flourish. 'From Atlantic, Georgia. The best in America.'

'Oh all right. Go away and leave me alone.' Sedgewicke sighed and poured himself a tasteless cup of tea as the Puerto Rican departed, tipless in spite of a series of spectacular bows.

Apart from the occasional trip to the South of France with Jamie, Sedgewicke had never ventured beyond the shores of Britain and disliked foreigners intensely. Nothing could have prepared him for the shock of America, the only knowledge of which he had gleaned from gangster films of the thirties. To Jamie's secret amusement, Sedgewicke had managed to find an excuse to remain in the hotel for hours on end and it had taken him two full days to venture beyond the sanctuary of its portals. His fists clenched tightly in his pockets – he expected to be mugged or gunned down at any moment – he had walked warily down Fifth Avenue past Bergdorf Goodman and admired the extravagant displays in the smart shop windows. He had crossed over to Tiffany's where the vulgar exhibition of large gems failed to impress him and continued down 57th Street to Madison Avenue.

Here he had gingerly entered a crowded coffee shop and taken the only empty seat at the bar in search of refreshment and refuge from the blistering heat.

'Morning Mac, what'll it be?' the thickset bartender demanded.

'How very observant of you.' Sedgewicke was amazed at the man's perspicacity. 'A cup of coffee and a pastry, if you please?'

'Danish?' The barman eyed him suspiciously.

'No, Scottish actually.' Sedgewicke was slightly bemused. 'I thought you realized.'

'What the hell are you talking about?' the man shouted. 'There's Danish, doughnuts or strudel. Make up your mind, I haven't got all day.'

'Oh well, er . . .' Sedgewicke said timidly, aware that he had become the centre of attention. 'Perhaps a little fruit cake then?'

'Fruit cake! You asshole, who the hell are you calling a fruit cake?' The bartender began to remove his apron menacingly. 'Get the fuck out of my shop, you dumb jerk. Before I throw you out.'

'Certainly,' Sedgewicke replied stiffly, 'with the greatest of pleasure.' And though scarlet-faced, he managed a dignified exist.

Now very hot as well as bothered, he beat a hasty retreat back to the Plaza, pausing outside a stationer's where he selected a copy of the previous day's London *Times* from the newsstand. Entering the dark and narrow shop with its overflowing boxes and cartons piled haphazardly to the ceiling, he located a fat, middle-aged woman who was squatting on a stool behind the cash register.

'Yeah, whaddya want?' she asked through a mouthful of gum.

'I'd like this newspaper please, madam.' Sedgewicke proffered a twenty-dollar bill.

'Twenty bucks. Twenty bucks!' she grumbled as she opened the till. 'Whaddya think this is, the Chase Manhattan Bank?'

'I'm most awfully sorry, madam.' Sedgewicke shook his head. 'This really doesn't seem to be my morning. I'm afraid I haven't anything smaller.'

'Yeah, yeah, Limey,' she huffed, counting out his change, 'just give me a break and buy your papers someplace else.'

'You can rely upon it, madam,' Sedgewicke said haughtily. He turned on his heel and left. He did not stop until he reached his hotel and had not been out again.

'Morning, Sedgewicke. Still having breakfast?' Jamie breezed into the suite, his limp barely discernible. 'Ah, pancakes. Glad to see you're getting into the spirit of things.'

'Yes, Sir James,' Sedgewicke groaned.

'Good, good. Rather you than me, though. Anyway, start packing, old chap, we're off to Newport for a while. You'll like it there too. But it's much more like England. Hope you'll be able to adjust!'

'I'll do my best, Sir James.'

'I'll leave you to it then. I'm just popping out to do a bit of shopping. We'll drive up with Mr Hamilton after lunch. See you about one o'clock.'

Jamie was gone as quickly as he had arrived and Sedgewicke lugubriously began to pack.

Jamie by comparison had been in fine form in New York. The frenetic pace of the city stimulated him, it suited his new life.

As far as he was concerned, a new chapter had begun the moment he set foot on American soil. He was determined to make something of his life. The gift that had ruined his grandfather and had dominated him, dictating and directing his every move, had departed. The manacles had been unlocked, the shackles shed. He was no longer captive to the cards, no longer a disciple of the dark. Less cold, less remote, totally uninterested in gambling, he could see clearly now. The scales had fallen from his eyes . . . 'freedom has a thousand charms to show which slaves, however contented, never know'.

He had been up at the crack of dawn every morning and had spent most of his time with Morton Hamilton at the Wall Street office of the bank in which he was still a major shareholder.

Hamilton and Partners had taken a severe beating but had survived. It was no longer a publicly quoted company, but Morton had brought about a modest rally. He had shut down the overseas network and was concentrating on traditional domestic services for those old clients who had remained loyal. A shorter, stocky version of his older brother, he had grown up in Greg's shadow and though lacking the latter's outgoing personality, had come into his own during this period of adversity. More insular in his outlook then Greg, he had joined the bank directly from Harvard and upon his father's recent death had calmly assumed the reins of responsibility. Since his teens he had idolized Jamie and was acutely aware of the business that Jamie's name and title could generate for Hamilton's. He was hoping to persuade Jamie to start a new life in America as an executive director of the bank.

Sedgewicke was not impressed by the drive to Rhode Island. The scenery improved gradually as they reached Connecticut, but although New England was reminiscent of the motherland of its settlers, its countryside contained a certain starkness that was not to be found among the warm, welcoming villages back home. He missed Scotland even more and the ultra-efficient air-conditioning of Morton's Lincoln Continental made the Plaza Hotel seem like a tropical island. Huddled miserably in the back of the car, be longed for their journey to end.

His misgivings, however, evaporated as they crossed the gleaming suspension bridge that linked Newport to the mainland. Even Sedgewicke had to admit the view was breathtaking. The bobbing boats criss-crossing the channel below, their gaily-coloured sails flapping in the wind; the bustling harbour with its quaint colonial restaurants and pubs peeping through a forest of wooden masts. The imposing grey mansions and palaces (for there was no other word for them) overlooking the sea contrasted markedly with the simple, white huts built by the original Portuguese fishermen that were dotted about the green hills on the other side. And beyond, on the distant horizon, like some sleeping leviathan, the faint, sinister outline of Cape Cod.

The drive to Hamilton House took them down Bellevue Avenue past the front of the grand homes Sedgewicke had seen from the bridge. It was the most extraordinary sight. French chateaux bordered on English castles which bordered on Italian palazzos – and all within a few hundred yards of each other. There was even a pagoda that had been brought over piece by piece from China by Cornelius Vanderbilt for the singular purpose of taking afternoon tea. Amazingly, this collection of excesses actually worked.

Hamilton House, palatial by most standards, was relatively modest and Sedgewicke liked it at once. It was a family home and old Gregory Hamilton I had built it as such. Morton's wife, Jackie – an attractive, matronly woman in her early thirties – and their three children greeted them in the driveway.

About an hour later, Morton's sister Jessica Turnbull threw a blue Ferrari convertible into a front-wheel skid and expertly negotiated the wrought-iron gates of Hamilton House. She accelerated again and then skidded to a halt, spraying gravel with deadly accuracy into the gaping mouths of the stone gargoyles that guarded the front entrance. Swinging her long, brown legs over the car door, she ran up to each gargoyle in turn, carefully removed the tiny pebbles from their mouths, counted them and threw them back into the driveway.

'Well, Quasimodo, got you again!' she exclaimed. 'Shit, Nikabrik, only six today! I'll get you tomorrow.' She ran into the house and up the stairs to her bedroom where she slipped off her tennis clothes and stepped into the shower.

When she emerged, her lithe body was wrapped in a thick, white bathrobe and a towel was tied turban-style round her sun-bleached blonde hair. Opening the glass doors to the terrace, she walked out and rested her elbows on the balustrade as she watched the reflection of the setting sun across the orange sea.

She had seen a great deal of life. A fun-loving, hard-drinking beauty, she had married two very different men. Jack Turnbull, the celebrated jungle explorer, was twenty years her senior when he swept her off her feet with tales of adventure that rivalled those of Rider Haggard. He taught her to drink Bourbon straight and drop her right shoulder in a punch. And she worshipped him. She had spent three blissful years on expeditions to the remotest corners of the globe until a rogue elephant in the forests of Hyderābād robbed her of him. It was a cruel twist of fate. Jack, who had practically been born on the back of an elephant, was the only casualty in the camp. He left her with an infant son and a treasure chest of unforgettable experiences.

Her second husband was the notorious South American playboy, Marcello Barbarosa. Impossibly good-looking and equally charming, life with him consisted of one long round of parties at every watering-hole of the international jetset, from Barbados to Bali. He had found her money and other women irresistible. The combination was fatal to their marriage, but they parted amicably – she to her son in America, he to his next wife in Cannes.

The sun was almost vanishing into the distant water and the first of the early-evening stars were beginning to appear. Since her childhood days she had sat on this balcony at this very hour, alone with her thoughts and dreams. She loved this house and she loved Newport but the people were too stuffy for her and the summer always seemed one month too long.

She was brought back to reality by the sight of a tall stranger standing at the water's edge looking out to sea. Straining her eyes through the gathering dusk, she watched him flick his cigarette into the surf below and walk, limping slightly, back towards the house. His fair hair was caught by the evening breeze and as he neared the lights of the guest cottage, she saw his face clearly for the first time. It was Jamie. Dashing into her bedroom, she pulled on a pair of jeans and a T-shirt and tore down the stairs, pulling the towel from around her head.

'Jamie. Jamie!' She ran towards him and jumped breathlessly into his open arms.

He hugged her tightly. 'Well, well, Jessica darling, let me have a look at you.' He held her at arm's length. 'My God, I heard you were beautiful, but that's the understatement of the century!'

'Oh come now, Jamie.' She touched her wet hair self-consciously. 'I'm a terrible mess . . . but you . . . you! You look really well.'

'And now that I've seen you, I feel it,' he replied. And he meant it with all his heart. He had been struck by a thunderbolt.

Love was a word that Jamie had never really understood. Yes, he had loved his parents and had adored his cousin, Lucy. Yes, he had loved Greg as if he were his own brother (after all, to paraphrase slightly, 'greater love hath no man than he should be prepared to give his life for his best friend'). But love for a woman had been to him the province of poets and troubadours, a land of milk and honey upon some distant shore. Distant of course because of that accursed gift, that damned gift which had not allowed him to be whole, which had deprived him of true happiness with a woman by forcing him to sublimate the depth of feeling that now came gushing forth. Although not forty years in the wilderness, the seas had parted and he had reached the promised land. That night Jamie made love for the first time.

Jessica, too, was seriously in love for the first time. She had adored old Jack Turnbull and would be forever grateful for the fascinating times and wonderful son he had given her. But she was an impressionable teenager when they met and he died too soon. Marcello had been a passing, if somewhat expensive, infatuation; and now, after a number of light-hearted affairs, she was ready for a real relationship.

Jamie was something of a legend in her family. From the age of fifteen she had heard nothing but stories about him. His recklessness, his gambling prowess, his extraordinary loyalty and the strange perceptiveness that Greg could never quite explain. But there was more. Beneath the refined good looks, the dry wit and worldly charm was a vulnerability she sensed he was uneasy with. It was, she supposed, like his limp, a result of his stroke and she found it irresistible. 'The guy's a lunatic, no question about it,' Greg used to say, 'but I'd give my life for him. He sure as hell would give his for me.'

For the next two months they were inseparable. Whether swimming off Bailey's Beach, dining by candlelight at the Black Pearl or sailing on the yachts of friends, they only had eyes for each other. At home it was the same. They were unable – much as they tried – to sustain conversations of any length with their hosts and could not even be distracted by the playful antics of the children. When they were not making love, Jessica would sit naked and cross-legged on the floor while Jamie dressed, pleading with him to tell her about his time in prison; and she would perch precariously on the side of the bath while he shaved – begging to hear more and more gambling stories, despite his obvious reluctance.

On the one occasion when Jamie accompanied Morton to New York, Jessica spent the day with Sedgewicke, pestering him to tell her stories of Lucy, whom she had never met, Jamie's parents and Kilpurnie. The normally taciturn Scotsman, having quite overcome his dislike of Americans, happily obliged.

Just when Jessica had decided she couldn't bear the suspense any longer and had made up her mind to take the initiative, Jamie asked her to marry him.

It was Labor Day weekend, the first weekend in September. The shutters were going up on the summer houses, the leaves were turning gold and the sea growing greyer. Jessica was driving them back at breakneck speed after a stupifyingly boring game of bridge at the mock-Tudor house of a local luminary whom Jamie had found as pretentious as his home.

'Some fucking bridge player you are!' She banged both hands furiously against the steering-wheel and glared at him.

'Now, now darling,' he laughed. 'Calm down, just keep your eyes on the road and your hands on the wheel.'

'Greatest card player of all time, my sweet fanny! When I open one no-trump with a sixty part score, I don't expect to be raised.'

'Sorry, darling,' Jamie laughed again. 'I was so bored, I completely forgot the score.'

'Do me a favour. Next time you play bridge, partner Nick the Greek!'

'Oh dear.' Jamie couldn't stop laughing. 'Oh well, you're acting like a wife so I suppose I'd better marry you.'

'What! What did you say?' She couldn't believe her ears.

'Nothing much,' Jamie said casually. 'By the way, wasn't the pheasant dreadful? Quite extraordinary really, cooking it in . . .'

'Now look here, you son of a bitch, what did you just say?'

'Quite extraordinary really, cooking pheasant in . . .'

'You bastard!' She slammed her foot on the brakes and brought the car to an abrupt stop.

'Jessica Turnbull, I am now deadly serious,' Jamie said, 'I am madly in love with you and I want to spend the rest of my life with you. Will you marry me?'

'Jamie Stuart, you're a no-good gambler and a jailbird with a run-down castle in Scotland. You've got some balls to ask me to marry you!'

'Yes, I quite understand. Silly of me, old girl. Forget I even mentioned it.'

'And miss the chance of being Lady Stuart,' she yelled. 'Of course I'll marry you, darling.' She threw her arms around his neck, smothering him with kisses.

CHAPTER 3

They were lunching at '21', finalizing the plans for their wedding, which was to take place the following week in Jessica's Park Avenue apartment. It was to be a small affair attended only by Morton, Jackie, Sedgewicke and Howard, Jessica's seven-year-old son who had just returned from camp in Maine. The bar was crowded and noisy when the sound of a familiar voice rose with startling clarity above the din.

'You jumped-up little waiter. I don't wish to discuss it. Just bloody well take this disgusting food away.'

'Jesus Christ.' Jamie paled under his tan.

'Darling, what's the matter? Are you feeling all right?'

'Yes, yes I'm fine. I've just seen an old friend. That chap over there with his back to us in the blue suit. See him?' He pointed.

'Absolutely. I noticed him when we came in. Very good-looking!'

'Hold on a second.' He let go of her hand. 'I'll go and get him.' Jamie left the banquette and worked his way through the tables.

'Excuse me, sir,' he said in an exaggerated American accent, 'I'm going to have to ask you to leave, we don't like rude Englishmen here!'

'What the hell . . .' Gavin Blunt swivelled around. 'Jamie! Jamie, what on earth are you doing here?' He jumped up and

213

embraced him. 'I heard some terrible story about you but you're looking really well. How are you?'

'I'm fine . . . never been better in fact. You're looking pretty good yourself.'

'Can't complain, old boy, can't complain. Who are you with, Jamie, where are you sitting? Come and join us. Sal . . .' He turned to the man sitting opposite him, 'this is Sir James Stuart, one of my oldest friends. Jamie . . .' He gestured towards his companion, 'meet Salvatore Bonetti, an associate of mine.'

'How do you do.' Jamie shook hands. 'I'm with that blonde girl over there. Er, actually, Gavin,' he said sheepishly, 'getting married in a few days. Why don't you two come and join us?'

'Well, well, well.' Gavin slapped him on the back. 'Congratulations! Who is she, Jamie?'

'Greg's sister, Jessica Turnbull.'

'She's terrific! You always were a lucky bastard. I'll be over in a few minutes.'

Soon afterwards, Gavin joined them.

'It's so nice to meet you at last, Gavin, I've heard so much about you,' Jessica said warmly.

'All of it bad, I hope.'

'Absolutely,' Jessica laughed.

'Good, good, wouldn't want to ruin a lifetime's work. Anyway you two, congratulations. Wonderful news! You must be my guests for dinner tonight.'

'We'd love to,' Jamie replied. 'I hope you'll be here for the wedding. It's on Thursday.'

'Of course, old boy, wouldn't miss it for the world. Now, Jessica . . .' He picked up her hand, his voice flooding with emotion, 'let me say how dreadfully sorry I was to hear of your brother's death. Greg was a dear, dear friend of mine. In fact, I was with him only a few days before that terrible accident. And . . .' he turned to Jamie, 'poor Lucy, I was absolutely devastated.' He sat quietly for a moment, shaking his head.

'Thank you, Gavin.' Jessica broke the silence. 'We all miss them very much. But about tonight, I'm afraid I promised my son I'd watch him in his school play. Why don't you two have dinner alone? I'm sure you've got a lot of catching up to do.'

'All right, darling,' Jamie replied. 'Where are you staying, Gavin?'

'I've got a town house on 62nd Street, between 2nd and 3rd Avenue. Why don't you come round for drinks at eight-thirty and we'll take it from there? Do excuse me, but I must dash now. See you later, Jamie; lovely meeting you, Jessica,' He kissed her on both cheeks and was off.

'Thank you.' Jamie took the drink from the silver tray.

'You're welcome, sir.' The black butler disappeared.

'Very nice, Gavin, you're obviously doing rather well these days,' Jamie remarked, admiring a particularly fine Cézanne.

'Ah yes, I won that in a game in Saratoga last week from a doctor who had a bit of a cash problem. Rather nice what?'

'Very.'

'I know what you're thinking, Jamie. Come and sit down. I owe you an apology and an explanation.'

'Yes, Gavin. But have the decency not to lie to me.'

'That bastard Virakis shafted us all. As you know, I never had anything to do with the running of the old company, Peregrine did all that. One night, though, after a poker game – you must have been in prison at the time – that slimy Greek came to me with a very interesting proposition. I'll spare you the details but I discussed it with Peregrine and it seemed to us too good an opportunity to miss. With hindsight,' he sighed, 'it was too good to be true. Basically Virakis was offering to help us finance the building of some new ships that we badly needed. Naïvely, we took him at his word – I thought he was a friend of mine. At the first possible opportunity, he pulled the rug out from underneath our feet by reneging on his contract and bankrupting both us and the shipyard. Just so that he could pick up our ships at less than half price. And he pulled it off brilliantly,' he said bitterly. 'I begged and pleaded with him to stick to the contract, but the bugger wouldn't budge and then he vanished, leaving me to deal with Hugo Robard. I even had poor Greg and that chap – what's his name? McKay I think, from the Union Bank – trying to bail us out. But it was too late, Virakis had done his work well and there was nothing any of us could do. Imagine how I felt. The first time I ever get involved with the company, it goes broke and that gangster, Brett, would have slit my throat as soon as look at me. What would you have done in my position, Jamie? I had to get out and get out fast. Peregrine was scared stiff, too. We put together all the cash we could get our hands on and took the first plane to Rio. I'd had a good run in London as you know, and I cleaned up in Rio. So we came here. And the games are very easy here too – you'd love it, even you couldn't lose!'

'Where's Peregrine now?'

'Took it all very badly. I've lent him some money and he's living out in Southampton. He's not well, poor chap.'

'What's the matter with him?'

'You know what he's like. Too many drugs and nothing left to live for now. And that's the story, there's nothing else I can say. I'm sorry that you got involved through Brett and even sorrier if you feel I let you down, but I think you'll agree I had no choice. I can't stand these Americans, but I'm stuck out here because of Brett, so I've just got to make the best of it.'

Jamie said nothing for a while. He very much wanted to believe him, but knew that it was all too glib. Typical Gavin. Oh what the hell, he thought, life's too short and we go back too far.

'Yes, I suppose so, Gavin,' he sighed, 'let's just forget the whole thing.'

'Thank you, Jamie, it's a great weight off my mind. Now, I've booked a table for us at the Veau d'Or and I've arranged for a couple of sensational models to join us here afterwards. Let's call this your stag night and have some fun like the old days.'

'Oh no,' Jamie groaned, 'I'll never get married with you around.'

And indeed it was rather like the old times, save that at the end of the evening, Jamie, after a quick nightcap, returned home to Jessica.

What neither of them knew was that the insignificant man with the fat lady at the table next to them was yet another of Spiros Virakis's informants.

CHAPTER 4

Yiorgio Necropoulos did not know how old he was. He knew only that he had been born shortly after the turn of the century on the sponge-diving island of Kalymnos during the Turkish occupation, which put him in his late fifties, though he looked ten years younger. He was not a tall man, but even as a child his might was legendary among a breed of islanders to whom feats of strength and bravery were commonplace. His niche in local folklore had been secured one stormy day at the bottom of the Aegean when, for over ten minutes and with no breathing apparatus, he had stood like Atlas, feet rooted to the sea bed, supporting on his shoulders a broken mast which would otherwise have crushed two injured fellow divers. It had taken three men to relieve him of the mast. That night his proud father took him to the brothel in the village where, at the expense of the management, he had lost his virginity and exhausted five of the house's most experienced girls. His voice had not yet broken.

The following year he had gone to sea to join another of the island's rising stars who had taken him under his wing. Apart from a few years in the Greek Commando Brigade during the war and a brief flirtation with the international motor-racing circuit, he had been with Spiros Virakis ever since.

Fastening the button on the ill-fitting jacket of his black suit, he tapped on the glass partition of the caretaker's cubicle at the Golden Gloves Gymnasium.

'Morning, Guv.' The old man put down his tattered copy of the *Sporting Life*. 'What can I do for you?'

'I would like to see Mr Dirk Brett?'

'And who are you, sunshine?'

'I am here on behalf of Mr Spiros Virakis.'

'Say that again, mate . . . Who?'

Yiorgio smiled gently, produced a card with Virakis's name on it and waited while the caretaker spoke into the telephone.

'He's not here at the moment, you'll have to come back.'

'That's all right,' Yiorgio replied pleasantly. 'I'll wait.' He sat down on the wooden bench.'

'He says he'll wait, Mike, what shall I do?' The old man listened for a moment.

'I'm sorry, mate, you'll have to go. Leave your number and I'll pass it on.'

'That's all right,' Yiorgio said patiently, 'I prefer to wait.'

The old man shrugged. 'He won't go, Mike, what do I do? . . . Yes . . . Yes, OK, I'll tell him.' He hung up. 'If I was you I'd go,' he said. 'Mr Brett's assistant is coming down and he's not a very nice bloke.'

Yiorgio smiled again and said nothing.

'Suit yourself,' the caretaker muttered and returned to his newspaper.

He had barely turned a page before the swing doors burst open and Brett's lieutenant, Mike, followed by an even larger leather-jacketed lout, stood in the hallway.

'Look here, you foreign turd, if you don't piss off, me and Jumbo are going to have to give you a bit of 'elp.'

'Most kind of you, young man,' Yiorgio said mildly, 'but I am not going anywhere.'

'Not going anywhere, you oily clown? We'll see about that. Come on, Jumbo.' They started towards him.

When asked afterwards what had happened by Brett, the old man was unable to say. It was all over before it had begun. Mike was lying on the floor nursing a broken nose and Jumbo was propped up against the wall spitting blood, his right shoulder dislocated. The softly-spoken Greek in the black suit did not seem to have moved and was still sitting on the bench.

Brett was in Virakis's nearby office in St Mary Axe. He had been furious with Mike for making him look a fool and for good measure had added a split lip to his broken nose.

'I must apologize,' Virakis began, 'for the unfortunate incident with your men. Yiorgio is a man of peace, but when provoked he forgets his own strength.'

'Don't worry, it'll teach them a lesson. They don't often come across someone they can't handle,' Brett replied. 'Now, your man said you had some information for me concerning Gavin Blunt.'

'Yes, Mr Brett. I believe you would be interested in his present whereabouts, eh?'

'Bloody right I would.'

'At the moment Blunt is living in New York City. Here is his address.' He handed Brett a piece of paper. 'He often spends his weekends at a place nearby called Southampton. Here is that address.' He gave him another piece of paper.

'It was a terrible thing he did to you and he must be punished. Of course . . .' He looked up slyly, 'he would never have got away with anything without the help of Sir James Stuart. He, my friend, is the one who has really made a fool of both of us.'

'Jamie. Made a fool of me. He's my mate, what do you mean?'

'Your "mate" eh? He is a treacherous man. Let me show you something.' Virakis took out an enormous bunch of keys, unlocked a drawer and took out an envelope which he passed across the desk.

'This document you will find is the original lease to the bordello known as Knaves where your dear niece, Miss Shirley, was so brutally attacked by that coward Blunt. As you see, it belonged, lock, stock and barrel, to Sir James.' He laughed demoniacally. 'But of course, you knew that. When he came, begging you to spare Blunt's life, he told you. Didn't he? Eh, Mr Brett. Eh!'

'No, he bloody well didn't.'

'Oh . . . I see . . . I wonder why? He must have forgotten. And when he pleaded for Blunt's life, did he not suggest that there must be some other way in which Blunt could make it up to you?'

'Yes, but . . .'

'And when,' Virakis interrupted, 'Blunt's business collapsed and you lost money, did not your "mate", Sir James, swear to you that he knew nothing about it and had no idea where Blunt was?'

'Yes,' Brett snarled.

'You see, my friend – and I am very sorry to have to tell you this – Sir James was in the plan from the beginning. They divided your money between them and they are both enjoying it in New York. Here is the final proof.' He unlocked another drawer and triumphantly extracted a newspaper clipping from which he read aloud: 'Heiress marries British aristocrat. Mrs Jessica Hamilton Turnbull of Newport, Rhode Island and New York City was today married to Sir James Stuart Bt, of Kilpurnie Castle, Scotland and London, England. Lady Stuart is the granddaughter of the late Gregory Hamilton I, founder and former chairman of Hamilton and Partners, the investment bankers. Sir James Stuart is the only son of the late Sir Archibald Stuart, formerly a British Member of Parliament. Lady Stuart was attended by her sister-in-law, Mrs Morton Hamilton. The groom's best man was Mr Gavin Blunt of London, England. The couple plan to reside in New York City.' He handed Brett the article with a flourish.

'Jesus Christ! . . . the bastards! . . .' Brett was speechless.

'Bastards.' Virakis nodded sadly. 'Yes, my friend, bastards. That is exactly what these aristocrats are. They look after only each other and to them people like you and me are no better than the dirt under their feet.'

'Right,' Brett said quietly. 'Thank you very much, Mr Virakis. I'll be on my way then.'

'A pleasure, Mister Brett. I wish you luck and may God go with you. Yiorgio will of course drive you back to your offices.' Virakis pressed the buzzer on his desk and rose to shake Brett's hand as he left.

'Excuse me, Spiro.' Hugo Robard stuck his head around the door in the wake of Brett's departure. 'Can I have a word with you about the BP contract?'

'Yes, yes, Hugo.' Virakis waved his arm expansively. 'Come

220

in, sit down. You see that man with the beard who just left?'

'Yes.'

'That man, Hugo, is the instrument of my revenge.'

'What, Spiro? . . .' He blinked. 'I beg your pardon?'

'The instrument of my revenge!' Virakis shouted. 'Are you deaf? Revenge against all those conspirators who are plotting, always plotting, against me.'

'Plotting, Spiro?' Hugo said in alarm. 'Are you feeling all right?'

'Yes, plotting, you fat fool!' Virakis shrieked. 'You fat, useless aristocrat. Do you think I don't know? Do you think I haven't seen you? What are you plotting, Hugo? Eh! Eh!'

'I can see this is a bad moment.' Hugo nervously gathered his papers. 'I'll come back tomorrow.'

'Yes, Hugo, I think you're right.' Virakis returned to normal. 'Please excuse me.' He held his hands to his temples for a moment. 'I've been working too hard. I'll see you in the morning. Please send Yiorgio in to take me home as soon as he comes back.'

Half an hour later, Virakis was sitting in the back of his car. He spoke in Greek. 'Well, Yiorgio, did he say anything?'

'Nothing, boss.'

'Good, good, that is an excellent sign. I am certain he will kill them both.'

'Yes, boss.'

'A good day's work, Yiorgio,' he exulted, 'because you see, my old shipmate, there is one most important fact that Brett does not know. Blunt is working for the Mafia. He is a most valuable front man at the moment for their casino licences in Las Vegas. When Brett kills him they will be most upset. He will never leave New York alive. What do you think of that, Yiorgio? Eh? All of them dead! Stuart, Blunt and Brett, eh! Yiorgio, eh! A perfect triangle.'

He began to cackle to himself as he watched the commuters hurrying home along the Embankment. So delighted was he with his fiendish scheme that he failed to notice the look of sorrow and revulsion on Yiorgio's face.

'Will you need me again today, boss?'

'No, Yiorgio, go home and relax. I am not feeling very well,

I shall stay in tonight. My *poutana* wife has already left for the theatre with her stupid girlfriends and I shall be alone with my son. Good night, Yiorgio.'

Virakis stepped wearily from the car and entered the house to the strains of 'Pomp and Circumstance'. He brightened at the sight of his son sprawled on a sofa enraptured by the music as he conducted an imaginary orchestra.

'Good evening, Daddy.' Andreas got up immediately and kissed him on both cheeks. He had his mother's colouring and was possessed of an easy, natural charm.

'Would you like me to turn the music down?' he asked. 'Perhaps it's too loud for you, Daddy, you look tired. Let me get you a drink.'

'Thank you, Andreas, an ouzo would be nice. But leave the music, I like it.' He slumped into his favourite armchair.

'Who is this composer?'

'Edward Elgar,' the boy replied.

'Oh . . . Elgar . . . Very good,' Virakis echoed proudly. 'Well, you obviously did not acquire your ear for music from your mother. The only ear she has is for diamond earrings. Eh, Andreas?' he chuckled.

'She does look very nice in them though,' Andreas said good-naturedly.

'Nice. Very nice? Nice and very expensive,' his father snorted. 'Bloody *poutana*!'

'Come on, Daddy, that's not the way to talk about Mummy.'

'Don't you tell me how to speak about your mother, Andreas. I'll say what I want,' Virakis said angrily. The boy was becoming too arrogant.

'If you'll excuse me, Father, I'm going out. I'll see you later.'

'Go out, go where?' Virakis barked. 'I wanted to have dinner with you tonight.'

'I'm sorry, Daddy, but I'm going to Oliver Barrington-Smythe's birthday party with some of the boys from school.'

'Fine, fine, go. Get out!' Virakis shouted after him. 'I don't need you, I don't need anybody!'

222

Yiorgio's loyalty to his master was, like Caesar's wife, above suspicion. He loved him in the way of a younger brother and had sacrificed his whole life for him. He had fought for him, he had stolen for him and on more than one occasion had killed in defence of him. Virakis in his turn looked upon Yiorgio in much the same way. From their early days at sea he had protected and carried him, and as a rich man he had kept his promise by financing his protégé's career as a racing driver. And Yiorgio was good. Very good. But an oil slick outside the Hotel de Paris during the Monaco Grand Prix had prematurely terminated his career and it had been of course Virakis who, within hours, had flown a plastic surgeon in from Brazil to restore his friend's burnt and broken face. Yiorgio had not left his side since and had been content to serve Virakis unquestioningly for the rest of his life. Until that day a year ago when Angela Virakis had come to see him in his little mews house around the corner.

She was crying hysterically, her body convulsed by sobs, a red weal livid against her cheek, and she poured her heart out to him.

'Yiorgio, he's mad, he's going completely insane. He thinks the whole world is trying to destroy him. He doesn't trust anybody, he has everybody followed and doesn't even trust the detectives. He's totally paranoid.'

Yiorgio was a man of few words and was not about to condemn his master, but did nothing to stem the outburst.

'I can't take it any longer. You're the only person I can talk to. The only one who understands him. What do I do? He can't stand having me around and treats me like dirt in front of everybody, including my own son. If I leave him, he'll kill me, and even if he doesn't I'll never see my son again. And why?' she cried out in pain. 'Why? I'm a human being too. What have I ever done to him? I've given him the son he's always wanted. I'm a good mother and I've always been a good wife. But look at me, Yiorgio. I'm a woman, a normal, healthy, ordinary woman. Do you know . . .' She grabbed his arm, 'he hasn't made love to me for four years. Four years, Yiorgio! He won't go near me, can't even bring himself to touch me – except to hit me,' she added bitterly. 'He calls me dirt, he calls me a slut and swears at me in Greek all the time. God knows, I may not have been an angel all my life, but I don't deserve this. Help me, Yiorgio, what do I do?'

Yiorgio nodded but still said nothing. He also thought that Virakis was going mad and had been worrying about it for some time. His loyalty was as unshakable as ever, but he knew that Virakis needed Angela and, even more, Andreas needed his mother.

The solution was not difficult. It was one that came naturally to the primitive mentality of the sponge diver. He gently reached out to the forlorn woman and taking her by the hand, led her to his bedroom. They had been lovers ever since.

Yiorgio parked the Rolls-Royce and walked sadly into his house where Angela, far from being at the theatre, was lying in bed waiting for him. The simple device of engaging a girl who resembled her to act as a decoy had been successful in keeping Virakis's detectives occupied. Yiorgio had briefed them himself and they had never seen the real Mrs Virakis at close quarters. The plan worked perfectly. Yiorgio had never considered his affair with her to be a betrayal of his employer. Rather the opposite. He saw it as the only way of keeping together the family which had become his own. Like all simple Mediterraneans, he was essentially a moral and religious man and his motives in the matter were pure.

It was this Greek-island morality that could not allow him to stand by idly while three men were murdered to satisfy the whim of a madman. Before returning home, he had gone to church where he knelt at the feet of the icon St Nicolas, the patron saint of seafarers, and asked for guidance. He lit many candles and St Nicolas had explained to him that such a betrayal was commendable in the sight of God. He had no choice. He would tell Angela everything, knowing that she could be relied upon to warn Sir James Stuart.

Chapter 5

Lennie Landau had never been on an aeroplane before. Yet here he was, halfway across the Atlantic in the first-class compartment of a TWA Clipper, sizing up the stewardesses and guzzling champagne. His feelings were a mixture of light-headedness at the novelty of the experience and apprehension at the mission that lay before him.

'Your job is to get to Jamie before Brett does,' Angela had ordered, as she stuffed his pockets full of cash. 'The next flight to New York leaves in two hours. Be on it.'

He gave an involuntary shudder at the thought of Dirk Brett close behind him and fervently prayed that their paths would not cross again.

'Stewardess,' he said with bravado, 'more champagne, please.'

'Certainly sir.' The trim blonde turned on her most professional smile. 'Are you staying in New York long?'

'No, my dear.' Lennie assumed the role of international businessman. 'I have a vital meeting on Wall Street this afternoon. With the chairman of a bank,' he added self-importantly. 'I expect to return tomorrow. Pressing affairs in London, you understand. But I'm free this evening, how about dinner tonight?'

'Well,' she hesitated, 'we're not supposed to date the passengers, but if you promise not to tell, I'd love to.'

'Good. I'm at the Carlyle Hotel, here's my card.' He handed the girl a garish, over-sized business card. 'I'll expect your call. Now my dear, if you'll excuse me, I must get some sleep. Got to be on top form this afternoon.'

'And this evening, I hope.' She wiggled her bottom cheekily as she moved off down the aisle.

Lennie awoke with a dull headache some time later and vomited violently when they flew through a small area of turbulence just prior to landing. The stewardess suddenly remembered a long-standing dinner engagement and after waiting for ages to pass through immigration he managed – with impeccable timing – to vomit again at the customs desk.

'For Chrissake don't tell me what else you've got to declare,' the disgusted customs officer said, and waved him hurriedly through.

He scrambled miserably into a yellow cab and dismissing with reluctance the idea of stopping at his hotel to change, he gave the driver the address of Hamilton and Partners.

'Mr Hamilton, there's a gentleman outside.' Morton's secretary wrinkled her nose in distaste. 'He insists on seeing you urgently. He claims it's a matter of life or death.'

'Who is he?' Morton asked in alarm.

'I've no idea,' she said primly. 'He's an Englishman in a horrible check suit and he stinks! Here's his card.'

'Leonard Landau Entertainments Ltd, Chairman and Managing Director, oh my God!' Morton exclaimed. 'Yes, Agatha, you'd better send him in.'

'Are you quite sure, Mr Morton?'

'Yes, yes,' he said impatiently, 'he was a friend of my brother.'

'Thank you very much, Lennie. Yet, I quite understand. Of course my wife will forgive you. She looks forward to meeting you another time. Please give our regards to Mr Hamilton and my love and thanks to Angela. Goodbye and have a good trip back to London.' Jamie frowned as he hung up the telephone and absently patted his pockets in search of his cigarettes. My God, he thought, this is the second life I owe to Angela. Thank goodness Jessica was over at Lyford Cay playing tennis and because of his limp he had not joined her. He was going to have to get hold of Gavin right away.

They had been married for two weeks and were honeymooning at her cousin Clifford's house on Hog Island in Nassau. Jamie had never been to the Bahamas before and was surprised at the Englishness of it all and the number of people that he discovered he knew there. They had been invited to dine soon after their arrival at Government House where he had run into an old friend and Oxford contemporary – Nicholas Wingate – presently on secondment as senior adviser to the Governor-General. Nicholas's wife, Penelope, had also been at Oxford with them and she and Jessica had got on famously. The four of them had spent several enjoyable evenings together, Penelope regaling Jessica with hilarious anecdotes of Jamie's and Greg's exploits at university.

'Oh my, yes . . .' Penelope had gurgled throatily at the end of one particularly salacious story. 'All us girls adored your brother Greg. Bit of a mouthful, though,' she nudged Jamie in the ribs.

They had spent their days much as in Newport – lazing around in the sun, water-skiing through deserted lagoons and making love on empty beaches. They had planned to move on to nearby Eleuthera for a week's fishing that evening. But it would have to wait until he reached Gavin.

'Operator . . .' Jamie picked up the telephone again, 'get me New York City, please, Regent 59005.'

'Mr Blunt's residence,' the butler's voice answered.

'This is Sir James Stuart. Mr Blunt, please.'

'I'm sorry, Sir James, he's out of town. Can I take a message? I'm expecting him back tomorrow.'

'Shit!' Jamie cursed. 'I need to reach Mr Blunt very urgently, where is he?'

'He's in Miami, Sir James, at the Fountainbleu Hotel. The number is Miami Beach 1973.'

'Thank you. If you should speak to him before I do, tell him to telephone me in Nassau immediately. He has the number.'

'Certainly, sir.'

Jamie broke the connection and waited impatiently for the operator to come back on to the line. When he eventually got through to Miami, all his threats and pleas were to no avail. Mr Blunt was in a meeting and could not be disturbed under any circumstances.

In desperation, he dialled Government House. 'Nicky, I need a favour. You may remember a friend of mine, Gavin Blunt. He's in Miami and in trouble. I've got to get there immediately.'

'Of course, old boy, how can I help?'

'I need one of the Governor's seaplanes.'

'You've got it. It will be ready to leave in half an hour.'

'Thanks very much. Two more things, Nicky. Please leave a message at the Fountainbleu Hotel and let Gavin know I'm on my way and please tell Jessica – she's over at Lyford Cay – where I've gone. I'll be back later tonight. Don't say anything about Gavin being in trouble.'

'Fine, Jamie, don't worry. Good luck, and have a good trip.'

The seaplane touched down three hours later outside the Fountainbleu and taxied over to the jetty where a crowd of excited children were watching. Pushing his way through them, Jamie walked up the beach and into the hotel. Gavin was waiting in the lobby. 'Welcome to Miami, Jamie. What's the panic?'

'It's Brett again,' Jamie said tersely. 'Where can we talk?'

To Jamie's surprise, Gavin seemed unperturbed. 'Oh how boring, I suppose he still wants to kill me. Come and have a drink.'

Gavin led the way to the main bar, waving back to a group of swarthy men in dark, bulging suits while Jamie quickly repeated the story that Lennie had told him on the telephone.

'So now he wants to kill both of us. What do you suggest we offer him this time?' Gavin asked maliciously. 'The deeds to Kilpurnie, perhaps?'

'Don't be so bloody cocky,' Jamie snapped. 'I've left my honeymoon to warn you. This is all your damn fault anyhow.'

'Yes you're right, Jamie, I'm sorry.' Gavin covered up quickly. 'And good old Angela, the old tart's certainly come through for us this time. What a common little turd that Virakis is! Anyway, no need to fret, old boy. It's my turn.'

'What do you mean?'

'I'll deal with Brett,' Gavin said coolly. 'Only this time it will really be taken care of. I promise you, Jamie, he'll never bother us again. I've got some very good friends over here.' He nodded in the direction of the dark-suited men. 'You go back to your wife, old man, and don't worry about a thing.'

'What about Peregrine?'

'Leave that to me,' Gavin replied. 'I'll get him out here now. He'll be safe with me.'

That Gavin Blunt should have gravitated towards the Mafia was very much in the natural scheme of things. He had soon tired of Brazil and Peregrine's constant company was driving him mad. New York was the ideal place to shake off his irritating cousin and, after London, the nearest thing to civilization. There he had passed his time as always – drifting between the racetrack and card games. He was a steady winner and it was not long before he cast his eye westward across the desert.

Las Vegas and Gavin Blunt were made for each other: the round-the-clock high-stake games, the unending stream of submissive showgirls. During a marathon poker session, he became acquainted with one Salvatore Bonetti. They struck up an immediate rapport, especially when Bonetti, after inviting him to dinner, introduced him to an exotic Morrocan belly dancer, who, lo and behold, possessed masochistic tendencies. The Sicilian further endeared himself to Blunt by suggesting that a man of such pedigree and obvious social credentials would be invaluable in his organization.

And thus it transpired that for a stipend of two hundred and fifty thousand dollars per annum, Gavin found himself, in name only of course – the successful applicant for the licences of a number of casinos yet to be built.

The town of Southampton rests on the south-eastern shore of Long Island, about a two-mile drive from New York City. Originally a sleepy fishing village, it has become a haven for the *nouveaux riches* who seek to escape the discomfort of long, hot suburban summers. Such people attract scandal and sensation much as sharks attract pilot fish and the inhabitants of Southampton were no exception. They gorge themselves on a daily surfeit of lurid divorce cases, drunken parties, attempted rapes and even the occasional suicide. But a murder was something else. Especially an unsolved one. Especially when the victim was a reclusive middle-aged Englishman who had been rumoured for some time to be a drug addict. And especially when the body had been battered beyond recognition. This was too much, they told each other over their dry martinis. Gave the place a bad name. Really most unfortunate.

Unfortunate, that is, to everyone except Gavin Blunt to whom the situation had been a heaven-sent opportunity. As the sole beneficiary of Peregrine's estate (which consisted entirely of their joint Swiss bank account) he could see absolutely no reason to take any steps whatsoever that might keep his cousin alive. He was later to tell Jamie that he had spent three desperate days trying to contact Peregrine, but alas to no avail; that he had telephoned Southampton every hour on the hour; that he had even, on the third day, sent the butler down from New York, but he had arrived too late.

'According to the police pathologist, he'd been in an opium stupor for days and would probably never have heard the phone or the doorbell.' Gavin had been in tears. 'I'll never forgive myself, I should have gone over personally. Poor dear old Peregrine, he was the only family I had.'

As for Dirk Brett, he was neither seen nor heard of again. If the truth be known, he had been picked up outside Gavin's 62nd Street townhouse and taken, as the expression goes, for a ride. A short ride. Along the Van Wyck Expressway – the latest extension of which he was now part of.

CHAPTER 6

In the weeks that followed Peregrine Blunt's widely publicized murder, Spiros Virakis attended very few business meetings. His entire attention was focused on the daily dispatches he was receiving from his informants in America and the copies of the more obscure Long Island journals with their emphasis on local gossip which his New York office sent him in their weekly pouch. Such was his early euphoria that he took the unprecedented step of inviting Hugo to lunch at the White Tower and even managed to avoid insulting him. This was as nothing compared to his behaviour towards his astonished wife, to whom he presented a diamond-encrusted azure Fabergé egg which had been specially made to commemorate the christening of Czar Nicholas II.

His mood darkened considerably, however, when reports began to filter through of Gavin and Jamie's return to New York, together with frequent sightings of them at all the leading nightspots. Still, Brett was a professional, Virakis kept telling himself, and it was surely only a matter of time before Stuart's new wife was a widow again. No harm though in sending Yiorgio down to the Golden Gloves to check things out.

'All right, Yiorgio, what's going on?'

'Well boss, it doesn't look good. I think he's dead. They haven't heard from him since he left, apart from one phone call in the first week. They are in complete panic and the other gangs are starting to move in on them.'

'Dead? Dead, eh?' Virakis whispered hoarsely. 'Yes, of course. There is no other explanation. Obviously. That snake, Blunt, he beat us to it.' He lifted his head. 'But how?' he said, almost to himself. 'Yiorgio, how did he know? Somebody must have tipped them off.'

Yiorgio shrugged and said nothing.

'And it could only have come from this office. Hugo! It had to be Hugo. *This* was Hugo's plot. I knew it! I saw him listening outside the door when Brett was here. Of course, he is even related to Stuart through that dyke who was married to Hamilton!' He clenched both his fists and banged them repeatedly on his desk like a child throwing a tantrum at mealtime.

'Yiorgio,' he shouted. 'Kill him! Go outside and kill him now! Now, Yiorgio, kill!'

'But boss . . . Come on . . .' Yiorgio was shocked.

'Do as I say, you peasant fisherman!' Virakis screamed. 'How dare you question me, I've kept you all your life.'

'No boss.' Yiorgio shook his head, his voice filled with sadness. 'No more killing. It is enough.'

'Then get out of here you ungrateful pig! Get out of my office, I never want to set eyes on you again . . . Eleni . . .' He pressed the intercom. 'Send Robard to me immediately.'

Seconds later, Hugo bounced in. 'Morning, Spiro. What ho, Yiorgio! Cheer up. You look as though you've just seen a ghost.'

Yiorgio was standing behind the door, head bowed in grief. He could not conceive of life without the man he loved.

'Ah, Hugo, come and sit down next to me here.' Virakis patted the armchair next to him, his tone betraying nothing. 'We must have a little chat.'

'Certainly, Spiro, what about?' Hugo made himself comfortable.

'About Gavin Blunt and the information you gave him.'

'Blunt? Information?' Hugo blinked in surprise. 'Don't know what you're talking about, old man. Fellow's a complete bounder. Haven't seen him since he disappeared with that degenerate cousin of his. Whoever killed that one did us all a favour if you ask me.'

The veins on Virakis's forehead looked about to burst. His whole face became horribly distorted and his mouth began to work crazily, low animal noises coming from deep within his throat.

'Traitor!' Without warning he hurled himself across the desk and locked his hands around Hugo's fleshy neck, his thumbs searching for the windpipe.

With one bound, Yiorgio crossed the room, grabbed Virakis like a rag doll and held him back down in his seat.

The shocked secretary rushed in. 'Eleni,' Yiorgio shouted, 'call a doctor, the boss is in trouble. Hugo, are you all right?'

'Yes . . . yes . . . I'll be OK,' Hugo gasped. His purple face was slowly regaining its natural ruddiness. 'What the hell's the matter . . . The man's gone insane . . . Look at him!'

Yiorgio by this time was cradling the sobbing Virakis tightly in his arms. '*Endaxi Spiro mou*, everything will be fine.' He smoothed his friend's fevered brow. 'You just need a long rest . . . We'll go home to Greece for a while . . . It's all right, I'm here. I'll always be here.' The tears were coursing down Yiorgio's cheeks. God had exacted a terrible retribution.

The doctor arrived within minutes, took one look at the broken man and gave him a massive shot of largactil. He then accompanied him to – irony of ironies – the London Clinic where for the next two days Virakis was strapped to his bed raving and foaming at the mouth. He was diagnosed as a paranoid schizophrenic. From the clinic he was transferred to a lunatic asylum where he was destined to spend the remainder of his days in a padded cell. He was officially declared insane one week before his son Andreas's eighth birthday.

BOOK FOUR

CHAPTER 1
BERKELEY SQUARE, LONDON, JUNE 1970

London was in the middle of a heatwave and at ten o'clock in the evening, the air was still warm. Jamie and Jessica had that afternoon cheered Nijinsky to victory in the Derby, but Jamie's mind had not been on the race. There were butterflies in his stomach as he strode purposefully across the square to the Dominion Sporting Club where Hugo Robard, the general manager, was waiting at the door.

'Evening, Jamie, nice to see you,' he said, mopping his brow. 'Follow me.' He led the way downstairs.

'Hello, Hugo. Terrific race today, don't you think?'

'So I hear,' Robard grunted. ''Fraid I couldn't make it this year. Too busy these days.'

They reached the bar and Hugo sat down panting at a table. A long-legged waitress dressed in a jockey's uniform and hot pants knelt at their feet to take their order.

'What are you drinking, old chap?'

'Scotch and soda, please.'

'Good evening, Sir James.' Jamie looked up at the smiling face of Paul Bishop, the assistant manager. 'How marvellous to have you back.'

'Thank you, Paul. You look well; how's life treating you?'

'Can't complain, sir. But it's not like the old days.'

'No, I can see that.' Jamie glanced around the casino.

Showgirls, fruit machines and piped music. It was Las Vegas in London. 'Times change.' He shrugged. 'Nothing any of us can do about it. Anyway, Paul, who's playing tonight?'

'Apart from the boss, I don't think you'll know any of them, Sir James. There's a new breed of poker player around these days.'

'And you're going to need every bit of your old luck,' Hugo butted in. 'I can tell you these chaps are no mugs. They'll skin you alive.'

'Really, Hugo. Just like you did?' Jamie winked at Bishop.

'This lot won't give you any trouble, Sir James,' the ex-dealer said in a soft voice.

'You always were a conceited little bugger, Stuart. If it hadn't been for . . .'

'Oh shut up, Hugo, you corpulent cretin.' Gavin Blunt joined them. 'Stop insulting the customers!'

'Really, Gavin, there's no need to be so rude,' Hugo said with surprising dignity and clambered to his feet. 'I must go. Got things to do.' He waddled off in the general direction of the restaurant.

'Is everything ready, Paul?' Gavin asked.

'Yes, Boss, but I'll just go and check. If you'll excuse me, Sir James, I'll see you later.' Bishop left them.

'Well, Jamie, what do you think of the place?' Gavin sat down. 'Awful, isn't it?'

'An understatement, old man.'

'Yes. Still, my partners are very happy. We're making a mint and I must say it does have its compensations.' He waved an arm and yet another lissom young jockey came tripping over. 'Caroline, my darling, bring us a couple more drinks in the private room. Come on, Jamie, the pigeons await! I've kept seat number six for you.'

Jamie got up and followed Gavin to the *salle privée*. It was his first poker game for fifteen years.

Gavin Blunt had just returned from his yacht in St Tropez and at forty-five had never looked better. The hair was still jet-black and his tanned face retained the striking handsomeness of its youth. His weight was unchanged since he left Eton.

Both time and fortune had been kind to him. Having persuaded his Italian associates to allow him to open a casino in England, he had returned home with relief some five years earlier. Still single (and self-indulgent) he lived in a four-storey house in Chester Square and in addition to his yacht owned a two-hundred-acre farm in Gloucestershire. The Dominion was the most successful casino in London. He had accurately gauged the mood of the times and there was no need for him to run it in any way other than legitimately.

To be fair, Hugo Robard was an efficient if unimaginative administrator and his honesty was beyond question. Dismissed by Angela Virakis shortly after her husband's committal with a golden handshake that should have lasted him the rest of his life, he had returned to the employment market around the time of the club's opening as a result of a series of spectacularly unfortunate investments. Gavin had snapped him up immediately. It had amused him to hire Robard as a flunkey and after all Hugo knew more about gambling (if not winning) than anyone else in town. Yes, life had dealt Gavin a pretty good hand.

'I bet twenty thousand pounds.'

'Up to you, Sir James,' the dealer said.

Jamie smiled. 'Young man, you've got three aces. I'm not going to call. Pass.'

The game was over. Gavin walked him to the door.

'Back with a vengeance Jamie, what? Like taking candy from a baby!'

'I suppose so. Not exactly the toughest opposition though.'

'No,' Gavin agreed. 'No one ever could hold a candle to either of us – but it breaks my heart to have to admit it, Jamie – you're in a class of your own. You always were.'

Jamie laughed. 'True, but you're a pretty good second. Anyway, must get to bed; I'm not used to these late nights. See you soon.' He set off across the square.

The gift had returned to Jamie six months earlier. He had awakened screaming with terror in the middle of the night at the vision of his grandfather's anguished face, the face he had not seen since his stroke. Demented and tortured, it was covered in a mask of blood.

'No, no. Go away, leave me alone,' he shouted and awoke, bolt upright, covered in sweat.

'Jamie, darling, what is it? What is it? Answer me. Answer me!'

The vision disappeared and his eyes gradually came back into focus. 'Nothing, darling,' he said in a strange voice, 'just a nightmare. An old prison nightmare. Go back to sleep.' He put an arm around Jessica, pulling her face to his chest. 'Go to sleep. It's nothing.'

'I was so frightened,' she mumbled, 'I love you so very much . . .' Her words trailed off as she snuggled up to him.

Jamie remained awake for the rest of the night. When dawn broke, he slipped quietly out of bed, pulled on a pair of corduroy trousers and a thick woollen sweater and walked down the great staircase to the study where he sat in his father's armchair and lit a cigarette. He was not surprised that his limp had gone.

Two hours later, he was equally unsurprised when Sedgewicke brought him a telegram from Sussex informing him that Clarence Stuart had died in the early hours of the morning. His life was about to change yet again.

They had gone straight to Scotland from New York and Jessica threw herself into the role of mistress of Kilpurnie with the joyous zest and total commitment with which she approached everything. It was infectious. As soon as they were settled in, Jamie reopened the great ballroom, which had not been used since the celebration of his birth, and gave a party for over a thousand people. The locals adopted the new Lady Stuart with delight. They cleared the floor and applauded wildly as she executed a series of perfect sword dances and when she toasted them with the words of Robert Burns's 'My Heart's in the Highlands', they gave her a standing ovation. Even Jamie, with his handicapped leg, gathered up the hem of his kilt and danced the first reel.

And slightly removed, overseeing it all, his own heart bursting with pride, was Sedgewicke. He had never been happier.

Jamie shrugged with resignation and sadness. The gift was back. There was nothing he could do. There was nothing he had ever been able to do. Ignoring the fact that it was seven o'clock in the morning, Jamie reached for the whisky decanter on the desk and poured himself a stiff drink. His mind returned to that joyous morning some six years ago, when Jessica first told him she was expecting their child. He had been sitting in this very armchair, pencil in hand, poring over the most recent draft of Hamilton's Annual Report for a board meeting in London that week.

'Would I be stopping Wall Street in its tracks if I were to distract its latest wizard for a moment?'

'Madam,' he replied with mock gravity, 'you do so at the peril of the imminent collapse of your family bank!'

'Well, screw you, you son of a bitch,' she said brightly, 'I'm pregnant. Sorry to have disturbed you. Just thought you might be interested . . .' She made as if to walk away.

'Christ Almighty!' Jamie jumped up, scattering papers all over the floor. 'What marvellous news, my darling! Are you sure? When did you find out? When is he due? Come and sit down!'

'Hold on, hold on,' Jessica grinned, 'there is a remote possibility that it could be a girl!'

'Oh . . . ah . . . yes, of course . . .' Jamie struggled to regain his composure. 'And I'd be delighted if it was! If it's a girl, we'll name her Lucy, a boy we'll call Gregory.'

'You've got no argument there,' she laughed. 'Now, to answer your questions chronologically. 'Yes, I am sure, Dr Finlay told me this morning, I'm two months gone, so I'm due just before Christmas and no, thank you, I won't sit down, I'm going riding.'

'The hell you are . . .'

'It's all right, honey,' she laughed again, 'I'm only teasing. I'm doing nothing more dangerous than going down to the church hall to discuss this Sunday's bazaar. We'll both be back for lunch! Love you, darling.' She blew her husband a kiss and left him speechless.

The very next day, and at Jessica's insistence, Jamie, with bulging briefcase, boarded the *Flying Scotsman* and set off for London. Arriving at King's Cross station in the late afternoon, he went straight to Berkeley Square. After an early supper, he telephoned his wife for the third time and went to bed. He slept like a baby.

The following morning he donned his bowler hat and, armed with *Financial Times*, sallied forth to the City and his business meetings. The evening was spent dining with Jeremy Hunter at Annabel's. Gently, but firmly rejecting Hunter's suggestion that they play a few shoes of baccarat upstairs at the Clermont, he got home soon after midnight and telephoned Jessica to tell her that his meeting would last another day and that his return to Scotland would be similarly delayed.

This was not true. At 9.35 a.m., Jamie once again boarded a train. But it did not depart from King's Cross. It was not bound for Scotland and it was not the *Flying Scotsman*. It was the *Brighton Belle*; it was going to Sussex and it left from Victoria. He was the only person to get off the train at the sleepy, rural station of Headingham.

Jamie felt a chill run down his spine at the memory of that day. Shakily, he poured himself another drink.

'I'm terribly sorry, Sir James,' the elderly physician had said, 'but he refuses to see you. There's no point in my trying to persuade him. I know him too well. Perhaps if you had warned me that you were coming, I might have been able . . .'

'Oh! Yes. I understand.' Jamie had been crestfallen.

'However,' the doctor added, 'your visit was not entirely wasted. He wrote this letter last night and asked me to give it to you.'

'What!' Jamie had said incredulously, 'you mean he knew I was coming?'

'Indeed, Sir James,' the old man said gently. 'He has been my patient for over forty years and nothing he does surprises me.'

Jamie had nodded dumbly and put the envelope in his

breast pocket.

'But since you've taken the trouble to come all this way, allow me to show you around. We're very proud of our grounds and at least you'll get a glimpse of your grandfather.'

Jamie had followed him through the conservatory and out on to the lawns.

'Look. There he is,' the doctor pointed, 'on the other side of the lake, feeding the geese.'

Jamie strained his eyes as the tall, stooped figure in the distance had deliberately removed his Panama and tipped it in their direction.

He did not open the letter until he was back in London. The immaculate handwritten script had read,

My dear James,

Please forgive me for not receiving you in person, but many years ago I made my position clear to your father. It is in all our interests that I have no direct contact with the family.

You have come, I perceive, because your wife is with child and you wish to know whether it will share our affliction. It saddens me greatly that I have been prevented from discharging the duties of a responsible grandparent – especially since the demise of your late father. It saddens me still further to be the harbinger of ill tidings, but you have come to ask and are entitled to know.

The child your wife is carrying will be stillborn and will thus escape the cross that you and I have had to bear. I appreciate that this revelation will deeply grieve you, but to be forewarned is to be forearmed and in our case remember, 'Even victors are by victories undone.' Give your wife every comfort and support.

Your loving grandfather,
Clarence

Jamie had destroyed the letter, returned to Scotland and said nothing. Six months later, Jessica had given premature birth to a dead baby girl. They were both devastated, if anything, Jamie the more so. He had been hoping against hope that Clarence might have been wrong.

Well, Jamie thought, as he finished off his whisky and lit yet another cigarette, time was a great healer and although Jessica had been strongly advised that further pregnancies would be dangerous, at least they had her son, Howard, of whom he was very fond.

The truth of the matter was that Jamie was relieved that the decision to have children had been taken out of his hands.

CHAPTER 2

'Should be a very interesting game tonight,' Gavin said.

Jamie and Jessica were dining with him in the restaurant of the Dominion Sporting Club. It had been almost a year since Jamie's return to the tables and – though hard to believe – his game had improved with age and experience. He was better than he had ever been before. He was untouchable.

'Who's playing?'

'Jeremy Hunter, Johnnie Radziwill, Raymond Lewis and two very big Greeks – Manoli Olympitis and Andrew Virakis.'

'Andrew Virakis? I didn't know he played. I ran into him at White's last week. Seems a nice boy.'

'Yes, he is,' Gavin agreed. 'Bloody miracle, though, with a whore for a mother and a raving lunatic for a father.'

'Is he any good?'

'Not bad. Plays with the same aggressive style that his disgusting father used to. Damned lucky to boot.'

'Well, boys . . .' Jessica was bored, 'I'll leave you to it. I'm going to play some blackjack; I feel outrageously lucky tonight.'

'Oh dear,' Jamie said seriously to Gavin, 'you'd better call Securicor to take her winnings home. She's been playing for twenty years and she's only just learned not to draw on sixteen against a six!'

'Shut up, Jamie, you silly twit.' She stood up and made to

245

hit him as he held up his arms, feigning terror. 'You tell me about blackjack when you've learned how to score at bridge! Gavin, honey, thank you for a lovely dinner.' She kissed him on the cheek. 'Darling . . .' She ruffled Jamie's hair, 'Good luck, I'll see you later. Love you very much.' She left and made a beeline for the nearest blackjack table.

Gavin laughed. 'Jamie, old friend, you're very lucky. She's a girl in a million.'

'Thanks, old man, I know.'

Andrew Virakis was a quiet, well-mannered young man who had inherited none of his father's temperament and, fortunately for him, little of his father's looks. He was tall, blond and had his mother's green eyes. He was also, Jamie thought, a fine poker player. They had not yet clashed, but Jamie had been watching him with interest for a number of hours and the young Greek had not put a foot wrong.

'Call and raise,' Virakis said confidently after Jamie had just bet the pot.

Jamie was surprised. He had a pair of kings and he knew Andrew only had a pair of tens. It was a very reckless raise. Jamie raised him back immediately.

'I call,' Virakis said.

The last cards were dealt and neither of them improved their hands. Jamie checked.

'I bet the pot.' He did not hesitate.

'Fifty thousand pounds to you, Sir James.'

Jamie stared into the piercing green eyes. There was no doubt about it. Virakis was bluffing.

'Call.'

'Three tens.' The young man turned over his hole card.

Jamie couldn't believe it. It just wasn't possible. But it had happened. That was it. And Virakis definitely hadn't cheated. What had gone wrong? He had been absolutely certain.

'You certainly walked into that one, Jamie,' Gavin said in surprise.

'Yes, I did.' Jamie's face showed none of his feelings. 'Well played, Andrew. Very well played. If you'll excuse me for a moment, chaps . . .'

Jamie left the room and walked over to the bar. He was stunned. He simply could not understand how he had been so sure yet so wrong. He sat on a stool, ordered a double whisky, took a large gulp, lit a cigarette and tried to pull himself together.

How could he have misread the cards so completely? Was his mind playing tricks on him? No. There was something uncanny about the strange boy with the familiar green eyes. Something buried deep in the recesses of his brain that he could not put his finger on . . .

It burst upon him like a shower of meteorites shooting across a darkened sky. Of course! It had to be! There was no other explanation. A great warmth enveloped him and he was filled with a deep, unrestrained happiness.

Drawing on the cigarette, Jamie noticed that his hands were beginning to shake uncontrollably. His eyes misted over and the room became a blur as the vision of first his father and then his grandfather appeared before him. A sudden excruciating pain exploded in his head, shattering his temples. He gasped and toppled off the stool. By the time he hit the floor, Jamie Stuart was dead.

Epilogue

Angela Virakis opened the drawer of the desk and handed the silver cigarette case to her son.

'Jessica Stuart sent this over. She thought you should have it.'

Andrew nodded soberly. He knew what was coming.

'Jamie was your father and this case belonged to his grandfather, from whom he inherited the gift. The same gift, Andrew, that you have inherited from him.' She stopped and wiped the tears from her swollen green eyes – she had been crying for days. 'I only hope it brings you better luck than it ever brought either of them.'

THE END